JORY STRONG

ZERAAC'S
FALLON MATES
MIRACLE

ELLORA'S CAVE
ROMANTICA PUBLISHING

What the critics are saying...

&

"If you like science fiction, erotica, and three-ways that are totally focused on the lucky girl, I would recommend Zeraac's Miracle," ~ *Romance Divas*

"Ms. Strong's writing never fails to capture my attention for many hours of reading pleasure. I highly recommend Zeraac's Miracle to anyone looking for a fantastic futuristic story. More Fallon Mates please!" ~ *Coffee Time Romance*

"It's an interesting journey into another world that will be sure to keep you guessing until the end." ~ *Road to Romance*

"Readers, be prepared to be in a constant state of arousal because each sexual encounter is mega H-O-T!" ~ *Fallen Angel Reviews*

An Ellora's Cave Romantica Publication

www.ellorascave.com

Zeraac's Miracle

ISBN 9781419955389
ALL RIGHTS RESERVED.
Zeraac's Miracle Copyright © 2005 Jory Strong
Edited by Sue-Ellen Gower.
Cover art by Willo.

This book printed in the U.S.A. by Jasmine–Jade Enterprises, LLC

Electronic book Publication November 2005
Trade paperback Publication October 2007

Content Advisory:

S – ENSUOUS
E – ROTIC
X – TREME

Ellora's Cave Publishing offers three levels of Romantica™ reading entertainment: S (S-ensuous), E (E-rotic), and X (X-treme).

The following material contains graphic sexual content meant for mature readers. This story has been rated E–rotic.

S-*ensuous* love scenes are explicit and leave nothing to the imagination.

E-*rotic* love scenes are explicit, leave nothing to the imagination, and are high in volume per the overall word count. E-rated titles might contain material that some readers find objectionable—in other words, almost anything goes, sexually. E-rated titles are the most graphic titles we carry in terms of both sexual language and descriptiveness in these works of literature.

X-*treme* titles differ from E-rated titles only in plot premise and storyline execution. Stories designated with the letter X tend to contain difficult or controversial subject matter not for the faint of heart.

Also by Jory Strong

∞

Familiar Pleasures

Carnival Tarot 1: Sarael's Reading

Carnival Tarot 2: Kiziah's Reading

Carnival Tarot 3: Dakotah's Reading

Crime Tells 1: Lyric's Cop

Crime Tells 2: Cady's Cowboy

Crime Tells 3: Calista's Men

Ellora's Cavemen: Dreams of the Oasis I *(anthology)*

Ellora's Cavemen: Seasons of Seduction I *(anthology)*

Elven Surrender

Fallon Mates 1: Binding Krista

Fallon Mates 2: Zeraac's Miracle

Fallon Mates 3: Roping Savannah

Spirit Flight

Spirits Shared

Supernatural Bonds 1: Trace's Psychic

Supernatural Bonds 2: Storm's Faeries

Supernatural Bonds 3: Sophie's Dragon

The Angelini 1: Skye's Trail

The Angelini 2: Syndelle's Possession

About the Author

෪

Jory has been writing since childhood and has never outgrown being a daydreamer. When she's not hunched over her computer, lost in the muse and conjuring up new heroes and heroines, she can usually be found reading, riding her horses, or hiking with her dogs.

Jory welcomes comments from readers. You can find her website and email address on her author bio page at www.ellorascave.com.

Tell Us What You Think

We appreciate hearing reader opinions about our books. You can email us at Comments@EllorasCave.com.

ZERAAC'S MIRACLE

๕ว

Trademarks Acknowledgement

ക

The author acknowledges the trademarked status and trademark owners of the following wordmarks mentioned in this work of fiction:

Big Mac: McDonald's Corporation

Conan: Conan Sales Co.

Happy Meal: McDonald's Corporation

Chapter One

∞

The fog rolled around and over Zeraac d'Amato, wet and clinging, coating his skin and clothing with its tears—a mirror of the damage that had already been done to his heart, his soul. He stood in front of the old apartment building, anxious to get this errand over with, and yet strangely reluctant now that he was on the planet known to its natives as Earth.

The image of his brother's human bond-mate, Krista, appeared in Zeraac's mind, framed there by joy and happiness. A smile found a small purchase place on his face, a tiny upward tilt that flickered briefly and then disappeared.

His heart lurched, remembering the expressions on Adan's, Lyan's and Krista's faces as they stepped out of the transport chamber—expressions rich with love, rich with the promise of a future with each other, the promise of children. The brightness of it was both a lightning bolt of happiness and a slow thunderous roll of pain in Zeraac's chest. A reminder of all that he'd lost when the Hotalings had found a way to invade Belizair, to let loose their bio-gene weapon and wreak havoc equally on both the Amato and Vesti alike.

None knew for certain whether the Hotalings had planned for their virus to kill everyone outright, leaving Belizair full of dead, perhaps believing that if no Vesti or Amato were alive, the planet would allow other beings to enter its atmosphere. Or perhaps they had planned just this, a vision of extinction, bringing the Vesti and Amato to their knees before reappearing from wherever they had gone and offering an antidote in exchange for access to the Ylan stones.

Even had those on Belizair been *willing* to offer access to the Ylan stones, they would not have been *able* to do so.

The Ylan stones were not a true stone at all, but almost a living entity. A power source—and so much more. Even the Amato and Vesti didn't fully understand them, though over time, they had learned to use the various types of stones.

It was the power produced by deep veins of certain types of Ylan stones that allowed them to transport between cities in any given region. To travel to Earth and back using the ancient portal in Winseka.

The individual stones on their wristbands allowed them to heal faster and move around, as well as to reduce their enemies into a million particles should they be threatened. The uses were endless, in part because there were variations in how the stones reacted to each individual.

For the Amato, they were sacred. For the Vesti, valued and treasured. But regardless of belief, neither Vesti nor Amato had the power to remove large deposits of Ylan stones from the planet.

How the Fallon had gotten the necessary Ylan stone off Belizair and onto Earth in order to build transport chambers was a mystery. The Amato and Vesti had never succeeded in getting any but what they wore in their bands. Ships could not escape the hold of the planet if they contained deposits of Ylan stone. Ships that didn't originate in Belizair would disintegrate if they persisted in trying to enter Belizair's airspace.

So even had those on Belizair been willing to give the Hotalings such a tremendous power source, they couldn't have. Nor could the Hotalings have descended on the planet had their virus succeeded in wiping out the entire population.

Zeraac's heart ached at the suffering—all for nothing. Nothing.

The Amato High Priests and Priestesses claimed that the Goddess, whose embrace surrounded Belizair, wept tears. And Ylan—whose form was Belizair itself, whose life force pulsed through the veins of crystals woven throughout the planet's soil just as blood pumped through the flesh of a man's body—counseled they would grow stronger for their suffering.

But Zeraac found no solace, no hope in the platitudes of the ones who claimed to hear the voices of the Goddess or her consort. Their words were empty and hollow. Their reports, meaningless.

It no longer mattered to Zeraac. There would be no children for him. No mate. Even a shared one.

Zantara's turning away from him once the scientists had declared him sterile—a rare result of the Hotaling virus, or perhaps he'd always been so—had shattered any dream of a family, even one that only included a mate. If she, who claimed to love him and had once pledged herself to him, was driven away by the hopelessness of a union with him, then how could he expect another, a stranger to bind her life to his?

Zeraac did not expect such a miracle.

The only thing he had to offer his people was his life. And as soon as he was done with this errand for the mate his brother shared with Lyan, then he would leave, following the trail of the Hotalings in the hopes of finding the place they called home, and learning something more about their bio-gene weapons.

So far the Council's own scientists had found only one way to defeat the Hotaling virus. Now the Council's agents searched among the humans in order to identify those females who had the genetic marker of one of the Fallon—the shared ancestor race of the Amato and Vesti.

All hope to avoid extinction rested on the unmated males, yet each male carried both the fear that there would be no match and the knowledge that it required a Vesti or Amato co-mate in order to produce offspring. Though the scientists couldn't reproduce the results in the laboratory with either an Amato or Vesti female, when it came to the human females carrying the Fallon gene, they theorized that the serum a Vesti male injected while mating somehow changed the female's chemistry, allowing for both the Vesti and Amato sperm to fertilize her eggs.

They'd stumbled on it accidentally, when an Amato in an experimental program was matched to a human, but elected to share her with his best friend, a Vesti. She'd become pregnant, the test results confusing as to whether her children would be Vesti or Amato, since the twins she carried contained the distinctive markers for both races.

Still, it was the first conception, the first time a woman on Belizair had managed such a feat since the Hotaling virus had struck. And since none of the earlier "experimental" matches between a human female and a Vesti or Amato had produced children, the scientists had gone to those pairs and urged them to take a co-mate. It had been a difficult undertaking, but eventually all of the couples had expanded to include another partner in their union, and now all were expecting children. Twins. The test results on the fetuses equally confusing, but the scientists were predicting a child of each race. Guessing that maybe the Hotaling virus had mutated the males' sperm in such a way that both needed to present in a human womb of one carrying the Fallon gene and that she also needed to be injected with the Vesti mating serum.

So the unmated males on Belizair worried, waiting for a match to be made, as they considered who they would choose for a co-mate. But for Zeraac, there was neither hope nor fear. Only resolve. He would do what he needed to do in order to aid his people.

His jaw tightened as he thought back to his encounter with his brother. There'd been worry in Adan's eyes and a pity felt but not spoken of.

Zeraac stiffened and turned away from those uncomfortable thoughts. It was because of Krista that he was here, and he would see this done so that she could move into a bright future with Adan and Lyan, so that her mind would be at ease and she could shed her life on Earth for one on Belizair.

Little did she know how valuable she already was to both the Vesti and the Amato. When word had come that Krista had witnessed the murder of a policeman, and that she feared her friends and her students would suffer after Lyan killed the murderer, there had been no shortage of volunteers, both Amato and Vesti, who had gained permission and rushed to San Francisco to guard those Krista cared about.

Long ago laws had been passed against interfering with cultures not as advanced as the one on Belizair. And even now, travel to Krista's world was still limited, still controlled. For the most part, only Council scientists and their agents, plus those who had been matched, along with whoever they had chosen as a co-mate were allowed to visit, and even then, they were urged to return as soon as possible. But the happiness of a bond-mate was paramount, and as a result it had been easy for Zeraac, as well as Lyan's brother and several others to gain permission and go to San Francisco in order to ensure that Krista would find happiness on Belizair. And so Zeraac stood surrounded by unwelcoming Earth buildings, with a task he now felt oddly reluctant to perform.

The sounds of a door opening and closing, followed by a long, hacking, choking cough, fought their way through the fog and found Zeraac. A child's thin voice followed. "Do you think it'll be different when I see Daddy the next time? Do you think he'll want to be with me if I'm not sick anymore?"

"Kaylee…" a woman's soft voice started to answer, only to be cut off by another rush of coughing, and a sob. "It hurts so bad, Mommy. If hurts so bad."

"Let's go back inside. Let me give you…"

"No, Mommy, please. I don't want a shot. I don't want to go to sleep. Please don't make me go to sleep."

A fist tightened around Zeraac's heart as another cough followed, long and painful, as though the child's lungs were so full of debris that there was no room for air, as though every breath was a battle for survival.

He was already moving forward by the time the sound subsided, his footsteps following the woman's voice instead of heading toward the apartment building where Colin Ripa's widow and child lived. He sensed others moving in the heavy fog, drawn to the sound of the woman and child as he was. And though he could not tell exactly where the others were, their intentions were broadcast in the silent menace they projected.

Zeraac followed for several blocks, the child's frequent coughing a beacon, the single steady rhythm of the woman's footsteps telling him that she was carrying the little girl, her soft voice weaving its way through him as she sang a song to her child.

"Almost there," the woman finally said. "I think the car is just up ahead."

Zeraac could sense the others speeding up, fanning out to close in and trap the woman. He increased his own pace, heading where he thought the woman had now stopped, the thick fog hindering him, making it harder to access which of the other threats should be addressed first.

And then there was no time to do anything other than react. A man's rough voice said, "Give me your car keys." Another said, "Let's have some fun with her first."

The woman's scream was cut off abruptly by the sound of someone being hit and a body slamming to the pavement. The child's cry was choked, a painful mew swallowed in the wet air.

Rage consumed Zeraac where always before he'd acted with the emotionless efficiency of a warrior trained to deal with criminals—quickly, effectively, justly. The three men who'd swarmed on the woman and child never saw what hit them, never had a chance against him as he rushed in, using his hands and fists to render them unconscious, wishing he could use the Ylan stones to finish what he'd started and destroy them so thoroughly that even the smallest particles necessary to recreate them would no longer exist.

He bound their wrists and ankles with the tape he found in one of their pockets. Then further secured them by tethering them together. Only when they were completely helpless did he turn his attention to the woman and her daughter. And as if ordained by whatever gods ruled the planet, a single muted shaft of sunlight pierced the grayness of the fog and illuminated them, making Zeraac's breath catch in his throat at the sight in front of him.

Both the woman and her daughter were delicate, finely boned, with hair that was spun silver to his gold, with eyes as blue as his own. But where the woman's skin glowed with health, the daughter's was pale, tight, so that her small bones stood in stark relief and her eyes commanded most of her face.

The woman's features spoke of exhaustion, of a pain none should have to endure. The little girl's expression held fear and yet a courage that reached deep inside Zeraac.

"Are you here to take me to Heaven now?" the child asked, her voice barely a whisper, her lips quivering and her eyes watering.

The woman's expression showed her surprise and her attention shifted to her daughter as she pressed her lips to the little girl's hair, gently gathering the child in her arms despite the angry bruise blossoming on her own forehead. But the child's gaze never left Zeraac's. "Are you here to take me to Heaven now?" she repeated, tears escaping and trailing down her pale, thin cheeks.

Zeraac's mind was a blank. He knew a little about Earth, but since this trip was unplanned, he hadn't studied, and so he had only a tourist's knowledge of this world. "Would you like for me to take you to Heaven now?"

The woman's gasp told him immediately that he'd said something wrong, but before she could say anything the little girl said, "We were going to the butterfly house. I'd like to see that first. And then I'd like to go somewhere special. Somewhere really beautiful. So it won't be so sad for Mommy when I'm gone."

A sob escaped the woman and Zeraac's heart felt as though it was being shredded as tears washed down her face. She hugged the child tightly, making no effort to get to her feet. The little girl's eyes moved to the bound men. "But I think we should call the police first, so those men won't be able to hurt anyone else. Then I'll be ready to...go."

"Kaylee...oh baby, please don't talk like that," her mother whispered.

"It's okay, Mommy. It's just like Kendall's mother said it would be. An angel would come down and get me when it was time to go to Heaven and be with Daddy."

The woman shuddered, her voice caught between a sob and a laugh. "Oh baby, this man probably saved our lives and he's an angel for doing it, but he's not the same kind of angel that Kendall's mother used to tell you about."

"Yes, he is, Mommy. Can't you see his wings? They're so shimmery that I can hardly stand to look at them."

Her words hung in the air, stopping Zeraac's breath and heart with their importance. Pinning him in place with what they might mean for Belizair.

The woman's eyebrows drew together slightly and for a moment he saw his true form reflected in her beautiful eyes, then she shook her head, dismissing the image, but leaving his heart thundering in his chest. Only those humans born with the Fallon marker could pierce the veil provided by the Ylan stones and see the Vesti and the Amato as they truly were.

She rubbed her head, wincing as her fingers skimmed over the bruise forming on her forehead. "Please," she said, "call the police."

"Do you have a phone?"

The woman shook her head slightly, but it was the child who spoke, pointing to one of the assailants. "He's got one on his belt."

Almost as soon as the words were out, she began coughing again, and Zeraac's heart filled with pain as he witnessed the woman's expression, as he read the anguish and helplessness there.

He quickly retrieved the phone, handing it to the woman—cursing himself for not taking the time to learn more about this world. But he'd never intended to stay more than a few minutes. To discharge his duty to his brother's mate by presenting himself to the policeman's widow and making sure that she and her daughter didn't lack for anything—save a husband and a father—but he was in no position to help them fill that void.

Now he found himself out of his element—a first in a long time. He was a bounty hunter, a lawkeeper, a man who protected his own people as well as providing his services to those on other worlds who could afford his price. Not since the days when he'd first begun training for such a profession had he felt so...unprepared.

And now his task had expanded. Not only did he have to find the widow and her child, but he needed to see to *this* woman and child.

His heart contracted as the little girl—Kaylee—coughed again, as he read impending death on her features. He needed to get a sample of her genetic material and take it to the Council scientists. She carried the Fallon gene within her—she must, or she wouldn't be able to see the folded wings laced with gold that attached between his shoulder blades, reduced to tiny particles by the Ylan stone so that they were more illusion than reality as he moved around on this planet.

A siren sounded in the distance and several of the men began struggling, diverting Zeraac's attention from the woman and child. He rose to his feet and moved over to make sure the men were secured, surprised to notice that the heavy wet fog seemed to be lifting, clearing as a breeze swirled it away.

Within minutes a police car pulled to a stop next to him, the doors opening and two men emerging, their hands resting on the butts of their primitive weapons. "What's going on here?" the younger asked, but it was the older man's question, the concern and familiarity in his voice, that sent an odd jolt through Zeraac's gut. "Are you and Kaylee okay, Ariel?"

Ariel. The name rushed through Zeraac, aiming for his soul and striking its target.

"We're fine, Peter, thanks to..." her voice trailed off, but the child said, "My angel."

"Your angel, huh?" Suspicion moved over the policeman's features as he looked at Zeraac, then at the three bound men at his feet, men who had been rendered helpless and secured by a professional, by someone who obviously knew what he was doing. "You a cop?"

"A bounty hunter," Zeraac answered, knowing that he'd be considered a policeman or soldier on Earth, but using the title from his own world because the meaning was different enough to avoid further questions. He offered a hand to the uniformed policeman. "Zeraac d'Amato."

"Peter Tyson."

The young policeman crowded in, radiating curiosity. "Nick Gaiman. You took them all down at the same time?"

"Yes."

Gaiman opened his mouth to say something else, but Kaylee's cough changed the direction of his thoughts, making him turn to his partner and ask, "You want me to put these guys in the car?"

"Yeah." The older cop knelt down next to Ariel. "You two live around here, don't you? Let's get you back to your place. I can take your statement there."

Kaylee's gaze locked on to Zeraac's and her lips began trembling, her eyes glistened with tears. "Not now. Please not now. If we go back to the apartment, I won't get to see the butterflies. Not ever."

The older policeman looked away from the child and Zeraac saw a hint of tears in his eyes before the cop cleared his throat. "Forget what I just said, Nick. Call for another unit. These guys can wait where they are. I'm gonna use the squad car for taking statements," he said, ducking his head and leaning over, silently offering to take Kaylee from Ariel's arms so that she could stand. But the little girl shook her head and struggled to her own feet, reaching for her mother's hand.

Emotion tightened Zeraac's chest and he couldn't stop himself from moving forward, from taking Ariel's arm and helping her to her feet, a jolt of recognition rushing through his body when he touched her, denial screaming through his mind even as the Ylan stones on his wristbands pulsed, coming to life in a way they'd never done before, not even in the presence of the one he'd once been pledged to. He let her arm go as soon as he could, moving away from her as if she was a fire that would burn him, trying desperately to close his mind and his heart to her. It meant nothing that the stones swirled to life in her presence, nothing, he told himself, other than perhaps a confirmation that she also carried the Fallon marker.

"We need a statement from you, too," the policeman said, misinterpreting Zeraac's retreat and thinking he meant to leave.

Zeraac nodded and followed as all but the young policeman and the three assailants moved to the car.

It was a tight fit, only made possible by Kaylee sitting on her mother's lap. But the policeman made quick work of getting the facts, though his expression grew more concerned each time he looked at Ariel, until finally he said, "I think I'd better drop you off where someone can keep an eye on you. You could be working on a concussion."

Before he could stop himself, Zeraac's hand cupped Ariel's face, turning it so that he could see her eyes. His other hand smoothed over the bruise on her forehead and around to a knot on the back of her skull, the stones in his wristbands pulsing again, as though they wanted to offer some of their healing ability to her. "She should go to a medical facility and be examined," he said and Ariel immediately tensed, pulling away from him, her words full of conviction. "No."

The policeman shifted in his seat, obviously ill at ease. "What about Colin's family…"

"Are we finished, Peter?" she interrupted, every inch of her body rigid, completely unaware of the turbulent assault of emotions taking place within Zeraac as he leaned forward to get a better glimpse of the paperwork the policeman had filled out, the information he'd already known and hadn't needed to ask about.

The arrow that had pierced Zeraac's soul from the first moment Ariel and her daughter had stepped from their apartment building, burrowed deeper inside him as he read their names. Ariel Ripa. Kaylee Ripa.

The wife and daughter of Detective Colin Ripa—deceased.

The wife and daughter of the murdered policeman.

The wife and daughter that Adan's mate, Krista, had asked him to check on.

Do you think it'll be different when I see Daddy the next time? Do you think he'll want to be with me if I'm not sick anymore?

Are you here to take me to Heaven now?

We were going to the butterfly house. I'd like to see that first. And then I'd like to go somewhere special. Somewhere really beautiful. So it won't be so sad for Mommy when I'm gone.

It's okay, Mommy. It's just like Kendall's mother said it would be. An angel would come down and get me when it was time to go to Heaven and be with Daddy.

The words assailed him, taking on new meaning, knocking down the barriers around Zeraac's own heart. "I'll stay with them today," he said, interrupting an argument between the policeman and Ariel that he hadn't even been aware was taking place.

The policeman scowled and demanded some identification. Zeraac produced it, handing it over without worry. The Council scientists and bounty hunters who monitored travel to Earth were expert in making sure the Vesti and Amato had what was necessary in order to blend in.

"Why are you in this area?" the policeman asked, writing bits of information down before handing the identification back to Zeraac.

"My brother's wife suggested I visit San Francisco."

A second police car pulled to a stop in front of the one they were in. A sole uniformed officer got out, joining the one guarding the three assailants.

Kaylee's cough filled the squad car Zeraac was in, ending in a whimper of pain. "Can we go now? The butterfly house is only open for a little while every day." Her voice was barely a whisper, her breathing rough and jagged.

The policeman looked at Kaylee, then her mother. "You shouldn't drive, Ariel. At least not until you're sure you don't have a concussion."

Ariel turned her attention to Zeraac. Up until now she'd been trying desperately *not* to notice him, not to think about him other than as a stranger who'd stepped in when she and Kaylee needed him, a stranger who would soon be on his way.

Oh God, he scared her. Scared her on so many levels, though none of them were physical.

"Zeraac already said he'd stay with us today," her baby girl said. "He can drive us to the butterfly house." And Ariel knew that with her head throbbing and the worry about a concussion, she had no choice but to let him into their lives, into these precious moments with a daughter whom the doctors could no longer help, with a daughter who had been released from the hospital for the last time. A daughter who'd come home to die.

Chapter Two

ɛɔ

Ariel's eyes watered as she looked at Kaylee, her mind trying desperately to capture the happiness on her daughter's face, to capture each fleeting second of joy and wonder as Kaylee stared intently at the brilliantly colored butterfly that had landed on her knee.

One day at a time. One moment at a time—intensely, painfully lived—the good moments hoarded away, held for a future that Ariel couldn't bear to contemplate.

She'd lived that way for so long now that she could hardly remember living any other way.

She could hardly envision a future past this day, this moment—though she knew there would be one. That somehow she'd survive and go forward. Just as she'd survived other losses.

But part of her would die with Kaylee. Part of her *wanted* to die with Kaylee.

God!

She rubbed her temple, wishing she could just close her eyes and go to sleep. The headache was making her weepy, maudlin.

She'd have plenty of time for that later…but not now. Not now. She'd never forgive herself if she…

"Your head is bothering you," Zeraac said, interrupting her thoughts, his voice stroking over her like a caress, making her heart jolt and her body ache in a way it hadn't done in years, not since the first part of her marriage to Colin—the part before guilt ate away at what they had and left a hollow, empty space.

"I'm okay," she said, the small lie escaping naturally.

He shifted on the wooden bench and his thigh touched hers, and then his hand was brushing the hair off her forehead, making her gasp, making her eyes flood with more unshed tears, his gentle touch and attention almost torture.

Not now, her mind screamed. Not now.

It was so, so wrong to feel an attraction toward him— toward any man right now. She had so little time left with Kaylee. Weeks maybe, if she was lucky. Or it could be over tomorrow.

His hand moved around to the knot at the back of her head, and she lowered her head, relief accompanying the strange warmth seeping into her as his fingertips made small soothing circles on her scalp.

It felt so good to be touched. To be this close to a man again. So close that she felt the heat from his body. So close that she could breathe in his scent and notice how good he smelled without any cologne at all.

For a second she yielded to temptation, imagining what it would be like to be held, just held, his arms wrapped around her, cradling her against his strong body, offering comfort and protection, companionship, an unspoken promise that he'd take care of her, that he'd be there for her, always.

It was such a sweet illusion that she lost control for an instant and the tears escaped, sliding down her cheeks as a sob burned in her chest, trapped there by habit and willpower. She squeezed her eyelids together, forcing the tears to stop, her face flushing with embarrassment, with mortification.

God! She didn't want Kaylee to see her like this. Or Zeraac.

Pain ripped through Zeraac. Helplessness assailed him, freezing him to motionlessness.

She was crying.

Every instinct urged him to take her into his arms, to kiss the tears away, then cover her lips with his, comforting and teasing her with the press of his mouth to hers, the rub of his tongue against hers, until she filled with want and joy instead of sadness and pain.

But he couldn't. Shouldn't. If she had the Fallon gene, then she would belong to others, to a Vesti and Amato who could help ensure that their races didn't become extinct by mating with her—to men who had more to offer a woman than he did.

He felt her regain her control, emotional steel making her body stiffen and then pull away from his touch, her head still bent as she turned and took off her jacket, surreptitiously wiping her eyes in the process.

He wanted to question her…about herself…about Kaylee. But he knew she wouldn't welcome his questions. That asking them would jeopardize the fragile truce that had allowed him into their lives.

If what he suspected was true, then they were important to his world, too important to let slip away—though his chest ached at the knowledge that he wouldn't share in their future. His heart no longer letting him maintain a distance by pretending that checking up on them was simply a responsibility he had to attend to.

His attention turned to Kaylee, who looked up at that moment as though sensing his gaze on her. "Come closer," she whispered and he answered her command, using his warrior's training to rise from the bench and move over to her without startling the butterfly on her knee.

"This one's called a Question Mark," Kaylee whispered. "And that one over there, the blue and green and black one, is called a rainbow skipper. Which one do you think is prettier?"

A smile filled Zeraac, though he kept his expression serious as he studied the orange-red butterfly with black and yellow spots on Kaylee's knee before moving to get a better look at the second one, his eyes straying to a third one instead. "I think this one might be even prettier than the other two."

"What kind is it?"

"I do not know."

Kaylee looked at him with consternation, her eyes going from the butterfly on her knee to the spot he was looking at. "I can't see it. And if I move, this one will fly away."

The smile Zeraac had been holding in escaped. "Let me see if I can bring it over to you then."

She frowned. "Be gentle. They're very delicate you know. You can't grab them like a baseball."

He laughed, the sound one he hadn't made in so long that it almost hurt as it forced his heart to open wider. "I will be very gentle," he promised, slowly extending a hand, willing the butterfly to let him show it to Kaylee. Surprised pleasure rushing in when it climbed on his fingers, so light that only the tickling sensation of its legs on his skin and the sight of it there confirmed its presence.

He moved slowly, returning to the bench where Kaylee was sitting. Her laugh making his own smile widen. "That's a Monarch butterfly," she said, her voice implying it was information he should have been in possession of.

"Are you sure?" he couldn't resist teasing.

She rolled her eyes. "Of course, I'm sure."

He made a show of frowning intently at the orange butterfly, thinking that the black lines on its wings gave them a fragile, segmented appearance while the thick black outline containing small white dots contributed to the beautiful, regal pattern. He could well understand how it got its name.

"Are you positive? Perhaps it is another kind of butterfly *pretending* to be a Monarch butterfly."

She giggled. "I'm positive. *Everyone* knows what a Monarch butterfly looks like. But I bet you didn't know this. The Aztecs believed that Monarchs were fallen warriors and the reason they were orange and black was because those were battle colors."

"Hmmm, you are right. I did not know."

Kaylee lifted a hand balled into a fist and placed it next to Zeraac's, the movement causing the butterfly on her knee to fly away, but she only glanced at it briefly before turning her attention to the one on Zeraac's hand. "I think you're right. I think this butterfly is prettier than either of the other two." The Monarch climbed from his hand to hers. "Did you know that they only live for about nine months from the time they're laid as an egg until after they change into a butterfly and make new Monarchs? That's a month for every one of the years I've been alive. I just turned nine." Her gaze shifted, meeting Zeraac's — so painfully adultlike that it was all he could do not to look away. "Don't they have Monarch butterflies in Heaven?"

"Oh baby," Ariel sighed, drawing Kaylee's attention to her and freeing Zeraac from the child's haunting eyes.

"It's just a question, Mommy."

"I know."

Ariel rose and joined them on their bench, wanting to gather Kaylee in her arms and hold her close, but not able to for fear of causing the Monarch to fly away. "Is that a swallowtail on the red flower over there?" she asked instead, preferring to divert her daughter's attention, admitting to herself that Kaylee's continued belief that Zeraac was an angel unnerved her.

Even as a child, Kaylee had rarely chosen to escape into a make-believe world, perhaps sensing from the very beginning just how limited her time on Earth was. She'd devoured books on nature, looking at the pictures so many times that the pages grew frayed from handling. The only television shows she'd tolerate were those dealing with the natural world. Zebras and penguins for a while. Lions, cheetahs and buffalo. Hawks and eagles and hummingbirds. And lately, butterflies.

"That's a swallowtail," Kaylee agreed. "Do you want to know what kind it is?"

Ariel pretended to think the matter over. "Don't I get a guess first?"

"If you want one."

"Okay, I say it's a yellow-and-black swallowtail."

Kaylee wrinkled her nose, her attention turning to Zeraac. "What do you say it is?"

"I agree with your mother. Aren't mothers always right?" He found himself smiling again as he thought of his own mother. She certainly seemed to think that *she* was always right — even now, when all her children were fully grown.

Kaylee rolled her eyes. "Mothers aren't always right. Especially not when it comes to butterflies. There's no such thing as a butterfly called a yellow-and-black swallowtail. That's a zebra swallowtail. It looks kind of like a tiger swallowtail, and some people might get them confused, but not me."

Ariel laughed, her eyes locking with Zeraac's in shared amusement. The emotion giving way to something else as her body came to life with a jolt, her nipples and clit jump-starting as though they'd been cold and dead for the past nine years. She hastily looked away, missing the startled look on her daughter's face, missing the glance Kaylee directed at Zeraac.

"I want to walk around for a few minutes," Kaylee said, the Monarch leaving the back of her hand as she struggled to her feet, her weakness suddenly obvious where it had been less so when she was seated.

"Do you want me to carry you?" Ariel asked, knowing how much her daughter hated to be helpless, especially out in public.

"No. I bet your head still hurts. Zeraac can carry me." A sly look crossed Kaylee's face. "But maybe you could hold his hand, just in case he stumbles or something."

It alarmed Ariel just how much she wanted to hold Zeraac's hand. How much she longed for it.

Until today, she'd believed the wounds left from her marriage were healed, but now she was learning that they'd only been scabbed over. The loneliness and need buried under day-to-day responsibility, under the heartbreak of having a child with a progressive, fatal disease.

She'd loved Colin so much in the beginning. And he'd loved her.

She didn't doubt that. Even now.

Their marriage wasn't the first to crumble under the strain of a sick child, under the guilt of knowing that their combined genes were the reason their child suffered, the reason she cried out, begging them to help her when the pain became more than she could bear. And even though they'd never divorced, never separated, as the years passed, Colin had spent more and more time "undercover" so that in the end he was hardly more than a stranger occasionally sleeping on the couch. Fulfilling his duty to them by turning over his paycheck.

Only after he'd been murdered did she learn the true extent of how separate their lives had become. His coworkers had been shocked to find out about Kaylee's condition, his supervisors uncomfortable with guilt for having assigned him to cases that would take him away from his family.

The pain of his death had almost been secondary to the pain caused by how completely he seemed to have purged them from the world where he spent most of his time.

Until his death she'd never allowed herself to wonder whether or not he was faithful to his marriage vows, but afterward the question had haunted her, filled her with agony. Chipped away at her until the thought of being involved with another man, of leaving herself vulnerable was almost unbearable.

It had been almost a year since Colin died, almost seven since the last time they'd slept together and he'd reached for her in the night, the quick coupling in the darkness so different from the leisurely lovemaking that had come before, that she'd retreated to the bathroom and cried afterward. When he'd elected to sleep on the couch the following night, and from then on, she'd closed off that part of herself that needed a man's touch, that craved it. She'd let it go cold and numb. Until now. When it seemed so wrong to even think about it.

Ariel rose to her feet, watching as Zeraac easily scooped Kaylee into his arms, her daughter squealing in delight as he gently tossed her into the air. Kaylee pleading for him to do it again, before a burst of coughing ended their play and brought Ariel to Zeraac's side, her hand going to his arm even as he curled Kaylee against his chest so that he could rub her back, his touch seeming to help, though Kaylee continued to cough and fight for breath for several long moments, until finally she sagged against Zeraac, her eyes going to Ariel's, silently pleading for a tissue so that she wouldn't disgust Zeraac by spitting out the thick, sticky mucus that filled her lungs and blocked her other organs, slowly killing her in the process.

Ariel fumbled in her jacket pocket for a tissue, handing it to Kaylee. "I'm okay now," Kaylee said after she'd handed the used tissue back to her mother. But she didn't sound okay. The energy that had buoyed her when they'd first gotten to the butterfly house was gone, leaving her sunken and frail-looking, her breathing shallow.

"Let's go home now, baby. My head is really starting to hurt," Ariel said, using her own injury as a sop to Kaylee's pride.

"I wanted to see more butterflies," Kaylee whined.

Ariel's heart was defenseless against the tenderness she saw on Zeraac's face, against the caring of his words when he promised, "I will bring you back here tomorrow, if you desire it, Kaylee. But only after I have had a chance to learn more about butterflies. I would not want you to find my company boring."

"You're not taking me away today?" Kaylee asked, her face tight and pinched.

Zeraac's eyebrows drew together. "I only intend to take you home now, so you can rest."

"To my apartment?"

"To wherever your mother directs me to go."

"Okay then. And tomorrow?"

"It will be the same as today, if you wish." His face lightened. "Though perhaps we can leave out the part where you and you mother are attacked and I come to the rescue. I am not sure your mother would like another knot on her head. What do you think?"

Kaylee's giggle was almost soundless. "I think you're right," she whispered.

Her struggle for breath was worse by the time they got to the place she called home. The fear of losing her raged through Zeraac, tempting him to break all the rules and take her directly to the Council scientists. But to do so was almost a guarantee that they would turn their backs, choosing to follow the law rather than their own hearts.

He insisted on carrying her into the apartment, on staying with her as Ariel took Kaylee's jacket and shirt off, exposing the sharp points of her bones along with the scars on Kaylee's chest, cuts healed over and left behind by a surgeon, the marks so primitive to Zeraac that he stepped back in reaction, then felt like crying when he saw the distress his action caused.

Without a word, he reached for Kaylee's nightgown, handing it to Ariel and then brushing his hand over the top of Kaylee's head before turning slightly in order to give them privacy so that the gown could be put on and the rest of the child's clothing removed. After it was done, he watched in awe as Kaylee herself fitted something around her head, answering his unspoken question by saying, "It's my breathing machine." She closed her eyes for a second, as though marshalling her strength. When she opened them, she asked, "Are you going to stay with me from now on?"

"Kaylee…" Ariel began but her words caught in her chest when her daughter reached out, tracing the air on either side of Zeraac and saying, "He's my angel, Mommy. He was sent for me and I want him to stay until it's time for me to go."

She began coughing, pain racking her frail body as she struggled for breath. Ariel rose and left the room, returning a moment later with a syringe. The sight of it made Zeraac jerk in reaction, just as the sight of the scars on Kaylee's chest had done.

Kaylee's tears fell more rapidly. "Please don't give me a shot, Mommy. Please," she whispered.

"Oh baby, let me do this for you. It's just a little bit, to help with the pain."

Kaylee's hand reached for Zeraac and he took it, squeezing it gently. Her voice was so weak that he could barely hear it. "You won't take me away while I'm asleep, will you?"

"No."

"Okay then. Okay."

Sleep didn't come easily, even after the shot, but finally it claimed Kaylee, leaving Zeraac and Ariel alone for the first time.

Ariel rose quietly and Zeraac followed, almost frightened to leave the child's bedroom. He was torn between the intense desire to stay with Ariel and Kaylee, and the urgent need to get the strands of hair in his pocket to the Council scientists for evaluation. There was no doubt in his mind that Kaylee carried the Fallon gene—she'd seen his true form in the fog, she'd traced the outline of his wings only moments ago.

"She will be okay tonight?" he asked.

"I think so," Ariel whispered, her head dropping, her shoulders tensing, moving forward slightly, as though she was trying to form a safe place where she could hide and avoid pain.

The sight of her like that struck at Zeraac's core. He moved into her, pulling her against his body, her presence in his arms thawing the ice-cold places in his soul.

Blood poured into his cock and it pressed against her abdomen. His hand stroked the long hair fanning out over her back, the crystals in his wristbands pulsing wildly, matching the beat of his heart, and hers.

For long moments he held her, offering her comfort, wanting to offer her more, but not daring to. "I need to run an errand," he finally said, "but you should not be alone." His finger went to the knot on the back of her head, circling it gently. "What if I get us something to eat and return in a little while?"

Ariel was torn, buffeted by emotion and logic and guilt, thrown into a kaleidoscope of conflicting needs by the feel of his erection against her belly and the answering wetness between her own thighs. It had been so long since anyone—since a man—had held her and offered the comfort of his arms.

She knew instinctively that Zeraac wouldn't take advantage of her. She guessed he wouldn't even act on his desire, not until she gave him some indication she would welcome it. That he wanted her, and yet wouldn't expect anything from her, felt like a miracle in itself.

Ariel smiled against his chest. Maybe Kaylee was right. Maybe he was an angel, coming into their lives when they needed him the most.

"Do you like Chinese food?" she asked. "There's a great takeout place a few blocks from here."

Relief surged through Zeraac. "Tell me what you want and I will provide it," he said, the words escaping from deep within him, a promise of more than food.

Chapter Three

∞

Every cell in Zeraac's body screamed that time was of the essence and he shouldn't waste it by using the primitive means of transportation on Earth in order to get to the Council scientists. And yet...he didn't dare *not* use the car loaned to him for the purpose of getting around San Francisco. To transport without it being an emergency was to risk that he'd be sent back to Belizair for breaking the rules and possibly drawing attention to the presence of the Vesti and Amato.

How foolish the strictly enforced rule seemed now. He could easily have transported without being seen. He was a warrior capable of stealth far more difficult than what was required in order to transport from one location to another. And even if he was so careless as to allow someone to see him disappear into thin air, they would simply convince themselves that they had imagined it. In his short time on Ariel's planet, he'd noticed how little the inhabitants saw, their attentions directed solely on the swift pace in which they seemed to live their lives.

But he couldn't risk breaking the law. And so he was forced to navigate through the tight, crowded streets, his frustration and anxiety building at each stoplight, with each suicidal pedestrian who took the right-of-way by stepping out into the street without regard for the cars there. He was gnashing his teeth and ready to do battle by the time he arrived at the Council house overlooking the ocean.

"Earth doesn't appear to suit you, Zeraac," Jeqon d'Amato said from where he lounged on a heavily cushioned couch, apparently doing nothing more than watching seagulls and fishing boats through the window that spanned most of the wall.

Zeraac stiffened at the sight of Zantara's brother, bracing himself against the memories that Jeqon's presence stirred up, against feeling once again the despair that had filled him when Zantara had said she no longer wanted to bind her life to his when there would never be a possibility of children.

What are you doing here, Jeqon? Zeraac asked, relieved to be speaking in the manner of the Amato and Vesti, though he knew the answer even before the question was completely asked. Unlike the warriors and bounty hunters of his own clan-house, the Lahatiel tended to be scholars and scientists.

What I can to aid us all, Jeqon said, his face and voice masking his thoughts, for which Zeraac was grateful. It was bad enough to catch glimpses of worry and pity in the faces of his own family members, it would be even worse to encounter them on Jeqon's face, a man he'd once looked forward to calling brother.

Jeqon rose from the couch and came to stand in front of Zeraac, extending his hands in greeting. Zeraac gripped the other man's forearms so that the wristbands they wore touched briefly before both men dropped their arms, Jeqon asking, *Is your business on Earth finished, then? Have you come to use the transport chamber?*

No, I came here seeking a scientist.

Jeqon grinned. *Then I am your man, and as you can see, I am available. What do you need?*

Zeraac hesitated, his chest suddenly feeling hollow now that the moment had arrived to turn over the silver strands of hair containing Ariel's and Kaylee's DNA. Once it was done, there would be no turning away from the results—and even the brief illusion that they could be a family together would be stripped away. Yet, what choice did he have?

The hollow place in his heart filled with worry and pain at Kaylee's suffering, at Ariel's anguish. The need to see that they were cared for swamped him.

What choice did he have but to turn over the samples of their DNA?

He pulled a strand of hair from his jacket pocket and handed it to Jeqon. *My brother's new bond-mate asked me to come here on an errand and while seeing to it, I think I have come across a mother and daughter who carry the Fallon gene.*

Truly? Jeqon asked, taking the strand of hair from Zeraac as if it were a priceless treasure.

Truly. That belongs to the daughter, Kaylee. She sees me as Amato. He retrieved a different strand from his other pocket. *And this one belongs to the mother, Ariel.*

Hang on to it, Jeqon said, starting to turn away, but then adding, *Give me one of yours as well.*

A black wave of despair rose from deep inside Zeraac. *What purpose is served by that? You know better than most that there will be no children for me.*

The child sees you, Zeraac. Perhaps it means something. We cannot always fathom the ways of the Goddess or her consort.

Denial coursed through him, a visceral rejection to the idea that Kaylee might be his match. *No.*

You would rather waste time waiting for one of the other scientists to return?

Anger flashed through Zeraac but he knew Jeqon would not bend now that he'd made his request. With an angry jerk, Zeraac ripped a strand of hair from his head and handed it to Jeqon before following him from the room.

Though the house claimed by the Council scientists was large, the area where they worked was small and filled with equipment that appeared as though it could be found on Earth. Jeqon took a seat on a stool and looked up, catching Zeraac's frown and answering it with a laugh. *Hard to believe a people who use such a primitive method of transportation and lock themselves in buildings that are little more than caves could have a technology that we would use instead of our own. But the Council ruled it would be safer to use what is here when we can, though we have modified it in order to speed the results.* He grimaced. *Still, it is slower than I'd like. You might as well take a seat.*

More than once Zeraac found himself rubbing the strand of Ariel's hair between his fingers, his mind replaying all that had happened since he stood outside the apartment building, his body growing hard with the memory of holding her in his arms as his hand stroked her silky hair and his cock pressed against her abdomen. It was sweet torment to imagine kissing her, to imagine slowly disrobing her—seeing her body for the first time, touching it, tasting it. Chasing away all the pain in her life and…

Zeraac's mind and heart jumped away from where his thoughts were taking him, even as his body and soul protested the abandonment of the journey. But he refused to return to dreams that would only bring him pain. Ariel would belong to another Amato, her life and Kaylee's intersecting with his only for this short period of time.

* * * * *

Ariel sat on the edge of Kaylee's bed, watching as her daughter's features tightened and cleared, tightened and cleared, the pain reaching her in her sleep, though the drugs kept her from waking. Kaylee's breathing was labored, the sound of it overriding that of the machine forcing air into her lungs. *Let her have one more day*, Ariel prayed, as she'd prayed so many other days.

She wanted to take her daughter's hand in hers, but she didn't dare for fear of waking her. Ariel's eyes moved to Kaylee's fingers, to the clubby tips caused by too little oxygen. Fingers that embarrassed Kaylee when she was out in public— though several times today she'd forgotten, tracing Zeraac's imaginary wings with them, offering her hand to him and letting him hold it.

The tears Ariel had been fighting all day escaped as the memories crowded in. Next to her wedding day, the day Kaylee was born was the happiest one in her life.

A lifetime had passed and yet it seemed as though it was only yesterday when she and Colin had sat on the hospital bed, staring down at their beautiful infant daughter, counting the tiny fingers and toes, perfectly formed miniatures of their own, and marveling that one day she'd be a teenager asking for the car keys and turning their hair grey.

It had all seemed so wonderful then. Two people who had found each other, and together created a third person, a miracle. The beginnings of their own family. One they would nurture and take care of better than their own had taken care of them.

"She's beautiful like you. The boys are going to flock to her. I think we'd better get working on a brother to help look after her," Colin had said, his husky voice making Ariel anticipate the day when she was completely healed and could feel his body on hers again, his cock thrusting in and out of her channel.

"Are you sure you can survive another visit to the delivery room?" she'd teased, enjoying the memory of how her macho policeman husband—a man who'd seen so many terrible, horrible things—had nearly passed out at the sight of his daughter being born.

"I can take anything you can dish out, and then some," he'd boasted, leaning forward and brushing his lips first across his daughter's downy-soft head, then Ariel's mouth, whispering, "But what happened in the delivery room is covered under the rule of husband-wife confidentiality. Right?"

Ariel forced her thoughts away from the past and wiped her tears, rising from the edge of Kaylee's bed and slipping from the room, not wanting Zeraac to have to knock too loudly in order to let her know that he was back.

* * * * *

"How old is the daughter?" Jeqon asked, choosing to speak out loud, his voice sounding casual though Zeraac was too well trained not to notice the tenseness of the other man's body.

"Nine Earth years."

Worry replaced the feigned casualness. "Let me have the other strand of hair. The mother's."

Zeraac made no move to relinquish it. "The child has the Fallon gene?"

Jeqon nodded, a brusque movement of his head. "But it's not a match to yours."

Zeraac rose from his seat and moved to the table where Jeqon was working, his gaze going to the glimpse of ocean and sky that could be seen through gauzy curtains. "Kaylee is ill."

"Dying."

This time it was Zeraac who nodded brusquely, pain seizing his heart at hearing the truth spoken out loud. "She thinks I am an angel come to take her to Heaven."

"That is the place where they believe they return to their god upon death, just as we believe the Goddess absorbs our souls while Ylan absorbs our bodies." Jeqon held out his hand. "Let me test the mother's hair."

"And if she does not have the Fallon gene?"

"Then the child will be lost to us. She is too young to be taken as a mate and we do not steal children."

"She could be healed and left here until she is old enough to claim."

"You know better, Zeraac. While these people have not progressed to the point of discovering other worlds and beings exist, their technology has advanced far enough that we can no longer cure them of their diseases or bring them back from the point of death as the Fallon and our own Amato ancestors once did. In those days such an event was a miracle not to be questioned or understood. But that is no longer the case on

40

very house whose pursuit of pleasure had infected Belizair with the Hotaling's devastating virus.

"Hear me out," Jeqon said, the sound of his voice reaching Zeraac, pushing through the agony now scouring his heart. "Hear me out, Zeraac. Komet does not involve himself in the pleasure business as most in his clan-house do. He is a scientist, a scholar, like I am. He is my friend and he is willing to accept that there may be no children. He is willing to be *your* co-mate, Zeraac. Ariel belongs to you. She's a match for you. And you need a Vesti co-mate in order to take her home to Belizair. Komet is well suited for the bond. He can help you deal with the scientists who will need to alter your daughter's genes so the disease won't begin its destruction all over again."

Zeraac almost staggered under the impact of Jeqon's words. Ariel was his!

A wild rush of love and longing and hope surged through him, only to be followed by the cold wash of despair as Zantara's words echoed in his mind, frozen in his memory for all time. *I cannot bond with you, Zeraac. Not now. I would rather wait until the scientists have an answer, or take another as a mate. It is better to have a small chance of bearing a child than no chance at all. No female wants to fail so miserably. To bind herself to a partner and then not see the fruit of their union in the form of a child.*

Komet d'Vesti watched the play of emotions on Zeraac's face, and even without knowing so much about the other man because of his long friendship with Jeqon, he could easily read Zeraac's thoughts. Sympathy moved through Komet, though he was careful to mask it. He could well understand Zeraac's emotions. Until Jeqon had appeared and told him about Ariel and Kaylee, Komet had given up the hope of ever having a mate and child of his own.

Who would take a member of his clan-house as a co-mate? And though the Council had ruled sanctions were not warranted on the Araqiels, that having to live with the knowledge they had brought such suffering to Belizair was

Earth. Scientists and doctors would race in if the child was suddenly healed. They would examine her and see if they could learn something that would help them cure others like her. You know the Council has long ruled we must have a minimal impact on this world, and we are not to tamper with the events and people here." He smiled slightly. "Only the fact your brother's human bond-mate was in mortal danger allowed Adan and Lyan to kill while they were here. Only the need to keep Krista happy swayed the Council so they allowed both Vesti and Amato alike to come here and ensure that those Krista cares about are protected and seen to."

Zeraac's face tightened with resolve. He had been willing to sacrifice himself for his people. To chase after the Hotalings, hoping to learn something that might aid the Council scientists in finding and offering hope to Vesti and Amato females alike, as well as to those who had bonded before the Hotaling bio-gene virus entered and overwhelmed Belizair. But was that any more noble an endeavor than giving Kaylee a chance at a future, even if it cost him his own? "And if I choose to heal her?"

Jeqon shook his head. "Even if the Ylan stones would migrate from your own wrists to hers, they do not have the power to cure her of this."

A heavy pain lodged in Zeraac's chest. "So it is hopeless? Even if Ariel also has the Fallon gene?"

"Not hopeless. The child's genes would need to be altered."

"It can be done?"

"Yes, on Belizair."

Zeraac handed the strand of Ariel's hair to Jeqon then turned and moved toward the window, pulling the thin curtain aside so he could look out at the flame-colored ocean and sky, the beauty of it reminding him of the red sands surrounding the city of Shiksa where those of his clan-house made their home. "If Kaylee can be cured on Belizair, is there a match for her?" he asked without turning from the window.

"No. But we are still gathering DNA samples. Not all of the Vesti or the Amato have reconciled themselves to taking a human as a mate, or sharing her with one of another race. And we have not looked at the male children yet."

Zeraac nodded and didn't speak again. Instead his thoughts returned to the apartment, his body filling with tension as Jeqon worked quietly behind him.

Only when he heard the sound of Jeqon's stool scraping against the wooden floor did Zeraac turn from his view of the now black sky.

"There's something I need to check. I'll return in a little while," Jeqon said, escaping from the room before he could be questioned.

Uneasiness moved along Zeraac's spine and gnawed at his nerve endings. He left his position at the window and moved to where Jeqon had been working, seeing almost immediately that the tests on Ariel's hair had been completed.

A hollow pit formed in Zeraac's chest, then filled with emotions so raw he immediately walled them inside, focusing instead on what was before him, but growing frustrated almost immediately. Science had never been his strong point. Almost from the moment he left his mother's breast he'd followed in his father's footsteps. He had studied the laws of Belizair and of the other worlds which most often hired the Amato to mete out justice and maintain order. He had studied the methods used to apprehend those who chose to break the law. But he'd had little interest in exploring or learning about the scientific world.

Zeraac searched the house, already knowing he wouldn't find Jeqon within—knowing instinctively that Zantara's brother had used the transport chamber to return to Belizair. To Winseka, the Bridge City. The sudden departure meaning Ariel had the Fallon gene marker and a bond-mate had been

found for her in the database containing information on all the males who'd been registered and sampled.

Pain breached Zeraac's barriers, slowing the time so it became unbearable. He wished he could simply leave the address where Ariel and Kaylee could be found and then transport away from Earth, but his heart was already involved and he knew he could never turn their care over to a stranger. He knew he would not leave this planet until they were safely on Belizair, where the healers and scientists could—*would*—attend to Kaylee.

He tried waiting by the window, looking out at a sky that was different than the one above his own world. But watching it gave him no relief from the agony of his wait and so he positioned himself outside the door of the transport chamber even though his pride and warrior's training argued it was foolish to wear his emotions so clearly, to show such a weakness. And yet his heart responded by urging him to let Ariel's future mate know that she had a champion, one who would make sure she was treated well.

With a curse, Zeraac began pacing. Before Krista sent him on this errand, he'd intended to follow the trail of the Hotalings and try to learn more about them, perhaps even capture one of them. They were a foreign, disruptive presence and yet despite their attack on Belizair, little was known about them. But how could he ensure Ariel and Kaylee were well if he was not in Winseka?

The hum in his wristbands and the vibration against his skin from being so close to the chamber signaled Jeqon had returned. Zeraac stopped in front of the door and braced himself for the emergence of Ariel's bond-mate. Given Kaylee's health, he didn't doubt that Jeqon had wasted no time in locating the other male. And yet even knowing that, Zeraac could not suppress his reaction.

No! It was a shout from the depths of Zeraac's soul when Jeqon emerged with a Vesti from the Araqiel clan-house, the

hardship enough, Komet wondered if either an Amato or Vesti scientist would ever acknowledge a match had been found for a member of his clan-house.

If he'd known about his family's plans to bring in hybrid beings, machines with a touch of humanoid-like DNA into Belizair, he would have argued against the idea. But, he hadn't been included in the discussion. Hadn't even known of their intention to bring the "companions" to their home city of Phlair in order to determine if a market could be created for the sexual playthings.

Perhaps they would have listened to him, perhaps not. But in the end, even the Ylan crystals that guarded the entranceway to Belizair hadn't recognized the threat posed by the hybrid beings, hadn't transmuted them to particles and allowed them to dissipate rather than reforming so that the virus escaped from hidden pockets inside them, rapidly spreading, a hidden enemy until several of the old had died, and the women newly pregnant had miscarried.

Only then did Amato and Vesti alike begin to question, to search for answers. Finding to their horror that where a direct attack by the Hotalings had previously failed, an indirect one had succeeded.

As Jeqon had claimed, Komet had never been drawn to the pleasure business, though for a while he'd studied the ritzca oil that the Vesti produced and sold throughout the galaxy, trying to better understand its sensory-heightening effects, and determine if it could be used for something beyond a pleasure aid and enhancer. But his lack of involvement in the pleasure business didn't spare him from being grouped with the others of his clan-house. And in truth, he would not denounce them. They had broken no law. Done nothing wrong by either Vesti or Amato custom.

Komet's heart swelled with the prospect of not only having a mate, but a daughter. He would not let this opportunity pass. Would not let pride stand in his way.

Stepping forward, he extended his arms in greeting. *What Jeqon says is true. I am a scientist and a scholar. What he has left unsaid is that I am a man without the hope of either a mate or a child, unless you extend such an opportunity to me by allowing me to claim Ariel with you, and to make her daughter my own as well as yours.*

Zeraac closed the distance between them, knowing in that instant it was foolish to cling to the course of action he'd decided upon before meeting Ariel and Kaylee. He already cared for them too deeply. He would never be able to walk away from them. And if Komet was willing to accept that there would be no children besides Kaylee... What other male would so quickly come to his side and join him in the claiming of a bond-mate?

His hands gripped Komet's forearms, the crystals in their wristbands touching briefly before their arms fell to their sides. *I accept your offer, but there is not much time to act. Kaylee's situation is dire.*

Jeqon told me as much.

They retreated to the room where Zeraac had first encountered Jeqon, choosing to converse out loud. It was Jeqon who opened the conversation, placing the most pressing of the issues surrounding Ariel in front of them as though it was a specimen put there for dissection, his voice making no pretense of expecting a positive answer as he asked Zeraac, "Is there time to get her to agree to both a binding ceremony and to returning home with you?"

Zeraac shook his head. "No. I would argue for transporting both Ariel and Kaylee immediately, now, but I can think of no excuse for having Komet with me when I return to their apartment or for luring them here tonight."

"You understand the risks involved if you take them to Winseka without following the Council's rules?" Jeqon asked, looking from Zeraac to Komet. "If the Council learns of it, then they have the right to set the bond aside."

"It is worth the risk," Zeraac said. "Kaylee is too precious to lose."

Jeqon nodded, expecting the answer he got, though his stomach still tightened with worry about the events to come. Zeraac and his clan-house had always been held in high regard. But many members on the Council knew there would be no children for Zeraac, and so it seemed inevitable that some would consider it a waste to allow him a human bond-mate when so far only a few females carrying the Fallon gene had been found. And to have Komet as a co-mate...that alone was cause for opposition.

Perhaps it was a mistake to suggest it...and yet, Jeqon couldn't regret involving his friend, in playing some small part in Komet gaining what he would never have otherwise. And while Jeqon had no intention of ever speaking of it to Zeraac, if there was to be even the possibility of children coming from the bond, then it would be because of Komet d'Vesti's interest in, and possession of, some of the rarer Ylan stones—stones said to have been formed from the tears of the Goddess herself—though the Vesti beliefs held no such claim.

"I am in agreement," Komet said. "The risks are worth taking. The child is too precious to lose and now is not the time to court the mother and convince her to accept two males into her life, especially since we are forbidden from showing our true forms until we are in the portal chamber and returning home." He turned his attention to Zeraac, deferring to his judgment by asking, "How do you suggest we proceed."

"I have promised to take Kaylee back to an exhibit of butterflies tomorrow. If you were already there, then it would provide an opportunity for them to meet you. And for you to be sure they appeal..."

Komet laughed. "I am already sure, and anxious for tomorrow to arrive. I do not doubt they will appeal to me, but I will wait until I see them rather than hear their description from you."

Zeraac smiled, unable to stop himself from saying, "Both of them are delicate, beautiful, perfect." He shifted his attention to Jeqon and asked, "When will the other Council scientists return?"

"You're in luck—somewhat. They will be back by noon. So if you hope to use the chamber unobserved, then the earlier the better." He grinned. "Most of those claiming human bond-mates seem to be choosing the bed in the portal chamber as the place to hold their binding ceremony, but I can remove the bed, since its presence might make Ariel and her daughter nervous."

Zeraac nodded, his words trapped in his throat at Jeqon's willingness to help despite the fact that he too might get in trouble for knowingly giving aid to those who were going against Council rule. Zeraac had thought once to call Jeqon brother, and yet now, to call him friend, seemed the higher compliment. "Thank you," he finally offered, and Jeqon nodded, acknowledging the deeper currents between the two of them before saying, "It's settled then, except for the wristbands. Since Zeraac needs to get back to Ariel and Kaylee, perhaps Komet can attend to that detail."

"That is acceptable to me," Zeraac said, surprised at how easy it was to give up the sacred task, to allow Komet to craft the bands that would go around Ariel and Kaylee's wrists so the Ylan stones could be coaxed into migrating to them.

Surprise flickered across Komet's face before he nodded. "I will attend to the task and return here. You will contact me in the morning?"

"I will contact you," Zeraac said, moving away from words and into images, showing Komet how to get to the butterfly house, finishing with a question, *Are you sure you do not wish to see Ariel and Kaylee?*

No, I want to savor our first meeting. To have my first memory of them be my own.

I will see you tomorrow then. And if all goes well, we will return to Belizair, to Winseka, with a bond-mate and a daughter.

Chapter Four

80

Zeraac followed Ariel into the tiny kitchen and set the bag of takeout food down on the counter, his heart tightening when he saw the way her hands shook for an instant as she pulled the containers out and placed the food onto serving plates before carrying it to a table set for two.

"You will allow Kaylee to remain asleep?" he asked, instantly regretting the question when Ariel's body tensed, as though he'd somehow implied a criticism.

Zeraac went to her, trying to undo the damage by placing his hands on her shoulders and pulling her back to his front, hoping the feel of his erection trapped between them wouldn't make matters worse. "She no longer eats well," he said, a statement of fact with only the merest hint of a question.

Ariel's head dropped in defeat, though her body yielded, flowing against his in acceptance of his offer of strength and comfort. "It's almost as hard to get her to eat as it is to get her to sleep."

"What do the doctors say?"

"That there's nothing else they can do for her except prescribe some medications to make her as comfortable as possible until it's over." Ariel's head dropped lower as she added, "I couldn't bear the thought of her dying alone in a hospital. It's the one thing she's always been terrified of, even early on, when she could still go to school and do some of the things other children can do."

Zeraac couldn't resist the urge to put his arms around her, to bury his face against her fragile neck and silky hair, to pull her more tightly against him. For several long moments they stood like that, until once again she tensed, saying, "If we don't eat, the food will get cold."

He let her escape, sitting when she directed him to do so, not objecting when the meal was eaten in relative silence, though he didn't find it awkward. Afterward he followed her into the living room, his attention captured by a collection of photographs he hadn't noticed when he was in the apartment earlier, his heart freezing with the realization that she might still love her dead husband, that there might not be any room in her heart for him.

Zeraac picked up a framed photograph, studying the expressions on Ariel and Colin Ripa's faces as they looked down at the infant daughter in Ariel's arms. It was a vision of what he would never experience for himself, a deeply held dream ripped from him before he'd had time to fully savor it.

He'd put off joining with Zantara for no other reason than he took his responsibilities seriously—as most of his family members did—indeed, as most of those on Belizair did. He knew that once he had a mate, and soon after, a child, then he would no longer travel so freely to other worlds and offer his services as a lawkeeper.

The Goddess and her consort blessed each Amato or Vesti family with only a small number of children, perhaps because Belizair was a small planet and none but those who wore the Ylan stones at their wrists could enter or exit, or live on their world. Even before the Hotalings let loose their bio-gene weapon, children were considered priceless, a gift of the Goddess and Ylan.

Zeraac braced himself against the emotion swirling inside him as Ariel joined him, taking the photograph from him, putting it back down on the small bookcase without saying a word. She ran her fingers along the top of the frame, then moved to the next one, a group photograph showing Kaylee smiling from ear to ear, a small stuffed koala clamped to one corner of the frame. "This is her kindergarten class. The girl on the right is Kendall. They were the only two "Ks" in the class, and best friends until Kendall and her mother moved out of the area." Ariel's smile turned sad. "Kendall had such a vivid imagination. She was always claiming to see imaginary beings—including an angel now and then. I didn't know until afterward that something wasn't quite right at home." Ariel rubbed her thumb along the small arm of the gray bear. "Kendall gave this to Kaylee."

"There was no father?" Zeraac asked, his attention caught by the thought that perhaps like Ariel and Kaylee, Kendall and her mother might also possess the Fallon gene.

"Not that I know of," Ariel said.

"Where did they go?"

Ariel shook her head. "I don't know. They were here and then they were gone without warning. Afterward I wondered if maybe they were in the witness protection program. Because thinking back on the conversations I had with Kendall's mother, I realized I didn't know anything about them really, not even where they'd lived before they came to San Francisco."

Zeraac picked up another photograph, Kaylee as a toddler, dressed up and in the arms of her policeman father, his uniform and expression giving the image a cool feel. It was the last picture in which he appeared.

Ariel took it from him, surprising him by putting it down so the image lay flat against the wood of the bookcase. "Colin was killed almost a year ago, while he was undercover, investigating a suspected mafia leader involved in selling weapons and drugs. The man's name was Alexi Sulemanov. The district attorney had a witness to Colin's murder, Alexi's girlfriend—a teacher named Krista Thomas—but she disappeared. And so did Alexi. They're probably both back in Russia, enjoying the good life now. Or maybe he killed her and fled the country."

Zeraac's fingers circled Ariel's wrist. "Alexi is dead."

She stilled, turning so she could meet Zeraac's eyes, probing them for the truth she heard in his voice. "How can you be so certain?"

"My brother—" Zeraac paused, uncertain how to proceed, how much to reveal. If they succeeded in getting Ariel and Kaylee to Winseka, they would soon encounter Krista as well as the other human bond-mates who now called the bridge city home.

"Your brother..." Krista prompted, her body language warning that suspicion would soon make her draw away from him, widening a gap he desperately wanted to close until there were no secrets between them.

"My brother, Adan, is involved in law enforcement. The man who murdered your husband was killed by Adan's partner, Lyan d'Vesti, in a cabin where Krista was being held prisoner. But rather than free Krista from fear, she knew Alexi's death would only make his family members want to avenge him, striking out at both her and those she cared about. She sought protection and my brother and his partner offered it."

Ariel could think of nothing to say. Her emotions were a confused jumble, her mind scrambling back to those moments when they'd been sitting in Peter's police car. Zeraac couldn't have known who she was then, and yet, it seemed more than coincidence that his brother knew of Alexi, had offered his protection to the woman who'd witnessed Colin's murder.

She rubbed her forehead and Zeraac's hand was instantly there, making small, soothing circles against her skin. And she let him do it, let him push away her feelings of confusion and her half-formed questions, let him ease her mind with his gentle touch.

In a perfect world, Alexi Sulemanov would have been tried and convicted, sent to jail where he would suffer for all the misery he'd caused—but in the real world, she suspected his money would free him from paying for his crimes.

"I'm glad Alexi's dead," she said, leaning into Zeraac's touch, not resisting when he lifted her into his arms and moved to the couch with her, sitting down and settling her on his lap, the hard ridge of his erection pressed against her buttocks. She closed her eyes, going lax against him, savoring his warmth, the security she felt when he was near. "But he didn't take Colin away from me. Or from Kaylee. The disease did that, a long time ago."

Zeraac acknowledged the comment by cupping her face and lowering his own, by whispering a soft kiss against her lips, teasing her with the gentle press of his mouth to hers, by the light stroke of his tongue. She whimpered and shifted, her arms going around his neck, her mouth opening under his, inviting him to deepen the kiss, to offer more of himself.

"Ariel," he whispered, his heart thundering in his chest, his body shaking slightly with the need to lose himself in her sweet scent and feminine flesh. There was no way he could turn away from what she was offering, especially now, when he knew she was his to claim as a bond-mate. His tongue delved into her mouth, dueling with hers even as he maneuvered them so she was lying underneath him, his thigh wedged between hers, his body moving against hers.

She whimpered into his mouth, pressing herself against him and eating at his mouth as though she was starving for the touch and taste of him. And he responded by pushing his hand underneath her shirt and the strange article of clothing that covered her breasts, by tweaking and tugging at her nipple, masculine pride surging through him at how responsive she was, how her body arched into his.

Pleasure ripped through Ariel. Longing. Desire. The need to be held, touched, loved by a man. Not just by any man. By him. He'd taken her emotions by storm. Awakened a part of her that slept deeply.

"Zeraac," she whispered. Wanting him to take charge. To take responsibility. To make her forget—at least for a little while. And yet even as she thought it, a part of her pulled back, knowing she wasn't ready to go any further with him.

"Easy," he whispered, as though sensing the beginnings of her panic and uncertainty. "Only this, Ariel. Just this."

She closed her eyes, unable to stop a soft whimper from escaping as he settled more heavily on her, the feel of his erection making her vulva swell, her clit ache for more than a clothing-shrouded rub, one body against another.

His hand speared into her hair, holding her in place as his tongue dueled with hers, pressing and retreating, coaxing and commanding, making her feverish with desire.

Tears of need escaped and she widened her legs, encircling his hips and pressing into him, rocking against him, her clit so engorged that she wanted to push her jeans down and beg him to suck it, to lave it with his tongue, to give her release.

But the words remained trapped in her throat and she let them stay there, accepting something less and grinding against him, arching into him until his hand moved from her hair, joining the other one under her shirt, both going to her nipples and as if sensing her desire for just a little pain with her pleasure, tightening on them, the extra stimulation enough to make her climax underneath him.

With a husky laugh Zeraac finally had to lift his head so that they both could breathe, and almost immediately the spell was broken. Heat rushed to Ariel's face. Guilt. And he knew her thoughts were on Kaylee.

"I...can't," Ariel started, but Zeraac leaned in and stopped her with a kiss, exploring her mouth in a leisurely fashion this time, gentling her, calming her as though the fury of what had just happened between them had not left him hard and aching.

When he lifted his lips from hers, his gaze was tender, soft. "I ask nothing more than just to be able to kiss and touch you."

Her face filled with uncertainty and embarrassment and something much more precious to Zeraac—trust and caring. "I've left you...hurting."

He laughed, unable to resist brushing his mouth against hers again and saying, "I'll survive. A little pain beforehand only heightens the anticipation and deepens the satisfaction."

But rather than laugh or tease him back, she tensed underneath him, filling his heart with heaviness and despair at how easily he seemed to find her weak spots and trample carelessly on them. "I'm sorry," he said.

She shook her head, a slight movement as the color on her face deepened. "You didn't say or do anything wrong." She met his eyes, hers skittering away several times before she took a deep breath and braced herself, holding his gaze and sending a wild, pulsing jolt of lust through his cock when she licked her lips and whispered, "There were things Colin and I liked to do, early on, before we were married, and then afterward, before we knew about Kaylee's illness. I think sometimes he blamed himself for her being born with a disease and having to suffer so much. He wouldn't talk about it, but I think he sometimes told himself it was God's way of punishing him for the things he—we—liked in the bedroom."

Zeraac could hardly breathe, could hardly think with so much of his blood in his cock and balls. For several seconds his imagination reeled with images—starring Ariel and *him*, and *not* Ariel and her dead husband. He desperately wanted to ask her for details, and yet some small kernel of rational thought prevented him from doing it. Now was not the time to explore what *they* would do together when they were bonded. Now was the time to build trust so the shock of what was to come wouldn't drive a permanent wedge between them.

And yet he couldn't prevent himself from asking at least one question. "And you, Ariel? Did you come to believe your god was punishing you for the way you and your husband loved each other physically?"

She relaxed underneath him, the movement causing him to moan, to drop his head and fight against the need to strip them of their clothing and bury himself in her wet sheath. His obvious arousal, coupled with his restraint, reassuring Ariel so her arms gripped him in a hug as she pressed a kiss to his chest.

"No. I never believed that," she whispered.

Zeraac speared his fingers through her hair, tightening them, her sharp gasp of pain and the widening of her legs an indication of her need. And when she arched into him, he rubbed the hard ridge of his clothing-covered erection against her equally protected mound, using his weight and strength to his advantage, overcoming the artificial barriers between them and once again showing her without words that he was capable of attending to her needs, even when flesh wasn't allowed to touch flesh.

"Let me please you one more time," he whispered, his mouth going to her neck, her ear, her lips, kissing and biting and sucking, the necessity of remaining silent in order to avoid waking Kaylee only making them both more desperate. "Ask me to please you, Ariel, ask me to give you release," he demanded, his free hand pushing aggressively underneath her shirt, his fingers once again taking her nipple, only this time, dominating and commanding rather than coaxing a reaction from her. She shuddered underneath him, getting him out of his shirt and pushing at the waistband of his jeans, begging him with her actions to break his promise to do no more than kiss and touch.

When he didn't give in, she whimpered, "Make me come, Zeraac. Please make me come again."

The fantasies of how and where he wanted to bring her to orgasm were endless, made more graphic by her earlier confession. It was all he could do to remain in control, to stop himself from ripping her pants down and shoving first his tongue and then his cock inside her. From mounting her repeatedly, her screams of pleasure and words of love the music he would carry deep within him until the Goddess and her consort reclaimed his spirit and body.

She writhed underneath him and his touch grew rougher, his body wilder as it surged against hers, rubbing roughly against the place between her legs, driving her higher as his fingers tortured her nipples and his tongue thrust in and out of her mouth, imitating what his cock would one day do as it buried itself deep within her cunt and claimed her.

Exquisite heat blossomed in every part of Ariel's body, and for the moment, it burned away any trace of guilt. It had been so long. Years of denying her own desire for love and comfort and physical intimacy.

She needed this so badly. Needed it with this man who'd come so unexpectedly into her life. Kaylee's angel and perhaps hers as well.

"Please," she whispered, a dark part of her thrilled that he was strong enough to take command, to require that she plead with him for release, to hold back his own need, making her fantasize about the day when his seed would jet into her body. "Let me come. Make me come."

He answered her by jerking her shirt and bra up roughly, his mouth latching on to her nipple, his touch dominant, thrilling, the sting of his teeth as wonderful as the hard pulls of his suckling, the way he ate at her hungrily.

She buried her fingers in the long strands of his hair, holding him to her, wanting to hold him there forever, and he rewarded her by moving to her other breast, by wedging his hand into her jeans, his palm covering her soaking wet panties and rubbing over her erect clitoris, taking her close to the edge and then backing off until she was shaking, whimpering, her body conveying the message that she was his—and only then did he let her climax.

For long moments afterward, Ariel trembled in his arms, unable to meet his gaze and acknowledge what had just happened between them. He shifted, positioning them so they were on their sides, her face buried against his neck as he stroked her back, her hair, pausing to gently circle the knot at the back of her scalp, before moving downward again.

His erection burned through their clothing and seared her belly, his cock seeming almost harder and larger than it had before. But he did nothing other than hold her as their breathing slowed to normal.

"I want to check on Kaylee," she finally said and he pressed a kiss to the top of her head, then tilted her face upward and brushed his mouth against hers. "Would you prefer I stay in here?"

Ariel's heart was defenseless against him. "No. Come if you want to."

He chuckled and she found she could laugh, too, the feel of his erection no less evident, and yet …

Before she could even complete the thought, they were both scrambling to their feet, as Kaylee's heart-wrenching cries filled the apartment. "Mommy, Zeraac. Help me! Help me! Please help me!"

Chapter Five

ⓢ

Never had Zeraac endured such a terrible night. A night spent praying to the Goddess and her consort as he'd never done before, not even when the scientists told him there would be no children for him.

Even now, still holding Kaylee in his arms as Ariel slept next to them, her arm draped over his and Kaylee's waists, he continued to pray that Kaylee be given time and strength. In a few more Earth-hours they would be on Belizair where the scientists and healers could begin their work, but until then...

He tilted his head backward against the headboard of Kaylee's bed and closed his eyes, reliving the terrible moment when they'd run into her bedroom and found the tears streaming down her face as she'd fought desperately to breathe, her features tight with a pain no child should have to endure. He'd scooped her into his arms, cradling her there with thoughts of racing from the building and getting her to the transport chamber.

"I'll get a shot for her," Ariel said, fleeing the room.

His gaze lowered, meeting Kaylee's terror-filled eyes and in that second, Zeraac saw death in her face, and knew she sensed it as well by her whispered plea, "Tell God you promised we could go back to the butterfly house tomorrow, Zeraac. Please don't take me to Heaven now."

He'd broken Council law then, letting the protection of the Ylan stones drop so that his wings shimmered into view, spreading out behind him, the white feathers with their glittering veins of gold momentarily chasing the fear and pain from Kaylee's face, changing her expression to one of wonder as his wings curled around to enclose them both in a soft cocoon.

He had no words other than a warrior's words. But he said them anyway, the tears streaming down his own face as he kissed the top of her silver-blonde head, "Keep fighting, Kaylee. Please keep fighting. Do not give up."

"I won't give up," she whispered, reaching out and touching the downy softness of a single feather, feeling it as it truly was before the Ylan stones at Zeraac's wrists pulsed, the wings dissolving into millions of translucent particles and recreating the illusion that he was human, in the seconds before Ariel returned.

Even with further medication, the night was long, exhausting. Terrifying. More terrifying than anything Zeraac had ever experienced, and there had been times when he'd witnessed the death of a fellow lawkeeper, when he'd nearly been killed himself.

His heart swelled with love and pride as his attention shifted to Ariel. He'd endured only a single night, she'd endured for years. He couldn't resist stroking her cheek, a smile settling on his own lips when hers turned upward and she shifted, nuzzling into his palm.

He wanted to lean down and kiss her, but with Kaylee on his lap, he couldn't. After he'd shown Kaylee his wings, she'd refused to let go of him, had insisted on staying in his arms. And so they'd all crowded onto her bed.

Zeraac closed his eyes once again, filling the moments until Ariel and Kaylee would wake by dreaming about their future on Belizair.

* * * * *

"Earth seems to disagree with you as much as it does Zeraac," Jeqon said as he watched Komet make yet another pacing loop around the main living room, the other man not even pausing to take in the sight of the sailboats on the bay.

"I expected to hear from Zeraac by now."

Jeqon shook his head. "The butterfly house does not open with the first light of dawn. In fact, few of the places I have observed here on Earth open as early as those on Belizair do, though there are some that remain open continuously."

Komet stopped pacing. "Continuously? Those living on Earth cannot plan ahead?"

Jeqon shrugged. "In many ways, they are not unlike some of the cultures that have formed on those planets we are more familiar with. They are not tied to the land as we are. In fact, often they seem oblivious to the natural world."

"They miss much then."

"True, though I'll confess, I find them interesting. I am actually anxious to explore their world more fully as I look for potential bond-mates. I think I will enjoy meeting and mingling with them as well as experiencing their culture."

Komet shuddered. "Give me the wide open spaces, or even the jungle with its carnivorous plants."

Jeqon laughed. "Spoken by one who spends his days studying everything living — except people — who he claims are not nearly as interesting as what flies, crawls, lopes or slithers."

"I have never said that!" Komet protested with a laugh, the familiar argument making him give up his pacing and sit down on the chair across from Jeqon.

He leaned forward and opened the crystal box on the coffee table, exposing the wristbands within it — one pair made for a woman, the other a small child.

Jeqon also leaned forward, admiring the craftsmanship, the uniqueness of the design incorporating both the device of Zeraac's clan-house and Komet's in each bracelet rather than isolating them on separate bands. But it was the small lavender Ylan stones with the sparkling color in their depths already present in part of each bracelet that made Jeqon's breath catch in his throat.

The Tears of the Goddess. Few had ever found them on Belizair, though many an Amato had looked. They were priceless—valued even by the Vesti, though because of their scarcity, and not because of their religious significance.

Jeqon felt privileged and honored that Komet had trusted him enough to share the discovery of The Tears with him. To show them to him once before, and now, again—on the wristbands meant for Ariel and Kaylee.

"Do you think Zeraac will hold to the agreement?" Komet asked, closing the box and restlessly getting to his feet. "Lyan d'Vesti's brothers and cousins are here. Zeraac would know them through his brother. Adan and Lyan have long been friends and now they share a mate."

Sympathy, not unlike what he felt for Zeraac, moved through Jeqon as he looked at his friend. Before the devastation on Belizair, Komet had been a much sought-after mate by many a Vesti clan-house. Even a number of Amato females, and males had openly chased him—not that relationships between the two races were forbidden, but they were fraught with difficulty, especially if the parties involved wanted more than a brief sexual liaison. Any children produced when the races mixed were always Vesti, regardless of which parent was of that race, and those children went on to produce only Vesti children, meaning the Amato clan-line was lost. For Komet, some had thought the loss was worth it.

Where most of the Vesti were created in shades of brown and black, with dark hair and dark, batlike wings, the members of the Araqiel clan-house had lighter skin, some of them only barely darker than the tanned skin of the Amato. And rather than always having dark hair, some, like Komet, had rich, golden-brown locks and wings to match.

Jeqon grinned. If he'd been one to love men, then he too, would have pursued Komet. Komet was desirable by any standard, and for the most part, completely unconcerned of his impact on others—his mind usually spinning off, analyzing some new fact he had recently learned about a creature few took any notice of. "Have patience, my friend, Zeraac will call soon, and before you know it, you will have a bond-mate and a daughter."

* * * * *

It was a battle for Zeraac to contain his anticipation and anxiousness. Up until the moment he'd carried Kaylee into the butterfly house, he'd been afraid something would go wrong, that he'd made a mistake in delaying.

He'd fully intended to forego this trip and take Kaylee and Ariel directly to the house by the ocean, but Kaylee had insisted he keep his promise of the previous day and return to look at the butterflies. And though she'd seemed weaker, frailer, the determination to keep fighting her disease had burned brightly in her eyes, making him think there was time to give her this.

"I need to stop by the ladies' room," Ariel said, squeezing his arm. "Too much coffee with breakfast."

He laughed, daring to lean down and brush a kiss across her cheek, "I told you that stuff was unfit for human...or even alien...consumption! Why anyone would choose to drink something so bitter..."

She laughed. "You'll wait here for me?"

"At the benches where we sat yesterday."

"Okay, I'll see you in a few minutes."

He moved forward, his mind reaching out and touching Komet's, directing him to the spot where he and Kaylee were heading, knowing immediately when Komet arrived.

"Zeraac!" Kaylee said, tugging his hair and pulling his face closer to hers before dropping her voice to a whisper. "That guy looks like a giant moth! Do you see him?"

A chuckle escaped and Zeraac's chest filled with relief at the lack of horror or panic or fear within Kaylee at the sight of Komet. "A moth?" he said, guessing Komet would know about such creatures, but deciding to enjoy his own ignorance. "Are they dangerous?"

Kaylee giggled. "Only to your clothing, and sometimes your food. I don't know as much about them as I do about butterflies. But once our apartment got infested with moths and they chewed holes in some of Mommy's favorite sweaters. And they got in the flour, which was gross. But some moths are really useful. Some of them are used to make silk."

Komet turned then, meeting Zeraac's eyes before shifting his attention to Kaylee and spreading his wings. They were visible only in Zeraac's mind's eye, but to Kaylee they must have appeared more real than imagined. Her arms tightened around Zeraac's neck and her heart rate jumped with the beginnings of fear.

"It is okay," Zeraac murmured against her hair.

"He looks like a bat now," she whispered.

"And bats are terrible creatures?"

"Some of them suck blood."

"Hmmm, I can see how that might frighten you. But I do not think Komet has a taste for blood. He is a friend of mine, from the same world I call home. Since I had no time to learn about butterflies, I thought perhaps he would be of assistance."

"Oh," Kaylee's grip loosened for a moment, her body relaxing, but then she once again tugged Zeraac's hair, forcing him to meet her too-wise gaze. "But he didn't come just for the butterflies, did he? He's here to take someone else to Heaven, isn't he?"

Zeraac hesitated, deciding to ignore the question for the moment as he moved to the bench where they'd been the previous day and sat down, settling Kaylee next to him on the wooden seat. Part of him hating the thought of using Kaylee to plot against her mother, hating the thought of using Kaylee's faith in him, using her belief that he would take her to the place where her god lived as a means of getting her to Belizair.

But the need to get them to his world was urgent and her health delicate. If she believed in him, in their destination, wasn't she more likely to survive until they reached the transport chamber?

What choice did he really have?

Join us, he sent to Komet, knowing it would be foolish not to take advantage of this unexpected opportunity to speak with Kaylee alone, to ease her fears.

Is the mother as beautiful? Komet asked, sitting next to Kaylee, the carved crystal box on his lap.

Yes. Kaylee has her looks.

Then I am doubly privileged to be included in this joining of bond-mates, Komet said, not bothering to hide his emotions or the fact that he was already drawn to Kaylee's plight, already felt protective of her. *You are right. She will not live much longer on this planet.*

I feared we would lose her last night. It was a close call. Zeraac turned slightly in his seat. "Kaylee Ripa of the planet Earth, this is Komet d'Vesti," he said, purposely making his voice teasing.

But rather than laugh at his introduction, her face remained somber and he realized immediately that his failure to answer her earlier question hadn't gone unnoticed. Huge tears welled up in Kaylee's eyes and her body trembled. "Are you here for Mommy?" she asked, her haunting gaze latching on to Komet and making it impossible for him to look away.

By the stars, it hurt his heart to look at her fragile beauty and think of the light inside her burning out before she could collect even a fraction of the memories and achievements that the old took with them when they died. Her gaze pinned him in place as surely as a butterfly in a collector's display. Trapping him without the possibility of escape, without the ability to avoid being examined.

For all they'd discussed and rationalized what they intended to do, Kaylee's distress at the question stripped away

Komet's justifications and left him raw at the thought of taking away their freedom of choice. The very freedom the Council had insisted on when they ruled bond-mates must agree to a binding ceremony and to returning home with their Vesti and Amato mates before they could be taken.

"Yes. I am here for her, as well as for you. Will you go with both Zeraac and me? Will you trust us?"

Her bottom lip quivered but she nodded. "It won't hurt will it? Mommy's not used to hurting, not like I am."

"It won't hurt at all."

Some instinct had prompted Komet to bring the box containing the wristbands. He opened it now, just long enough to remove the pair he'd crafted for Kaylee. "You will need these to go where we are going," he said, handing one bracelet to Zeraac.

Kaylee's eyes lingered for a moment on the wristbands that both he and Zeraac wore, and then she held out her arms, her face solemn. "Will Daddy be waiting for us when we get there?"

Komet's panic collided with Zeraac's for an instant, but it was Zeraac who answered, "No, his duties are elsewhere."

"Oh. I understand. That's the way it was when he was alive, too."

Zeraac's heart wrenched at her simple words. He leaned forward, brushing a kiss against the top of her head before pulling the sleeve of her jacket back and waiting for Komet to do the same at her other arm. Then they placed the wristbands on her, the Ylan stones swirling to life at the contact with her skin, the bracelets melding, tightening, becoming almost a part of her flesh.

When Kaylee would have taken the time to examine them further, Zeraac murmured, "Later, Kaylee. Your mother cannot see them now. It is too soon, and I do not want her to worry or be afraid." Kaylee nodded, her arms going lax as she allowed Zeraac and Komet to pull the sleeves of her jacket over the bands.

Ariel joined them moments later, her expression growing uncertain when she caught sight of Komet. "It's okay, Mommy, Komet is a friend of Zeraac's," Kaylee said, reaching out and taking her mother's hand, squeezing it, rushing ahead when Zeraac and Komet would have gone more cautiously. "They want to take us somewhere."

"Where?" Ariel asked, confusion on her features – but not suspicion.

Relief filled Zeraac and he stood, taking Ariel's other hand. "What Kaylee says is true, Ariel. This is my friend, Komet d'Vesti. He has access to a house with a garden full of exotic flowers and beautiful stones, and has invited us to go there."

"Won't there be animals?" Kaylee asked, her small features drawn together in a frown.

Komet laughed. "Not in the first room I will show you, or even the second that you will see, but there will definitely be animals in the third place."

"Is it far?" Ariel asked, concern in her voice, her eyes meeting Zeraac's.

"Not far at all," he said, squeezing her hand. "I think you and Kaylee will both find value in going to this place. A short car ride and we will be there. It overlooks the bay."

Ariel's eyebrows drew together and she shifted her attention to Kaylee. "We only just got to the butterfly house…"

"It's okay, Mommy, I think this other place will be better." She began coughing then, the same horrible choking struggle for breath that Zeraac had witnessed before, but Komet hadn't. And yet his instincts were the same as Zeraac's, his hand going to Kaylee's back, rubbing, trying to soothe her, leaving only to retrieve a handkerchief and press it to her mouth, urging her to spit even as his words flowed into Zeraac's mind, *We must leave!*

The coughing passed, but Kaylee was noticeably weaker. She tangled her fingers in Zeraac's hair, letting the weight of her hand and arm pull his face down to hers. "I'm trying to fight," she whispered, "but it's getting harder."

He scooped Kaylee up in his arms before once again taking Ariel's hand in his, squeezing it when he saw the argument for taking Kaylee home forming on her face. Knowing it was too soon to ask it of her, but also knowing it was too late for any other course of action. "Trust me, Ariel."

Chapter Six

&

It scared Ariel that she trusted Zeraac so much, that she wanted so desperately to cede control to him, to let him take charge, to make the decisions and be the one to carry the weight of responsibility. She'd been strong for so long, but now, when the end was so close, when she needed her strength the most, it was a struggle to face each new moment.

Kaylee had once again fought off death, a miracle this time, a small one wrought by courage and paid for by Kaylee's pain. But as much as Ariel longed for an end to her daughter's suffering, she couldn't bear the thought of her dying.

Heartbreak ripped through Ariel as she looked at Kaylee sitting on Zeraac's lap in the front seat. The emotional pain was followed by a wild rush of love, by gratitude at having had this much time with Kaylee. And today, the heartache and love and gratitude were also followed by an anger directed at Colin, for not being able to cope with Kaylee's disease, for not rising past his own disappointment and guilt and keeping the promises he'd made, to be a better father to his daughter than his father had been to him.

She'd never guessed how much her daughter wanted a father, needed a father, until Zeraac had come along. But now it was obvious.

Kaylee had always been outgoing, and yet she'd latched on to Zeraac, emotionally and physically, fearful of even letting him out of her sight, insisting that he be the one to hold her, to carry her. And Ariel couldn't find fault with her daughter's instincts. She too had trusted him from the start, letting him into their lives, and she didn't regret it. The image of him standing with Kaylee in his arms last night, his cheeks wet with tears, had burned into her heart and mind and soul.

When she'd rounded the corner in the butterfly house and seen Zeraac and Kaylee sitting with a stranger, her own first thought was a selfish one. She'd wished that he would go away because she didn't want to share Zeraac's attention with anyone other than her daughter. But later, when Kaylee had started coughing and Komet had immediately responded with compassion, rubbing Kaylee's back, pressing his own handkerchief to her mouth and urging her to spit, seeming to understand without being told about Kaylee's embarrassment, then Ariel's desire for him to leave had disappeared, and her appreciation of both his looks and his manner had begun.

It was difficult not to compare the two men. Zeraac was stunning with his long blond hair and warrior's body. Even if he hadn't taken down all three of the men who'd assaulted Kaylee and her in the fog, she would have pegged him for a vice cop. It was even easier to see him as a bounty hunter.

Komet on the other hand... His hair was a golden-brown and like Zeraac's, it fell below his shoulders, but where Zeraac's was straight, Komet's was somewhere between wavy and curly. Where Zeraac's eyes were blue, Komet's were light brown. And even though the two men were similar in physique, somehow...

Stunning didn't capture what Komet was. Even gorgeous was too tame a word. The only one that might even come *close* was desirable. Heart-stopping, soul-stealing, body-pleasing desirable, and yet it wasn't any single one of his features that made him so beautiful to look at, it was how all of them had come together on an exquisitely masculine form.

A touch of humor found Ariel when she noticed that Kaylee's hand had crept over and was now covered by Komet's. She couldn't help smiling, approving wholeheartedly with Kaylee's taste in father figures. The smile widening as she thought back to the moment when they'd reached the car and her daughter had become a small general, ordering her into the backseat while insisting that she and Zeraac needed to sit in the front so that she could be close to Komet. *I'll share them with you when we get where we're going, Mommy. But right now, I need both of our angels.*

Komet found navigating the streets of San Francisco, while using the human means of transportation, more harrowing than wading through a maze of carnivorous plants. Several times during the short trip, Zeraac's mentally shouted *Pay attention!* had nearly caused him to wreck.

But how was he to focus on the other vehicles or the crazed pedestrians who made a game of stepping out in front of him when Ariel and Kaylee were present in the car? By the stars and the Goddess of the Amato, if he could have conjured up a mate, then she would have looked like Ariel. From the moment he'd seen her, he'd known there would be no other for him, that the reason he'd found it so easy to resist anything more than a casual liaison with other females, was because he'd been waiting to find her.

He rubbed his chest as he pulled into the driveway of the Council's house, relieved this part of the journey was almost over. He didn't expect that Ariel would fall into his arms as easily as others had, and he didn't care. He had a lifetime to woo her, to gain her trust and love, and he didn't doubt that he could do it. But first the binding ceremony must be completed so they could travel to Belizair, immediately.

Panic threatened to fill his chest when he was forced to drop Kaylee's hand in order to get out of the car. While his hand had covered Kaylee's, he had felt the Ylan stones in her wristbands pulsing with agitation and warning, drawing on the healing ability in his own bands and sending a message to hurry.

Like almost everyone who lived on Belizair, Komet had studied the Ylan stones since the days of his childhood. They were a mystery most spent their entire lives exploring and appreciating — and never fully understanding. For the Amato they had come to be enmeshed in their religion — the Goddess' consort taking physical form. For the Vesti they were part of the natural world, yet another gift of their one god, a wandering god who had created them and then traveled on to create other worlds. No doubt both religions had roots in yet another belief once held by the ancient Fallon, but lost long ago, just as the ability to shapeshift into other winged forms had been lost.

Wherever the truth lay, the Ylan stones protected and aided the people of Belizair. Some of the stones operated the same way every time, but the results of using others were varied, and some, like those he used in crafting the bands for Kaylee and Ariel, were so rare that little could be claimed about them, except that they would cause no harm to one with a link to the Fallon.

Jeqon opened the front door and stepped out, sending a message as he did so. *Go around back. Not the first door, but the gate through the garden.*

We need to get to the transport chamber. There is no time to sightsee and ease into this, Komet said.

There is even less time than you know of. My uncle has arrived. I will keep him busy while you slip into the transport chamber.

Fear settled in Zeraac's chest at the mention of the Council member. *Why is he here?* he asked, taking Ariel's hand and detouring to the path leading around the house.

Who knows? I have managed to avoid letting him ask me questions, and will continue my efforts. All should be ready for you on the other end. One of Lyan's brothers was here earlier and since you are now related by Adan's sharing of a bond-mate, I asked him to help prepare for your arrival on Winseka. Both a Vesti and Amato healer are waiting to take Kaylee.

A lump formed in Zeraac's throat. *My thanks, Jeqon.*

Mine as well, Komet said as they disappeared around the corner and found the garden, hurrying through it despite Ariel's laughing protest about it being the reason for their visit.

Only when they got to the transport chamber and sealed the door behind them did they relax, and only then, just a little bit. *You know them better than I, Zeraac,* Komet said, *I will follow your lead.*

Zeraac nodded slightly, heading for the center of the chamber with Ariel in tow and Komet following. Usually a bed or a couch rested inside the multiple rings of Ylan stone, but today there were four pillows in a tight circle. His wristbands were pulsing and he knew that Kaylee also felt the power. "Almost there," he whispered, glad her face was full of nervous excitement and not fear.

Men! Ariel laughed silently. *Insist you have to see something, then hurry you along!*

Still, what she could see was beautiful. The ceiling was see-through to allow the sun to shine on an exquisite collection of flowering plants. Beneath her feet were colorful stones arranged in complex exotic patterns. And in the center of the room, where Zeraac seemed determined to go, were four cushions set amid a spectacular pattern of crystals.

She could probably spend a week just studying the rocks and crystals in this room alone, and probably the same on the ones they'd raced by in the outside garden. Unlike Kaylee, who'd always been fascinated by any living creature, Ariel had once been a passionate rock collector. No mountain too high to climb in order to find something unique, no cave too deep to explore.

Zeraac came to a halt and lowered Kaylee onto a gold cushion, the color of it catching Ariel's eye because it matched the stones in Zeraac's wristbands.

Komet stopped next to her, a crystal box in his hand. Ariel's heart jerked and raced, noticing for the first time that he had bands similar to the ones around Zeraac's wrists, only instead of molten gold, the stones Komet had were blue with flecks of green.

"To fully appreciate the room, we must all sit here," Zeraac said, his body language urging Ariel to take a seat.

She lowered herself to a cushion, her heart rate accelerating when Zeraac stripped his shirt off and tossed it outside the circle of crystals before kneeling on the cushion between her and Kaylee. Her stomach turned over when Komet also dispensed with his shirt, exposing more of a body she was finding it increasingly hard to ignore, as he knelt on a cushion at her side.

"Mommy needs wristbands, too," Kaylee said, the mix of emotions in her daughter's voice suddenly filling Ariel with uneasiness. An uneasiness that grew when Kaylee pulled back her jacket sleeves and exposed her wrists.

Zeraac's soft laugh eased some of the tension inside of Ariel. "Never fear, Kaylee. Komet and I have not forgotten such an important matter." He brought Ariel's hand to his mouth and pressed a kiss against it. "What Kaylee says is true. Humor us by wearing the bracelets."

"This is shades of the sixties," Ariel said, wrinkling her nose but finding no reason to protest.

Komet opened the engraved box and handed Zeraac a bracelet, repeating with Ariel what they'd already done with Kaylee, their minds open to each other as they watched for Ariel's reaction when they slipped the bracelets on her wrists and the bands tightened, becoming a part of her until she died, the crystals swirling to life, giving and receiving in a symbiotic relationship that none truly understood.

We will show her our true forms before we transport, or afterward? Komet asked, relieved that Ariel seemed more fascinated by the crystals than concerned by the tight bands.

I do not know which would be best. Once we are a bonded family unit, the stones will reduce the danger to Kaylee. But perhaps it is best not to linger here. Ariel is strong, and Kaylee has already planted the idea that we are angels from their Heaven.

Uneasiness swirled through Komet. *And you will fit that mold, while I will appear to her like a demon from their Hell.*

Stunned surprise trapped Zeraac into speechlessness. Though he hadn't let himself dwell on it, one look at Komet and a part of him had feared Ariel would cease to want *his* touch after meeting the other man. And though she had done nothing overt, he had sensed her attraction to Komet, had caught her glancing at the Vesti while they were in the car, and had watched her eyes dilate when Komet had removed his shirt. And yet her easy laugh, the way her hand softened in his, the way she'd trusted him, all served to chase away his not-fully formed fear.

Zeraac raised his eyebrows. *You do not think you can coax her into looking beyond your wings? You do not think you can use the Vesti mating fangs in such a way that she will come to crave your bite?*

Komet's answering frown was fierce. *Of course I can.*

Then why do you delay our trip to Winseka with worries about your appearance?

A small laugh escaped and Komet reached for Ariel's free hand, his other taking Kaylee's. *Why indeed.*

Let us proceed then, first with the binding, and immediately after, with the trip to Winseka, Zeraac said, closing his eyes and focusing on the Ylan stones at his wrists, knowing that Komet was doing the same—both men prepared to will a part of their Ylan stone into both Ariel's and Kaylee's wristbands. But there was no need to force the transfer.

Zeraac knew by the sudden heaviness of his own bracelets that the Ylan stones were swelling, growing in mass, pulsing, synchronizing themselves not only to the stones at Komet's wrists, but with those in Ariel's and Kaylee's bracelets as well. By all that was holy to the Amato, Zeraac was still reeling from the knowledge that Komet possessed Tears of the Goddess and had fashioned them into the bands for Ariel and Kaylee.

It was a gift beyond measure. An act of generosity Zeraac would not have dreamed of. A surprise. He had never heard of Ylan stones being present in a bracelet first placed on a human.

And yet the stones had immediately reacted to Ariel and Kaylee, claiming them both for Belizair. He doubted that they even required the stones from Komet's or his bands in order to transport, but he would take no chances, and even given a choice, he would still want to go through with the binding ceremony which would make them a family. Because of the circumstances, because of Kaylee's presence, the first binding wouldn't be sexual, wouldn't be as deep as a first joining usually was, but later, when he and Komet were alone with Ariel…

Kaylee's hand tightened in Zeraac's as the power swelled in the instant before the stones found a common rhythm, and then an unheard language whispered through each individual, making them strain to hear the words, making them lose themselves in a timeless, unseen place — returning abruptly when the common rhythm became more like a bolt of lightning passing from wrist to wrist, making the circuit three times before ceasing and leaving them dazed.

Ariel gasped, making Zeraac curse his lapse, the sudden awareness of both his own and Komet's wings all the urging he needed to initiate the transport sequence.

This time it was the stones around them that began to pulse in a sequence of light and color, the air in the chamber becoming charged, the crystals in their wristbands pulling on the energy around them. Both men tightened their grips on Ariel and Kaylee, sending reassurance and images of what was about to happen, even though they knew neither the child nor the woman was yet aware of the ability to communicate mind-to-mind.

And then it was done. Between one heartbeat and the next, they were on Belizair, though in the chamber room, all appeared to be the same.

Ariel's heart thundered in her ears, rushing so hard in her chest that she was afraid it would stop suddenly. Her wrists still throbbed and pulsed with a beat she had no control over. Just as she had no control over the thoughts and emotions pressing in on her, words and feelings—images and explanations that weren't her own, but belonged to the two men who still held her hands in theirs.

A jolt went through her as she turned her head to either side, seeing the wings again. Not shimmering into view this time, but solid. As real as her own body.

It was Kaylee who spoke first, her voice quivering as she pulled her hands away from Komet and Zeraac, pain and disillusionment in her words, in the tears on her face. "I thought it would be different in Heaven. But it's the same." Her voice broke on a sob. "I still hurt."

For the first time, Kaylee stiffened and resisted when Zeraac tried to take her into his arms, the rejection like a blade piercing through his heart. Komet interceded, cupping Kaylee's face. "Even here, on Belizair, such matters take time, Kaylee. There are healers waiting outside this chamber for you. After you have spent some time in their care you will be able to run and play and do all that you have ever desired, but it will take our scientists to truly rid you of the disease." He used his other hand to wipe the tears from her cheeks. "You say you still hurt, but is it the same as when you were on Earth? Can you not already breathe easier?"

Kaylee sniffed, her small face becoming a study in concentration, until finally she nodded. "You're right, I'm already a little better." She turned her attention to her mother and opened her arms, an invitation for a hug that Ariel hurried to answer, pulling Kaylee tightly against her body.

Ariel closed her eyes and buried her face in Kaylee's hair, not sure who was getting comfort and who was receiving it. The wild, confusing mix of emotions still leaving her feeling nearly paralyzed, even as a scattering of *her own* memories and thoughts assailed her.

Can't you see his wings? They're so shimmery that I can hardly stand to look at them. And she *had* allowed herself to see them in the fog, for an instant before rational thought took over and the image dissolved.

Then later, when Zeraac held her in his arms, hadn't she wanted to believe that he was an "angel", coming into their lives when they needed him the most?

Heat rushed to Ariel's face when she thought about what she and Zeraac had done on the couch, about the look of desire on his face, his sexual dominance and fierce erection.

Confusion followed the images and her mind skipped ahead, leading her to an answer before the question had fully formed.

My brother, Adan, is involved in law enforcement. The man who murdered your husband was killed by Adan's partner, Lyan d'Vesti, in a cabin where Krista was being held prisoner. But rather than free Krista from fear, she knew Alexi's death would only make his family members want to avenge him, striking out at both her and those she cared about. She sought protection and my brother and his partner offered it.

Komet's words of comfort a moment ago. *Even here, on Belizair, such matters take time, Kaylee. There are healers waiting outside this chamber for you. After you have spent some time in their care you will be able to run and play and do all that you have ever desired, but it will take our scientists to truly rid you of the disease.*

Belizair. It was a puzzle piece sliding into place. A shifting of Ariel's beliefs so that they meshed with the images and explanations that weren't her own. Not Heaven. But a different world. Not angels or demons, but something else entirely. Though there was no denying what her eyes had told her or what she could feel. Wings. The feathery texture of Zeraac's as it brushed against her arm, the soft, suedelike texture of Komet's as it brushed against her other arm, both men close, their scent and heat, and presence a protective cocoon. Their voices in her head — unless she was going insane, Ariel thought, managing a touch of humor — offering further explanation, but in that moment Ariel thought of the healers waiting for Kaylee and found she was willing to delay her own questions. The promise of seeing Kaylee run and play, of knowing her daughter would truly *live*, filling Ariel with courage and a willingness to face whatever challenges lay ahead.

She lifted her face from Kaylee's hair, meeting first Komet's eyes and then Zeraac's. "You can cure her?"

Pride filled both Zeraac and Komet at the strength and courage of their bond-mate. "Not us, but others who live on Belizair," Komet said, not sure whether or not she had accepted his earlier thoughts and images, and so he chose to speak out loud rather than give Ariel yet something else to adjust to.

Zeraac's hands went to Ariel's arm and back, relief surging through him when she didn't flinch away from his touch, but let him help her to her feet, Kaylee still held against her in a hug. "Komet is a scholar and scientist, he will be able to explain much of it to you, but we must leave the transport chamber in order for Kaylee's treatment to begin."

When Ariel nodded in acceptance, Komet's hand went to Kaylee's back, lightly stroking along her spine. "Our ways of caring for the sick and injured are different from yours. There are no doctors or hospitals. There are no visitors to witness the healing. What is done remains private between the healers and those they heal. No harm will come to Kaylee, on this Zeraac and I will swear a solemn oath. Children are valued here beyond all else. But Kaylee must go alone with the healers who will care for her."

A sob caught in Ariel's throat, trapping her instant denial before it could escape. It was Kaylee who answered for them both. "We can both be brave, Mommy. I'll go with the healers. You'll have Zeraac and Komet with you. It'll be okay."

Zeraac laughed softy and bent over, pressing a kiss to Kaylee's forehead. "It *will* be okay. You will learn much about our world from the healers while Komet and I will remain with your mother."

"Okay then. I'm ready. What about you, Mommy?"

Ariel's laugh was shaky, and there was no hiding the hint of tears in her eyes, but she said, "I'm ready."

Zeraac and Komet each put a hand on Ariel's arm, guiding her footsteps toward the door which would lead to the outer chamber, both of them casting a glance at the wooden chest just inside the doorway, both longing to be out of the uncomfortable Earth garb.

It will seem odd when we emerge dressed as we are, Komet said, a new concern starting to build in his gut. From the very first moment Jeqon had presented his plan for helping Komet obtain not only a bond-mate, but a child, he had worried that something would go wrong, that the chance would be snatched from him.

I know, Zeraac said, letting Komet feel his own uneasiness. *But there is no help for it. So far it has gone better than I dared hope it would.*

True. Komet took a deep breath as they got to the door, then gave the command for it to open.

I feared you were never going to emerge, Kaleaf d'Vesti said as he pushed away from the wall, his eyes going to Ariel and Kaylee, his sharp intake of breath audible to all. *By the stars, they are both exquisite.*

"Ariel, Kaylee," Zeraac said, hoping the others in the chamber would take the hint and use the human manner of speech. "This is Kaleaf d'Vesti. He is related to me through my brother Adan's mate-bond." His attention shifted to the elderly healers—the man Amato, the woman Vesti—who had risen from a crystal bench. Two girl children, both Vesti, rising with them.

"We thought your daughter might enjoy the company of our grandchildren while she was with us," the elderly man said.

Zeraac bowed his head slightly. "Your thoughtfulness is greatly appreciated, Healer." His hand moved to Ariel's back, but he didn't need to coax her into releasing Kaylee. After the initial embarrassment of being in the presence of females whose only clothing was haremlike pants, and men who wore little more than a loincloth fashioned from the same material, Kaylee was now completely focused on the children, and already signaling that she wanted to be put down.

"How long will she be with you?" Ariel asked, her face flushed with color at the exposed breasts and lack of a blouse on the elderly woman healer, her harem pants and the minimal covering on the men around her. God! This was going to take some getting used to! Ariel's color deepened when her mind leapt forward, presenting her with a picture of *her* parading around in public with so little clothing.

The woman healer shook her head. "There is no way of telling, but the suns will rise several times before the scientists can begin."

The male healer smiled gently. "Try not to worry about her, she will be safe and well cared for." He gestured with his hand toward where the three little girls, all about the same size, were already conversing quietly.

The tears that had threatened to escape earlier slid down Ariel's cheeks, drowning both Komet and Zeraac in emotion. "All will be well, beloved," Zeraac said, pulling her into his arms.

"I know," she whispered, encircling his waist as her tears dampened his chest. *Feeling* his reassurance. His absolute belief that Kaylee would be safe, well cared for, healed.

Joy raced through Zeraac at her touch, at her acceptance of his comfort, and he savored it—until he looked up and read the pain and longing in Komet's face. *Join us,* he said, finding a measure of humor in Komet's small step backward even though he understood its cause. The Amato had always bonded in whatever variation was agreeable to those involved. But the Vesti took only one mate.

Join us, he said again, *or it will look like we are not what we claim to be.*

81

Komet joined them, his own sense of humor returning as his hands rested on Ariel's shoulders. *This is difficult in a manner I had not yet imagined.*

We will find a way.

We will. But I, for one, long to do so in the privacy of our own living quarters. Komet's mind reached for Kaleaf's. *You have arranged a place for us?*

Yes. His words grew heavier. *But not without others learning of the match. If I were you, I would transport directly to your living quarters and not risk an encounter, especially dressed as you are.*

Where have you settled us? Zeraac asked.

I thought your bond-mate might find Krista's companionship comforting, so I found you quarters near where Adan and Lyan have settled. He grinned as he passed on the coordinates of their particular place. *But I would not rush to make introductions. Despite the fact that I was bringing news of your match, both your brother and my own were testy when I interrupted them from their "duties" to their new bond-mate.* His eyes dropped to Ariel and his voice dropped also. *I know you find yourself in a delicate situation, the details of which I do not wish to know for fear of being questioned, but I would urge you to see to your "duties" and make her your bond-mate in truth. Quickly.*

Zeraac nodded slightly. *Thank you for your efforts on our behalf.*

Kaleaf shrugged. *You are both family and friend now. And with any luck, I will soon join your ranks with a bond-mate of my own.*

You return to Earth?

Yes. Your bond-mate's belongings need to be dealt with and the impact of her disappearance minimized.

There was no time to mention this to Jeqon, but Kaylee had a young friend who claimed to see "angels" walking among the humans. You may find traces of her DNA on a small toy animal. Zeraac quickly replayed the earlier conversation with Ariel, pointing out Kaylee's kindergarten picture with the koala clinging to its frame.

I will leave now and tell Jeqon. Kaleaf grinned. *And then I will volunteer my superior services as a bounty hunter for the task of finding this child and her mother.*

As Kaleaf slipped into the transport chamber, the male healer said, "We should be leaving as well."

Ariel's heart jerked in her chest and she took a second to gather her composure before pulling away from Zeraac and Komet. Kaylee met her halfway, her bottom lip trembling even as she said, "It'll only be for a little while, Mommy. We can both be brave."

"I know, baby, we can be." Still, she gathered Kaylee into her arms and hugged her. "We can be brave, and the next time we see each other, we'll think of something to do that we've never been able to do before."

"I love you, Mommy."

"Oh baby. I love you so much."

"You're not going to start crying are you? 'Cause if you do, it'll make me start crying."

Ariel gave a little laugh, the tears streaming down her face yet again. "Of course not, neither one of us is going to cry. But I think maybe I'm allergic to some of these plants in here, because my eyes are watering."

"I think maybe I am, too."

She hugged Kaylee tighter, kissing the top of her head and whispering. "I love you so much. But you'd better go now. The sooner you go, the sooner you'll get back."

Kaylee returned the hug, then kissed her mother without commenting about the wetness on both of their faces. Her back straightened and her steps were sure as she walked over to the elderly healers. "Are we going to fly?"

The man scooped her up in his arms. "Not today, little one. But perhaps on the return trip we will travel in such a manner."

"You've never dropped anyone, have you? Because I don't have wings."

The healer chuckled, joining his hand to the elderly woman's, their grandchildren coming to stand next to them, taking each other's hand, one of them also clasping her grandmother's. "I have not dropped anyone…yet," the elder teased before all of them disappeared in the blink of an eye.

Chapter Seven

✂

Ariel looked around the room she suddenly found herself in, her heart jumping in her chest, her stomach telling her she'd been on a roller-coaster ride, while her mind tried to process the fact that they were no longer standing outside the transport chamber. "How did we get here?" she asked, trying not to be overwhelmed, wanting to do something that felt normal, to see something that might reinforce the idea that she hadn't completely lost her sanity. That she wasn't lying in a hospital bed on Earth, full of drugs because her mind had snapped. Because Kaylee had —

"Kaylee's with the healers," Zeraac said, feeling powerless when his words sent another burst of wild emotion through her.

"You can read my mind."

Zeraac grimaced. "Beloved, you're practically shouting." In truth it was closer to a panicked scream.

Ariel took a deep breath, catching a whisper of his thought. The image of herself becoming a hysterical female like the countless women she'd encountered in the hospital over the years doing a lot to help her regain her resolve. She was not afraid. She was not crazy. She was just in a new place with a different set of rules. "How did we get here?" she asked again.

Komet answered. "The Ylan stones, in combination with something you might think of as microcomputers which are part of our wristbands, allow us to transport short distances. Kaleaf provided the coordinates and so we were able to move between the two points."

"What is this place?"

"This is our home for now," Zeraac said, letting go of her and moving away as Komet did the same, both of them somehow knowing she needed space and time in order to find her balance.

Ariel rubbed her arms, then moved to the window—or rather the wall, since the entire room appeared to be formed of crystal—and looked out at a landscape of desert, with mountains far in the distance. "Where do the healers live?"

"In the mountains," Komet said, coming to stand next to her. "The mountains call to those with the talent to heal and they answer, separating themselves from the cities, living in small enclaves and serving all who ask for their help."

"Does everyone here on—Belizair—have wings?"

"Yes. I am Vesti, Zeraac Amato. Once we were a single race of winged shapeshifters known as the Fallon, but over time, we became separate races."

"The angels of God who came to Earth and mated with the sons and daughters of man and were kicked out of Heaven for doing it."

"That is one of your legends. One of your people's ways of interpreting our presence among them. The Fallon were attracted to humans and bred with them. You carry such a gene inside of you, as does Kaylee." He touched her wristband, his heart stilling as he noticed for the first time not only the change in her band, but the change in his own as well. *Zeraac!* he sent, momentarily distracted from the conversation.

Zeraac joined them at the window. His eyes widening when Komet pointed out the wristbands. Though the devices engraved on each pair were different, the combination of Ylan stones looked the same.

"By the Tears of the Goddess," Zeraac murmured, knowing no other way to explain why his own solid gold stones now contained the blue and green of Komet's as well as a hint of the sacred crystals that had once been on Ariel and Kaylee's bands.

"It has to be," Komet said, knowing as well as Zeraac did that when a bond was formed among two males from Belizair and a female from Earth, the stones from the males' bands migrated and combined in a swirling pattern on the female's wristbands, but did not change themselves.

"What's going on?" Ariel asked, unsure of whether or not to be worried by whatever was consuming Zeraac and Komet's attention.

Zeraac turned and stroked her cheek. "The stones in our wristbands have changed, perhaps it is a sign the Goddess and her consort have found favor with our match."

"Match?" Ariel cringed at the way her voice rose almost to the level of a squeak.

Zeraac stilled, cursing himself for having brought this conversation on, and yet strangely relieved at the same time. He took her wrist in his hand. "You are bonded to both Komet and me. You are our wife. Our bond-mate."

Ariel's eyes widened with shock, her gaze darting between the two men. "Wife?"

Komet's fingers encircled her other wrist, his thumb stroking over the stones in her band. "When our Ylan stones moved to your wristbands and Kaylee's we became a family group. After we...after the three of us...there will be more later, a deepening of the connection...not the tie of a family group but the bonding of adults who would be considered "married" in your world. If there had been time, we would have courted you on Earth, Ariel, let you get to know us, accept us as lovers, as mates, as fathers for Kaylee. But..." He shrugged. "There was no choice but to proceed as we did. The situation was dire and we were afraid Kaylee would be lost to all of us if we delayed. Binding you to us as our mate was the only way we could bring the two of you to Belizair."

Her mouth was dry, her womb fluttering traitorously, and yet she forced the words out, unable to keep her heart from racing and her face from flaming with color. "You intend to share me?"

Komet nodded, his face bearing testament to his own discomfort. But Zeraac's body tightened at her lack of horror, at the way she continued to let them hold her wrists captive, his cock filling so rapidly that he almost doubled over. "Yes," he said, images of the previous night assailing him, her whispered confession ringing in his ears, urging him to take charge as he had before, to consummate their bond and reduce the risk it could be challenged. "You belong to both of us now, Ariel. You are ours to pleasure and protect."

Zeraac sent only the briefest warning of his intentions to Komet before turning from the window and heading toward the sleeping quarters with Ariel's wrist still in his hand. She resisted, but only enough to make him anxious to get out of the confining clothing he'd been forced to wear, anxious to claim his bond-mate. She would do as they commanded, she wanted to do as they commanded—he knew that from what had happened on the couch in her apartment, from the way her face was flushed, her eyes showing a mix of feminine fear and desire. She longed to be with a man who would take charge and see to her needs, but they had to be firm with her now. They had to take control from the very start.

Already she'd proved herself to be strong and brave, adaptable. And Zeraac saw no reason to delay, to put off the deepening of the bond that would occur once they consummated the union, he and Komet touching their bands to hers as they coupled with her in a true joining. A true bonding.

Beads of sweat coated Komet's chest by the time they stepped into the sleeping chamber. In the span of a heartbeat, the Vesti mating fever had swamped him with heat, with instincts primitive and foreign to his nature.

He'd been prepared to woo Ariel, to take his time, to wait for her to invite him into her bed. But now...

Every cell in his body urged him to mate with her, to pound in and out of her until she acknowledged his dominance and accepted his protection, until she craved his touch as much as he needed hers.

He couldn't shed the uncomfortable Earth garments fast enough, couldn't wait to devour her body and feel her mouth on his. Couldn't wait to sink his mating teeth into her and inject the serum of his race into her body, making it impossible for her to ever escape him.

He'd thought he would loathe sharing a mate so intimately with another male, such was not the way of the Vesti, and yet now he found Zeraac's lust for their bond-mate only fueled his own. The unspoken competition between them becoming a way of giving their mate pleasure beyond any she could imagine.

"Take off your clothes, Ariel," Zeraac demanded. "We will dispose of them later. From this moment forward, when you are not naked, then you will wear what we provide."

Her eyes widened and Komet thought for a minute that she would defy Zeraac's command. His cock pulsed in anticipation, forcing his hand down to the painfully engorged organ, the movement causing Ariel's eyes to follow and her breath to come out in a shallow pant even as more blood rushed to his swollen penis.

By the stars. It had never been like this before!

Ariel's fingers shook as she slowly unbuttoned her shirt. God! She'd never thought to have this again. To have a man strong enough to command her. To take charge as Colin had in the early days. She'd never thought it possible that she'd have a man strong enough to command that she give herself to another man while he was present.

It was a fantasy of hers, fueled by the play with Colin, when he'd fuck her with a dildo at the same time he took her with his cock. And yet she'd never expected to experience it, to have the attention of two men, of two *husbands*.

She had no reason to doubt what they said, had caught traces of their thoughts and feelings though she tried to block the unfamiliar intrusion from her mind, finding it disorienting and confusing, more than she wanted to handle on top of everything else. She knew instinctively that it was pointless to protest their claim, and she was honest enough with herself to admit she didn't want to. *Husbands.* The word curled around her heart. She'd been so alone for so long that to be here like this came close to reducing her to tears.

Almost every day for the last nine years had been a struggle, a fight to find the strength to make it through one more day, to endure, to love, to give Kaylee what she needed. And now that burden was lifted. Her daughter would have a chance to live as she never had before.

Ariel would have yielded her body to Zeraac and Komet for that alone. But she knew this was no payment of a debt. This was a claiming.

Her shirt dropped to the floor and her bra followed. Feminine satisfaction roaring through her at the way both men moved closer, their eyes riveted on her tightly beaded nipples, both men wearing identical expressions of lust, their hands on their cocks, their bodies covered with a sheen of sweat, their wings quivering slightly.

She couldn't keep a small moan from escaping, couldn't stop herself from arching, from thrusting her breasts forward in a silent plea for approval and attention.

They responded immediately, pulling her to them and going to their knees, Komet's mouth latching hungrily onto her right breast while Zeraac attacked her left, the earlier command to take her clothing off forgotten as they struggled with what remained themselves, stripping her so that she stood before them naked, arousal coating her thighs, her bare mound finally drawing their attention away from her breasts.

"By the Goddess, I have never seen anything as beautiful as this," Zeraac whispered reverently before running his tongue along her slit and sucking her clit into his mouth, then moving back so that Komet could do the same.

Komet's mouth zeroed in on her heated skin, his senses overwhelmed by the feel and taste of it. *We must put her on the bed!* he said, knowing even as he said it that it would take all of his strength just to lift his face away from her hot, wet, flesh.

Agreed, Zeraac said, rising to his feet, the movement sending Komet's tongue stabbing aggressively into Ariel's cunt as he swallowed hungrily, the nectar of her arousal feeding the Vesti mating fever, making him growl and protest when Zeraac tried to pull her away. But he yielded, panting as he rose to his feet, already focused on burying his face between her thighs once again and exploring her smooth perfection.

Ariel was drowning in sensation, unable to put up even a token resistance as Zeraac positioned her on the bed, his lips covering hers, forcing her to taste herself as he speared his tongue in and out of her mouth.

His hand fondled her breast, his palm and fingers working her nipple, alternating between pain and pleasure, demonstrating his dominance, demonstrating his knowledge that he knew what she liked.

He held her upper body down as Komet's hands urged her to spread her legs. Rewarding her with the sounds of his pleasure when she obeyed, offering herself to him and arching upward, crying into Zeraac's mouth when Komet's tongue thrust in and out of her cunt, the moans he was making as he probed and sucked and ate her arousal sending her out of control, driving her higher and higher.

Komet was lost the minute his mouth once again reclaimed her cunt. Her whimpers were music to his ears, her scent a perfume more wonderful than the most exotic of flowers, and her taste…he would never get enough of her. He would forever desire her.

He tightened his grip on his penis, forcing himself to hold steady and not to pump through his closed fist until he came.

His tongue retreated from her sheath, the in and out thrusting testing his control, making his cock jerk and pulse and ache to spew.

Instead he moved to her swollen folds, licking over the skin and sucking at her cunt lips, enthralled by something he would never have imagined. Something that he would never have longed for. But something he would desperately crave from now on. A bare mound. A cunt kept ready for a man's mouth and tongue. For his pleasure.

She was hot to the touch, burning him, making him ravenous. With a groan he lifted his face, staring at her wet, flushed pussy for a long moment before his mouth covered her clit, sucking wildly, as though he would swallow her whole.

Zeraac moved to her breast, latching on to a pale nipple, biting, suckling, his actions timed to coordinate with Komet's assault on her clitoris. Satisfaction roaring through him at the way their joined efforts had Ariel writhing and pleading, the stones in her bands pulsing in time to theirs. Already he and Komet were attuned to each other. Their actions perfectly synchronized, choreographed with only one purpose, to please and claim their mate. And claim her they would, separately at first, and then together, becoming so closely bonded that it would seem as though there was no barrier separating them from each other.

He tightened his grip on her wrists when she began thrashing, arching, tears streaming from her eyes as she pleaded for release. But neither he nor Komet was ready to give it to her.

They drove her up, backing off when she was about to climax, slowing their assault, leaving her whimpering, shaking, so submissive that both men were covered in sweat, their cocks huge and full, their balls tight against their bodies, nearly ready to fight with each other in order to mount her.

"Please Zeraac, please Komet, one of you fuck me, please!" Ariel finally cried, shaking so desperately that she thought she'd die if one of them didn't stick his cock in her.

You take her first, Komet said, moving from between her legs, his hand tightening on his shaft, unsure whether or not he could keep from coming at the sight of Zeraac thrusting into her and bringing her to orgasm. By the stars, no wonder the Amato often bonded in arrangements that held more than one partner. Or perhaps the intensity of this experience was because they were bonded mates. Whatever the truth was, he'd never dreamed it would be like this, and yet now, he would never wish for anything less.

Zeraac urged Ariel to her hands and knees, sending Komet an image that had him closing his eyes and gritting his teeth. But he didn't turn down the offer to participate.

Ariel whimpered when Komet shifted position, moving so that his cock was near her face, his wings spread out behind him like some powerful beast from a legend. So far they hadn't let her touch them beyond spearing her hands in their hair and eating at their mouths. "Please," she whispered again, unable to take her eyes off Komet's penis. "Let me please you."

His laugh was husky, a sound of pure male satisfaction and anticipation as he tangled the fingers of one hand in her silky hair and pulled her head down to his erection, teasing them both by limiting just how much of him she could take in her mouth.

Ecstasy burned through Komet's veins, making him hunch over, his wings quivering with eagerness as her wet mouth and sinful tongue sucked and laved the head of his cock, stripping him of all vestiges of being a scholar and a scientist, reducing him to his most primitive form. His breath came in short pants, his hips jerked as he fucked her mouth, letting her have more and more of him in reward for her whimpers and mews of pleasure.

By the Goddess, Zeraac wasn't sure who was getting the better deal. The sounds of their pleasure had drawn his eyes away from her wet slit and erect clit, leaving him hungry for the feel of her mouth on *his* cock.

The fantasies he'd entertained those few moments on her couch were nothing compared to the reality of being with Ariel in this way. He had shared women before, though he had never imagined he would want to form a bond that would require it, but watching Ariel with Komet…it excited him, made his cock swell even larger, satisfied him even as it made him feel more savage.

Zeraac's attention returned to the sight that had transfixed him from the moment they'd gotten her clothing off her—the smooth, flushed skin of her bare cunt with its plump, swollen lips. He had never seen such a sight on an adult woman, would have cringed had someone told him it was alluring—but the sight of it now, the knowledge that it belonged to their bond-mate…he couldn't resist the temptation to lean forward, to press his mouth to her slick folds, to lap at her clit and slip his tongue inside her. His blood roaring in his head as the scent of her filled his nostrils, as the taste of her seduced him thoroughly. She arched her back, offering herself to him, pleading with her body for him to take her any way he wanted to, and he couldn't resist.

He rose to his knees and fitted the head of his cock to her opening, nearly coming at how small she was. A part of him thrilling at the realization it had been a long time since any man had penetrated her. And now she belonged to him, to them, to pleasure and protect.

Zeraac felt lightheaded, as though every drop of blood had gone to his cock by the time he was fully sheathed inside her. Every muscle in his body was taut, the edges of his wings rigid with the struggle to stay still as the tight, hot, pulsing squeeze of her inner muscles urged him to move, to thrust in and out of her violently.

He held steady for as long as he could, savoring the first mating, wishing he could draw it out. But even as he thought it, she pressed backward, forcing him deeper, drowning him with her arousal, and he couldn't fight the lure of her anymore, couldn't do anything other than see to her needs, and his, to take her hard and fast, dominantly, possessively. Komet's shouts of pleasure erupting before his own, the other man's cock leaving her mouth so that Zeraac could pin her down more forcefully, her whimpers and pleas letting him know how much she enjoyed what he was doing to her, her needs feeding his own until her cry of orgasm triggered his own lava-hot release.

The most primitive part of him wanted to stay on top of her, to remain buried in her channel, but he felt Komet's presence at his side and knew without looking that the Vesti mating fever was raging through the other man. With a groan, Zeraac rolled off Ariel, coming to a rest on his side, and watching as Komet immediately covered her, thrusting his cock all the way into her dripping cunt with a single stroke. Making her cry out and grab at the bedding, even as she changed the angle of her body, inviting Komet to go deeper, to slam against her cervix.

What they were doing to her, doing with her, was beyond anything Ariel had ever allowed herself to fantasize about. Every nerve ending in her body felt as though it had been created just for this purpose.

Her head dropped to the mattress, her arms strained, burned as she held herself in position, relishing the way first Zeraac and now Komet had mounted her, riding her fiercely — making her feel protected and cared for, stripping away her inhibitions and doubts in the process, leaving her bare and exposed and vulnerable, and yet more powerful for it.

She reveled in the way Komet was panting above her, craved his hard thrusts and the way he gave her more of his weight, dominating her as Zeraac had done. Making her plead for more and beg for release.

She shivered when his mouth moved over her shoulders and neck, his body hot and hard and forceful. "Bite me," she whispered and he did, sending her careening out of control and leaving her limp, sated, deeply content—satisfied beyond just the cravings of the flesh.

Komet rolled off her and Zeraac moved to her side, pulling her back against his front and kissing her shoulder while Komet pressed against her front, his mouth covering hers, their arms and legs shifting, entwining, tangling, their wings settling, trapping the heat of their bodies and drying their passion-wet skin.

Ariel explored Komet's golden-brown wing with her fingers, enjoying the texture, so like him—a smooth play of skin over firm muscle. She smiled when she realized she'd been so enthralled with the rest of him—of them—that she hadn't actually touched their wings before. He shivered under her touch, his cock hardening against her belly, and her body responded, coating her inner thighs with a fresh rush of arousal. "You like that," she whispered.

Very much so.

Her hand stilled, the beat of her heart accelerating. His thought clearer now. Easily understood. So real the words could have been spoken.

Zeraac laughed softly, his palm covering her breast, his mouth teasing her shoulder and neck before moving to her ear. *Easy, beloved, you will find there are advantages to speaking in this manner rather than the one you are accustomed to,* he said, proving the point by probing her sensitive channel with his tongue as he spoke.

She shifted restlessly between them, torn between her body's desire to have them again and her mind's need to adjust to this new reality—one she'd put of examining earlier.

Let us show you how natural it is to speak in this manner. How much better it can be. Let us give you release, Komet whispered, his thoughts in alignment with Zeraac's as they both moved, easing Ariel to her back, one of Komet's hands going to her wrists and pinning them to the bed, the fingers of his other tightening on her nipple as his mouth covered hers, his tongue gentle and yet demanding at the same time.

Zeraac slid down, latching onto her breast and suckling, his hand going between her legs, his palm gliding over her erect clit, circling it, teasing it so that the hood pulled back and exposed the most sensitive part.

Without even realizing she was doing it at first, Ariel's pleas sounded in their minds as her body writhed underneath them. They answered her with their hands and mouths, with their words of praise and caring, driving her higher, making her beg, leaving her no choice but to speak directly to them in the manner of their kind until she was sobbing, asking them to fuck her, to let her come, the words tumbling from her mind to theirs.

This time it was Komet who took her first, shoving his cock inside her as his tongue continued to dominate hers, his wings forming a dark cave where they lost themselves in ecstasy.

She could only whimper when Zeraac followed, settling over her, his face taut with need, his cock hard and hot as he pushed into her, and yet he was gentle this time, his strokes agonizingly slow, his kisses tender, thorough, loving, as he brought them both to orgasm, leaving her with tears streaming down her face from the sheer beauty of having this after being needy for so long.

Rest easy, beloved, we will always give you what you need, Zeraac said as they once again positioned themselves so that all three of them were cuddled together, warmed under the cover of soft wings.

Does everyone speak telepathically? Ariel asked, silently agreeing with their earlier comments, already seeing the benefit of it. She felt too lazy and sated to bother moving her lips.

Yes, though we also use our voices, Zeraac said, and Komet added, *We will have to teach you control though. For us, this is normal, something we do without thought from birth. But I have heard that some bond-mates struggle with it, inadvertently "saying" things to others that were meant to be private thoughts.*

Ariel laughed, then teased, *That could be embarrassing. Especially if I was mentally stripping someone of their skimpy little loincloth!*

Both men growled in reaction, swooping down to bite at her shoulders and neck, the sensitive outer shell of her ear, Zeraac reduced to the human means of communicating, "We'd better not catch you undressing any other male, with your hands, your eyes or your mind!"

She laughed again, enjoying the teasing. "Hmmm, I suppose the two of you could keep me suitably entertained."

We will make it our life's work, Komet said, his mouth covering hers in a quick, sweet kiss.

They settled once again, Ariel's thoughts going to Kaylee, a fist clamping around her heart in response.

"She will be okay," Komet said, knowing somehow that she needed to *hear* the words.

"Will they let us know how it's going?"

Zeraac's finger traveled down her nose and traced her lips. "No, they will return her when they think she is strong enough for the scientists to begin their work."

Ariel's heart jerked and Komet said, "The healers can only restore her organs, but without the intervention of the scientists, the disease would simply begin its assault again, reclaiming her cell-by-cell since its root is in her genes. The only way to completely heal her is to alter her genes, to make them healthy."

Questions bombarded Ariel's mind, but she suppressed them, not wanting to contemplate anything beyond the moment when Kaylee would return from her visit with the healers. When her daughter would be able to run and play and *live* as she'd never been able to do before.

They lay together for a long while, content, lightly dozing, until Ariel's body made her aware of how long it had been since she'd attended to its other needs. They rose, her face flaming as Komet showed her how to use the facilities by providing her with an imagined picture of her doing just that.

"A verbal explanation would have been better!" she shouted from the safety of the other side of the door and heard his answering laugh.

Someone had been thoughtful enough to leave a pair of pants similar to what the Vesti healer and her grandchildren had been wearing, though unlike the black they had worn, the outfit left for her was a combination gold and blue with green flecks, done in the exact shades of the odd stones in her wristbands. Ariel couldn't help smiling when she slipped the pants on. Men! Regardless of the species, if they could get away with dressing their women in easy-to-get-out-of clothing created using fabrics which teased, both concealing and revealing, they would. But she had to admit, she loved the feel of the material against her skin, and when she left the bathroom, the expressions on both Zeraac's and Komet's faces sent a sensual shiver through her body, making the touch of the cloth as it whispered over her bare cunt and clit almost painfully arousing.

Beautiful, Zeraac said, moving toward her as if he were unable to stop himself from doing it.

Exquisite, Komet murmured, also coming to stand in front of her, his erection and Zeraac's equally obvious, despite the fact that they'd also gotten dressed, the cloth the same, but Zeraac wore gold while Komet wore the blue with green flecks.

Ariel assumed the colors had some meaning, but she couldn't find it in her to open such a discussion. Instead she reached out, taking their cloth-covered cocks in her hands and teasing, "I don't know why you even bother with the pseudo loincloths. They don't leave very much to the imagination."

Both men laughed, pulling her against them, Zeraac saying, "I can see we have our work cut out for us, Komet. Our bond-mate has much to learn. The first lesson being that when we go out in public, her eyes should not drop to any other male's loin covering nor should her imagination follow!"

Ariel snickered, but before she could make a comeback, the room filled with a chiming sound and both men stiffened. *What is it?* she asked.

Someone pays us a visit, Komet answered. *You will answer it, Zeraac? Perhaps it is your brother.*

Perhaps. Though his voice did not sound as though he believed it.

Zeraac walked to a place in the dark crystal wall which looked just like the rest of the room they were in, save the side with the view of the desert and distant mountains. Without a word or gesture on his part, the wall seemed to dissolve and form a doorway.

The breath caught in Ariel's throat, not only at the sight of the sudden opening in the wall, but at the woman standing in the doorway. Her red hair and red-veined wings made Ariel think of an avenging angel and had her scrambling as best she could not to project her thoughts, especially when their eyes locked and Ariel could sense burning emotion beneath the beauty.

"So it's true," the woman said, not bothering to hide her disdain and disgust when her gaze moved to Komet. "You have taken someone else's chance at having children and have done so with one from the Araqiel clan-house."

"She is my match, Zantara, and who I ask to join me in the bond is my right by law."

Bitterness edged Zantara's voice when she said, "She is wasted on you, and he does not deserve a mate at all. Our scientists have not yet found enough of these human females to know for certain whether or not there is more than one possible match for them. It was wrong for you to claim her so quickly."

"She is mine and I have claimed her, as has Komet."

"And you think the Council will let this bond stand when there is no hope of children?"

Zeraac tensed. "You have had your say, Zantara. And because we were once a committed-pair I have allowed you to do so, but this is my binding day, and I would end this interruption now."

Without another word the wall reformed and Zeraac turned, Komet's somber voice seeming to fill the entire room. "The trouble begins."

Chapter Eight

ຄ

"Ex-wife?" Ariel asked, trying to keep her voice light despite the sudden ache in her heart.

"No, we intended to bond but didn't," Zeraac answered, his own voice holding a wealth of emotion, the intensity of it making Ariel return to the window and focus on the desert and distant mountains, on Kaylee.

Ariel pressed the pain and uncertainty deep inside herself, stiffening her spine and gathering her courage with the memory of her earlier resolve. She would face any challenge that lay ahead if it meant Kaylee would run and play, would truly *live* as a child should do. If Zeraac stilled loved another... She would find a way to cope. To deal with it.

She rubbed the wristbands, sorry now that she hadn't asked more questions before going to the bedroom with them. She felt foolish, uncertain—vulnerable. The old doubts about Colin's faithfulness, the insecurity of being married and yet always alone, suddenly assailing her.

It had seemed so right, so natural. But what did she really know about their customs? What did she know about their reasons for bringing her here?

Zeraac's shoulders slumped as he felt Ariel's pain and confusion and fear. *Go to her*, Komet urged, though the raw ball of emotions in the pit of his stomach, the dread of explaining his family's role in the devastation on Belizair, kept him from taking even the smallest step toward the window.

We are in this together, Zeraac reminded, stiffening his own spine and taking a step forward. Reminding himself that regardless of what might happen in the future, he—they—had accomplished something worth any sacrifice—they had

102

managed to get Kaylee to Belizair and into the hands of the healers.

Ariel felt them moving toward her. When they stopped on either side of her, she purposely used the spoken word in order to avoid breaking down and crying under the onslaught of all their combined emotions. "I've had to handle a lot of bad news. I'd rather you tell me what's going on. The truth, not some sugarcoated lie you think would be best for me. I've learned to deal with things rather than pretending everything is all right. In the end, pretending only hurts worse."

Zeraac couldn't stand so close to her and remain separate. He put his hand on her back, bracing himself to feel her flinch away, his heart easing when she didn't. "What do you wish to know?" he asked, feeling overwhelmed by the task of explaining *everything*. He was a warrior, better suited to actions than words.

A trace of humor fought its way into Ariel's thoughts, a touch of poignancy at hearing in Zeraac's voice something she'd heard in Colin's in the days when their marriage was whole, when she sometimes asked him for more than he thought he could give of himself—something that required words instead of actions. Explanation rather than demonstration.

He'd often managed to dodge her questions, to avoid looking too deeply into the roots of why he was the way he was, by luring her in to bed, by telling her he loved her, by showing her how much he needed her. And in the end, maybe it was because he couldn't look inside himself and change what needed to be changed that he hadn't been able to cope with Kaylee's disease.

But years of asking hard questions of the doctors treating Kaylee had made Ariel tougher than she'd once been, less able or willing to overlook an evasion or let someone escape without telling her what she wanted to know.

Still, Ariel started with the easiest, the least important question—for her. "What did she mean when she said there was no hope of children?"

Zeraac immediately stiffened, closing his eyes against the pain of what she'd asked, forcing the answer past lips that hated to hear the words spoken out loud. Hated acknowledging he was unable to perform perhaps the single most important task the Goddess and her consort had set out for him. "I am sterile. Made so by a weapon set loose upon Belizair by the Hotalings."

Ariel's eyebrows drew together. "You are not allowed to marry—" No, they didn't use that term. "You're not allowed to form a bond on this planet unless you can produce children together?"

Komet took pity on Zeraac, rushing in, prepared to face the pain of his own confession. "Until the bio-gene weapon was let loose on our planet, bonding was a private matter— and even now it remains so among the Vesti and Amato—but not when a match is made with a human female who carries the Fallon gene."

Now it was Ariel's turn to stiffen as she remembered Komet's earlier words. *The Fallon were attracted to humans and bred with them. You carry such a gene inside of you, as does Kaylee.*

A fresh wave of pain rushed through her, along with anger, and a terrible sense of betrayal. "That's why you and Zeraac were on Earth. That's why you brought Kaylee and me here. Because…" Her words tumbled to a halt in confusion— Zeraac's confession and the image of him standing with Kaylee in his arms, his cheeks wet with tears, leaving her confused, unable to make sense of the conflicting information.

She sagged, needing them to hold her, wishing she could let them get away with telling her everything would be all right.

As if sensing her willingness to listen, to remain calm, to consider their words and withhold judgment, Komet said, "Let us sit down, Ariel. The things Zeraac and I have to say are painful for us. It would be easier done if you would allow us to..." *to hold you.*

Ariel nodded, not resisting when they guided her to a piece of furniture that could have easily been an elegant, outrageously expensive designer bench on Earth—its frame done in crystal, its cushion some type of fabric that matched the color of the stone flooring, though the seat was higher than what she was used to. She took the middle position with Zeraac and Komet flanking her, their wings relaxed behind them, the tips just short of touching the floor. They each took one of her hands while their thighs pressed against hers, the heat of their bodies providing comfort.

Komet began, his voice pained when he said, "There will be time later for you to learn more about my clan-house, but for now, what is important for you to know is that some of its members were responsible for bringing in a virus that has left both the Vesti and Amato females unable to bear young. For now our scientists have determined that the only way either race will avoid extinction is if those males who are not yet bonded join in a mate-bond that includes a Vesti and Amato male and a human female. One who carries the Fallon gene. You are such a female, Ariel, and the marker you carry is a match for Zeraac. Because you are his match, it was his choice as to who his co-mate would be. He honored me by allowing me to join with him in claiming you." Komet squeezed Ariel's hand, not making any attempt to hide the intensity of his emotion, the joy that binding with her had brought him. "Even though there was no official sanction on the Araqiels, even though I have always been uninvolved in the business matters of my clan-house, I held little hope of a mate until Zeraac accepted me."

Tears welled up in Ariel's eyes—not for herself, but for him. "Komet," she whispered, pulling her hand out of Zeraac's so that she could spear her fingers into Komet's golden-brown locks and pull his face to hers, so that she could press her lips to his in a kiss that conveyed acceptance, the beginnings of love.

He groaned, leaning into her, deepening the kiss, finding all that he would ever need or want in her arms, in the softness of her body, in the way she touched his soul and claimed his heart with her generosity of spirit, her acceptance. Only reluctantly did he allow her to escape, to pull away and turn to Zeraac, offering the same to her other bond-mate.

Zeraac held her to him, his cheeks wet with tears, his heart glad they were in the privacy of their own quarters, his mind glad Komet was not the macho warrior his brother's Vesti co-mate, Lyan, was—though he would still have preferred Komet not witness such a show of emotion. "You are at peace with…" Zeraac could not force himself to say the words again, to admit his failure by speaking it, by letting the words hover in the air, as vile as the curse that had made him less than he once was.

"Zeraac," Ariel said, her voice so soft it was almost a sigh. "I'm not so quick to give up on miracles as you are. Your coming into my life when you did is proof enough for me that they happen. But, if we never had any more children, if Kaylee was our only child, I wouldn't care. Just to have her healthy, to see her grow up…to be able to do all the things with her that we've never been able to do before. That's enough for me. There's never been any room in my life to even think about wanting another child. I would have given my life for hers, Zeraac." She squeezed both of their hands, suspecting she already knew the answer, but wanting them to admit it—both to her, and to themselves. "If she's the only child we ever have, will she be enough for you? Or will you grow angry and bitter?"

Zeraac's laugh was shaky as he brought Ariel's hand to his mouth and kissed the back of it. "You know she captured my heart from the very first. I, too, would have given my own life if it would have spared her suffering and saved hers."

Komet leaned over and nuzzled into Ariel's neck. "I am equally smitten by our daughter. And if what Zeraac tells me is true, then I can hardly wait to show Kaylee our world and introduce her to the life forms that reside here."

Ariel smiled, turning her face so she could brush her lips against Komet's. *I suspect you have no idea what you're getting yourself into. Kaylee has an insatiable appetite when it comes to learning about wildlife.*

"I believe I am up to the task," he murmured, his voice going husky. He deepened the kiss, turning as he did so, rising and resettling his legs on either side of the bench before pulling her so that she straddled his lap. Zeraac positioned himself in the same way behind Ariel, then began trailing kisses along her bare shoulders as his hand wedged between Ariel's body and Komet's in order to cover her breast.

Ariel whimpered, amazed at how quickly the need could build, not just for any man, not just for sex after years of abstinence, but for these two men, for the joy and closeness she felt when she shared herself with them.

For several long minutes she was content to be held between them, to be touched and petted, worshipped with their hands and lips, with the hot feel of their naked torsos against her own bare chest and back, with the sounds of their increased breathing and the way their hearts pounded in sync with the rapid beat of her own.

"I need you both," she whispered, letting them see the true depth of her need, the desire to have them both at once as she'd only fantasized about before.

Zeraac groaned in response, his hand tightening on her nipple, his cock surging against her back, the thin fabric of their clothing serving only as a minimal barrier. He pressed a kiss to the juncture of her neck and shoulder, lingering, finding it hard to stop touching her long enough to move to the sleeping quarters—where the ritzca oil produced by the Vesti would ease the way and heighten the pleasure of taking her at the same time.

Komet caught the flavor of Zeraac's thoughts and his own cock jerked in response, anticipating not only the dual joining with Ariel and the opportunity to bind them more closely together, but the use of the ritzca oil. *Pick her up and carry her to our private chamber*, he said, moisture beading on the tip of his penis, his own need to penetrate Ariel rapidly growing beyond what he could endure.

Zeraac needed no further urging. In one smooth motion he slid from the seat and pulled Ariel into his arms, his steps already moving toward the sleeping quarters.

She laughed, her lips going to his, her tongue coaxing his to rub and twine and make love in the warmth of their mouths, just as it had been doing with Komet's only seconds before. She expected Zeraac to toss her to the bed, but instead he slowly lowered her to her feet, the slide of her body against his, arousing.

Beloved, he whispered in her mind, *you fill my heart as no other has ever done.*

She stilled, ending the kiss and pulling away just far enough so she could look up into his face. She could *feel* the truth in his words, she could *see* it in his face, but the image of the beautiful avenging angel — Amato — with her red-veined wings, her statuesque body and well-formed breasts, intruded on Ariel's happiness and brought with it a touch of doubt. *Even Zantara?*

"Ariel," Zeraac whispered, closing his eyes, the question and the memories it brought with it scouring his soul, savagely burning him as if he were standing in the desert when all three suns were at their highest point in the sky.

But he didn't turn away from it, instead he shared the most painful moment in his life with Ariel. Letting her hear the words Zantara had spoken to him.

I cannot bond with you, Zeraac. Not now. I would rather wait until the scientists have an answer, or take another as a mate. It is better to have a small chance of bearing a child than no chance at all.

No female wants to fail so miserably. To bind herself to a partner and then not see the fruit of their union in the form of a child.

And when it was done, Zeraac opened his heart and his mind further, letting her truly feel how her acceptance of him affected him, how profound his joy was at not only having a bond-mate to share his life with, but at having Kaylee for a daughter.

Komet moved in so that Ariel's body was pressed between his and Zeraac's, the earlier rush to take her giving way temporarily to softer, gentler emotion, to the need to simply savor the closeness, the bond neither man thought to have.

For long moments they stood near the bed, soaking in the warmth, the trust, the beginnings of love—content until the needs of the flesh to act on those feelings rose within and between them. But even then the desire wasn't fierce and urgent, but more like the slow filling of a well—deep and sustaining.

Zeraac's hand went to Ariel's face, his knuckles skimming cheeks still wet from the tears she'd shed when he shared his memory with her. *I would experience it again and again if the pain would lead me to you, Ariel*, he said before his knuckles moved to her mouth.

Her lips parted and her tongue reached out, caressing his skin, making his eyes darken as the mood shifted between them. Komet's mouth went to Ariel's neck, his cock once again ravenous as images of burying himself in Ariel's small channel, of having it tighten on him as Zeraac pushed into her back entrance, filled his thoughts, spilling over to the other two, making Ariel shiver and Zeraac pull away so they could get on the bed.

Komet stripped off his clothing then cupped Ariel's hips and slid her pants down in one smooth sweep leaving them pooled around her feet. "You are so beautiful," he whispered, knowing what hearing the words did to her, unable to stop himself from pressing his naked body to hers, from lowering his mouth to her shoulder as his hands moved around to cup her breasts, to tug and tease her sensitive nipples before going lower, to explore slick feminine flesh so alluring it almost made him dizzy any time he looked at the exposed folds. He longed to sink his mating fangs into her, to once again feel the rush as serum flowed through them in the exact moment his seed erupted from his testicles and burned through his cock.

Zeraac stepped back from them, stripping out of his own loin covering and moving around to retrieve the ritzca oil from a hidden compartment at the side of the bed, guessing from Komet's earlier thought that he would prefer to take Ariel's cunt this first time, but sending the question anyway.

Komet answered by moving away from Ariel long enough to lie down, his wings spread out like a soft brown comforter on the bed, Ariel's body an erotic contrast as he urged her to straddle him. As he commanded in a voice made raspy by desire, "Put my cock inside you, Ariel."

Ariel shivered, responding to the sight beneath her, to the dominance in his voice. She took his penis in her hand, whimpering at the hot, hard feel of it, at the way it pulsed against her palm, growing even larger and beading with moisture. She couldn't resist using her thumb to spread the drops of arousal over the silky head, her heart racing with pleasure when he groaned and arched upward, his face flushing with extreme pleasure even as he gritted his teeth and renewed his command in a harsher voice. *Put my cock inside you, Ariel. Now!*

She obeyed, but not with the speed or thoroughness his words demanded. She allowed only the tip of him to feel her wetness and heat, intending to slowly let the rest of him slide into her channel. But he had no intention of letting her tease and play with him in such a manner.

Komet drove upward, ramming through the fist of her hand and thrusting all the way into her, the force of his penetration making Ariel cry out in ecstasy and fall forward onto her hands, her breasts both an offer and a temptation that he couldn't resist. With a groan he latched onto a flushed, hard nipple, sucking and biting even as his hands smoothed and palmed her buttocks, waiting for Zeraac to get into position.

When Zeraac joined them, Komet gave Ariel's nipple one more sharp bite before releasing it and letting Zeraac force her down so they were lying chest to chest, his heart soaring when her lips immediately sought his.

Now, Zeraac urged, his own cock so hard that it raged at him to hurry up and penetrate her, the need becoming almost unbearable when Komet spread her buttocks and his eyes latched on to the small pink pucker of her anus. Still he hesitated, not wanting to shock or hurt her despite her desire to have this. *Have you done this before?* he asked, the question escaping though he immediately hated the image she gave him in response—a quick flash of her husband using both a cock and a toy on her at the same time.

This will be better, he growled, knowing it was foolish to feel competitive against a memory, and yet still wanting to make this experience so good for her that it would erase any memory of previous ones.

Without another word, he spread the ritzca oil on his fingers and began preparing her entrance for his cock, the oil heating up with the contact to skin, lubricating, heightening the need by making each nerve ending more sensitive, more aware.

Ariel was panting within seconds, spreading her legs wider and arching, writhing against Komet and pleading as the oil slid downward, working itself into her vagina and coating her clit.

Hurry! Komet urged, his own control nearly nonexistent as both Ariel's thrashing and the ritzca oil's assault on his penis demanded that he rush wildly toward release.

Almost there, Zeraac said, his face taut, his features strained, his wings spread over them, rigid from the effort to remain still. The fire of the oil was almost unbearable as he slowly worked his cock into Ariel. It was almost more than he could stand in combination with her tiny opening.

By the time he was fully seated, held tightly in her body, Komet's cock lodged against his own, separated by an almost nonexistent barrier, he was panting, left with no will, no thought other than to fuck, to merge completely.

With a groan he urged Komet to take her hands, to position them on the bed so that their wristbands touched, and as soon as it was done, Zeraac's hands meshed with theirs, his bands touching theirs, the Ylan crystals feeding on the connection, pulsing, singing an erotic song, weaving them together more tightly than had been done in the transport chamber, intensifying their feelings for one another, and reinforcing the rightness of their joining.

In perfect unison the three of them moved together as though this particular dance had been choreographed just for them, as though they had always been together in such a way, their movements synchronized, the sounds of their combined pleasure filling the room, filling their hearts, bonding them together so deeply it felt as if not only their bodies were joined, but their very souls. In unison they came, shuddering in a long, exquisite release.

Afterward they lay together in contentment, a mix of wings and arms and legs. Ariel smiled with the realization that she could easily start purring, she felt so languid and well satisfied. She reached out, her fingers stroking and exploring Zeraac's wing as her mind drifted to their earlier conversations.

"Komet said that the Fallon were once a single race of winged shapeshifters who eventually evolved into separate races. Can you change in to something else?"

Zeraac rubbed his cheek against her hair. "No. That was lost to us long ago. The wings are all that remain. If legend is to be believed, different clan-houses among the Fallon began to favor one form over another, breeding for that particular form and considering any others as lesser, until eventually they became separate races, warring among themselves until there were few pairs left of any one race. And so they bred outside their races, but in the process they lost the ability to shift form. The Amato once called the high peaks of the mountains home. Living there as birds of prey similar to your eagles. The Vesti were batlike in their alternate form, claiming the caves where the healers often settle now."

Ariel's hand traced over Zeraac's collarbone. "So all that's left of the Fallon are two races. The Amato and the Vesti?"

It was Komet who answered, nibbling at her shoulder before doing so. "Here on Belizair, yes. But there are those whose ancestors favored forms other than the eagle or bat, as well as planets other than our own."

"What other forms?"

Komet's arm rested on her side, his hand moving to cup her breast. "On Earth, they appeared in your myths as dragons, or faeries, or ancient gods." His fingers drew her nipple to a tight point, making her pussy clench in reaction. She laughed, still sated, and yet she could already feel the need building again. Her hand went to his, her fingers entwining with his, a jolt going from their joined hands straight to her clit when their wristbands touched, turning the laugh into a small moan. "The stones didn't do that before," she said as Komet gave her a sucking bite on the shoulder, his cock stirring against her buttocks, Zeraac's stirring against her belly.

"We weren't bonded mates before," Zeraac said, touching his wristband to theirs, sending another pulse of recognition, connection, unity, through their bodies. "As Komet said earlier, because of Kaylee's presence, the initial binding ceremony formed a family bond, much as would be done upon the birth of a child." His laugh was husky, utterly masculine as he leaned in and kissed Ariel before adding, "But what we have done together in bed...that has changed the nature of what we are to one another."

Her gaze dropped to where their bracelets touched. "I think I could spend a lifetime studying the Ylan stones."

Both men laughed. Zeraac said, "Then you will fit in well here. They are a fascination all on Belizair share. A mystery we all explore. When there is time, I will bring the stones in my collection here for you to look at."

"As will I," Komet said, the discussion triggering memories Ariel wouldn't have summoned, allowing an old sadness to invade her heart as her thoughts briefly flickered to the past, to Colin and the collection of rocks she'd once been so proud of. Many of which had been sold when money became tight, the few she couldn't bear to part with placed in a box and put away, for a time when she could look at them and remember without sadness or pain.

Beloved, Zeraac whispered in her mind, using the more intimate method of speech. *What is wrong?*

Ariel forced the memories aside, concentrating instead on the other items that had been left behind, items equally priceless to her—the photo albums and framed pictures chronicling Kaylee's life. "What will happen to our things on Earth?"

"They will be gathered and the things you truly desire will be brought here," Zeraac said.

"And our sudden disappearance?"

"The bounty hunters working for the Council will do what they can to minimize the impact." Zeraac shrugged. "Perhaps they will make it appear as though you have taken a trip, then decided not to return to San Francisco. In your world, it seems an easy thing to arrange for someone to leave and not be seen again."

"Too easy," Ariel agreed, thinking of Colin's parents, who lived in California, emotionally distant, estranged, even before their son had been murdered, and her own—one dead, but unavailable even when she'd been alive, the other missing since childhood.

As she'd done before, Ariel forced her thoughts away from the things that couldn't be changed, that weren't worth reflecting on, especially when she found herself in bed, between two gorgeous men who considered themselves her husbands.

Husbands. Plural. Their cocks, one against her buttocks, one against her belly, both standing straight and hard, making her think of huge exclamation marks emphasizing the point.

A small snicker escaped from Ariel, and then a laugh. She suddenly felt too playful to lie still. To cuddle.

She wriggled, making them groan as their penises jerked. "What about a shower?" she teased, remembering the large area in the bathroom which she'd guessed was used for that purpose.

Zeraac grinned, his gaze meeting Komet's, the silent, masculine exchange making Ariel suddenly wary about exactly what she'd suggested, especially when Zeraac rolled from the bed and then scooped her up in his arm. "It is our duty to see to your pleasure, Ariel, Komet and I can do nothing else but attend to your needs—in the bathing chamber."

She smiled despite herself, knowing that whatever they had planned, she could trust them. Even without the influence of the Ylan stones, she would have trusted them not to hurt her. But with the stones...she shivered, her body tightening in anticipation, the intensity of the shared emotions and sensations that came with the bond making each touch so much more.

Zeraac set her on her feet in the center of the shower stall—though stall was a misnomer. The area looked as though it had been built so that two could easily shower together with their wings expanded. Komet joined them and with a command, a hidden door moved into place, forming a seamless wall just like the one in the living room.

Ariel's breath caught when a second command was issued and the crystal walls began to fill with smoky color, grey-white at first, then darker, then silver, until they shone like mirrors, capturing and reflecting the image of her standing naked with Zeraac and Komet, her nipples tight, her vulva swollen, her skin flushed.

"Both the Amato and Vesti are a sensuous people," Zeraac murmured, moving to stand behind Ariel, his hands cupping her breasts.

This time it was he who gave a mental command and Ariel jerked, her gaze going to the ceiling where two thin ropes were descending from fixtures she'd assumed were shower heads. But before she had time to react further, Zeraac had the ropes around her wrists, their softness surprising her even as they reversed direction, rising, holding her hands above her head. Restraining her.

Ariel's heart thundered in her chest. Her womb fluttered wildly with the racing beat of her pulse. A whimper escaped and her body flooded with desire.

Had Zeraac guessed this was one of the things she had done with Colin? Allowing him to handcuff her. To take complete control of her physically. Sometimes even to punish her.

She shivered, meeting Zeraac's gaze in the mirror and seeing the dark hunger there, as though he knew what she was remembering and wanted to obliterate every memory of sex before she was his.

Komet moved to stand in front of her, his wings opened, relaxed, his cupped hand going to a dispenser on the wall, filling with liquid soap before he knelt as jets of warm water pulsed from the sides of the stall. Zeraac's hand also filled with soap, his voice husky when he repeated what he'd said in the bedroom. "It is our duty to see to your pleasure, Ariel, Komet and I can do nothing else but attend to your needs."

She moaned as Komet began soaping her legs, moving slowly upward to a pussy that was already screaming for his touch, while Zeraac's hands went to her shoulders, down her arms and around to her belly before moving upward toward breasts that were full and heavy, aching.

It was heaven and hell. Pleasure and pain. To be touched but unable to touch back. To be taken to the edge of release time and time again, but not allowed to come. The sensations magnified not only by the bond the Ylan stones had forged, but by the images captured in the mirrored walls. Not just of them bathing her, of their hands on her body, on her breasts and bare mound, but of them each kneeling in front of her, spreading her legs, positioning her so that she saw what they saw as they looked at her flushed, swollen cunt, the lips already open, exposing pink flesh. The images of their tongues and mouths as they'd eaten her, making her thrash and scream, were forever burned in her mind, carved on her soul.

She was shaking, whimpering, barely unable to stand when Zeraac released the ropes, guiding her to her hands and knees, the pulsing jets of water following them. "Now watch as your mates take you," he growled, covering her body with his, plunging his cock in with a single thrust, pounding into her, his wings spread out behind them.

And she watched, mesmerized, enthralled, her own desire raging, cresting, not just from the feel of him inside her, but at the sight of his winged body covering hers, at the sheer eroticism of being with a man who looked like he did, one whose face showed every nuance of pleasure as he fucked her. A pleasure that was echoed on Komet's face when he mounted after Zeraac slid from her body. His cock thrusting into her, renewing her need so that her channel tightened on him, hungry for his claiming, hungry for his seed, their bodies moving against each other in a timeless dance toward completion.

"Does dressing and feeding me fall under the 'attending to my needs' category," Ariel asked, still feeling nearly boneless after the water had turned into streams of air so that they emerged from the shower stall dry.

Zeraac chuckled. "If it were left to us, you would remain naked."

Ariel shook her head. Men!

Komet pulled her back to his front, hugging her to him in a gesture of companionship. "To dress you would mean our hands moving up your legs again, drawing near to a place that fascinates both Zeraac and me beyond all imagining. Such a thing would delay us from eating our first meal together." He pressed a kiss to her neck. "And if we are going to continue to see to your needs, I for one need some food to sustain me in my efforts."

Ariel placed her arms over his, their wristbands touching and sending tingles of pleasure through them both. "Food it is then." She grinned, feeling playful, thinking that after they'd eaten she just might turn the tables on *them* for a change. "Perhaps when we're done eating, I'll tie you down one at a time and coat your cocks with some of that oil, then tease you like you've teased me, until you're begging for me to let you come inside me."

Both men laughed, husky sounds indicating they weren't afraid to put themselves in her hands. Zeraac leaned in, pressing a brief kiss to her mouth. "It might be necessary to get stronger ropes, beloved, even without the ritzca oil, the desire to couple with you is enough to break what restraints we have here."

Ariel laughed, amused, her heart overflowing. "Food first, then we'll see whether or not your claims hold up."

They returned to the bedroom, the men trying to convince Ariel that she didn't need pants, but she insisted, sliding them on, once again noting how the colors matched the stones in their wristbands. "Do we wear these colors every day?" she asked after they'd returned to the main living area, moving over to the section that served as a kitchen.

"No, today is our binding day, it is tradition to wear the colors found in our bracelets—though Lyan's brother could not have known that Komet and I would need clothing to match *your* bands," Zeraac said, surprising Ariel by opening a cabinet door built into the wall, this one actually on hinges.

"How come the cabinet door doesn't just appear like the one leading outside or the one in the shower?" Ariel asked, diverted.

"Those require a certain amount of energy, but aren't opened and closed as many times during a day as a cabinet might be." He pulled out ceramic plates, putting them on the table. Pausing to give her a quick kiss. "Sit. We will see to the meal."

Ariel sat on something resembling a wide stool, grimacing. They were going to have to make some adaptations to the furniture if she was going to live with men who had wings. She wanted to sit on something with a back to it!

Komet prepared a tray of fruits and bread, placing it on the table, retreating to collect a pitcher of water and another that probably contained juice, though its color made Ariel think of sloe gin. For a while they ate, the men offering her tiny slices of fruit, feeding it to her as they gave her a name to go with it, chuckling when she teased them by nibbling and touching her tongue to their fingers. When they were finally full, Ariel's thoughts returned to her earlier line of questioning. "Are the colors of the Ylan stones significant?"

"Sometimes," Zeraac said, his gaze going to his wristbands, awed all over again at seeing the blue and green of Komet's Ylan stones as well as a hint of the sacred crystals woven into his own gold.

Komet traced a finger along Ariel's band, pleased that she was fascinated by the Ylan stones. That she would enjoy hunting for them as he did. "In some ways, they are similar to the gems you treasure on Earth. Some are rarer than others. Some have different qualities than others, though all are a source of power. When we are born, a portion of the Ylan stones belonging to our parents migrate to our wristbands, serving and protecting us until we move into the beginnings of adulthood. When we reach a certain point, they begin to fade and we choose our own stones."

Ariel leaned forward. Fascinated. "How?"

Komet laughed. "I can speak only for myself, and to a lesser extent, for the Vesti. We are all collectors of Ylan stones. Some stumble upon the stones they will claim in adulthood through trading, some gain them as a gift, others, like me, by discovering them as they explore Belizair. As soon as I unearthed them, I knew that when it was time, I would touch the Ylan stones I'd discovered to the bands and let them fill the place where my parent's stones had been."

"How do you know when it's time?"

Komet shook his head. "You just know, Ariel. It is almost as though the mountain calls you—like it does the healers—and you have no choice but to go. Though you also have no choice but to leave once the old stones fade and the new take their place."

Ariel turned her attention to Zeraac. "Was it the same for you?"

"Only in that I also went into the mountains. For the Amato, the choosing of the stones we will wear until we die is a sacred task the Goddess and her consort set before each of us. When we enter the mountains on the cusp of adulthood, our parents' stones leave us, so we are unprotected, freed, alone to contemplate who we are, to set a course for our lives and find grace with the Goddess. Some stay in the mountains for only hours before finding favor—the consort's own life force—in the form of the Ylan stones. Others remain for a week, or more."

Ariel shivered. "And some never come out of the mountains at all?"

Zeraac brought her hand to his mouth, pressing a kiss to it. "In my lifetime that has not happened."

"But it has happened."

He nodded and a sliver of fear wedged itself into Ariel's heart. "Will Kaylee have to go into the mountains when she gets older?"

Komet took Ariel's other hand. "We can not know for certain since she is the first human child brought here. But there are many years to prepare her, and her love of the natural world will make the task a pleasure for all of us. Do not worry needlessly. In our lifetime, no one entering the mountains as part of their passage into adulthood has been lost."

Ariel nodded, forcing the fear for Kaylee away, chiding herself gently as she did so, and yet also marveling at the miracle of Kaylee having a future beyond the next minute, the next hour, the next day to worry about.

Zeraac nibbled at her knuckles, his eyes dancing with mischief. "Now beloved, I believe you have set forth a challenge. Shall we return to the bedroom and test the strength of the ropes in the bed drawer?"

Ariel's body responded instantly. Her nipples answering for her, puckering into hard, tight knots, and drawing the men's attention to them so that they both leaned over, taking a pink bud in their mouth and sucking. She arched into them, her fingers weaving through their hair as she held them to her breasts for long moments, until she was nearly ready to pull her own pants down and position herself on the table so they could take her there.

A tempting idea, Zeraac said, letting her know her thoughts had escaped, again.

One I would certainly explore further, Komet agreed, giving one last pull on her nipple before he stood.

Zeraac also rose, pulling Ariel to her feet. A laugh escaping from her when their hands went to her hips as though they planned to push her pants down and proceed to take her on the table. But before they could do more, the living

121

area filled with the muted sounds of chiming, instantly killing the playful mood.

Komet strode toward the wall containing the hidden door while Zeraac and Ariel followed, stopping in the middle of the living area. Dread suddenly filling Ariel—a conviction that nothing good was waiting on the other side. She shivered, crossing her arms over her breasts, her near-naked state making her feel vulnerable where seconds before it had made her feel powerfully feminine.

Chapter Nine

ʂɔ

The doorway once again formed where there was no obvious opening and Ariel's chest tightened at the sight of the three people standing there, all with somber expressions on their faces. Zeraac stiffened next to her and she asked, *Who are they?*

I do not know the male, but the Amato and Vesti female both work for the Council.

The Amato male looked uncomfortable as his gaze swung to Ariel and then to Zeraac before saying, "Forgive me for the news I bring on your binding day. I am Galil d'Amato. A protest has been lodged against this union and the Council has sent me to both inform you and to gather some samples."

Komet stepped out of the way, the movement inviting Galil and his two companions inside, but Galil shook his head. "Again, I am sorry. This is not of my doing. But before I enter your dwelling I would disclose that until the matter of whether or not the mate-bond will stand has been settled, your bond-mate Ariel is to be housed separately. You will be allowed to visit her each day, either separately or together, but the Council recognizes that the bond will only deepen and her dependence on you will grow if she remains with you. So they have set limits in place."

Fear pulsed through Ariel, pushing away her discomfort at having her breasts exposed, so that she uncrossed her arms and reached for Zeraac's hand, desperately wanting him to say everything was going to be okay, but he didn't say *those* words. Instead he said, *Trust me, beloved, no harm will come to you on Belizair.*

"Where do you intend to take her?" Komet asked.

Galil indicated the women who were with him. "She will stay with Shiraz d'Vesti and Paraisio d'Amato. They will see to her safety and ensure she is comfortable here."

No! Ariel's heart and mind screamed in protest. "And if I refuse to go?" she said, unable to keep a slight tremor out of her voice. "Will you haul me out of here like a prisoner?"

A flash of sympathy appeared on Galil's face, and perhaps on Shiraz's as well, but he didn't answer Ariel's question directly. Instead he said, "It is not a punishment. And as I said, Zeraac and Komet will be allowed to visit you each day. You are also free to explore Winseka as long as you are accompanied by Paraisio or Shiraz. There are other human females here. They can arrange for you to meet and spend time with them if you desire."

"Who brings the complaint and what is the exact nature of it," Komet asked, redirecting the conversation. His voice full of resignation, making the fear settle more thoroughly in Ariel's chest.

"Raym d'Amato. He questions first whether or not Ariel is indeed a match for one of you and requests a retesting of DNA samples gathered here on Belizair. He questions secondly whether she came here willingly, accepting both of you as her mates before being transported here—as is required by Council law." Galil shifted uncomfortably. "Thirdly, he argues it best serves both races to set a bond aside in the event a human female with the Fallon gene is matched with a mate who…if there is no possibility of children coming from the bonding."

Pain speared through Ariel and she squeezed Zeraac's hand, wanting to turn to him and hug him, to reassure him once again that *he* was enough for her, and Komet a wonderful and welcomed bonus, that she didn't need to bear a child to be happy with them both.

Thoughts of Kaylee filled her with a new worry, making her words sharp, fear making her attack even though she knew Galil was only the messenger and not the force behind what was happening. "So the only interest your people have in mine is as broodmares? Whether or not we're happy here doesn't matter? Are we disposable once we've served our purpose?"

True horror flashed across Galil's face and he took a step backward. Zeraac interceded then, saying only, "Perhaps it would be best if you allowed us a few moments to talk with our bond-mate."

"We will wait underneath the trees," Galil said, relief in his voice.

The crystal wall reformed and Komet joined Zeraac and Ariel, taking her hand in his. "We will fight this, Ariel. There are twelve members on the Council, six Amato and six Vesti. Zeraac's clan-house has always been held in high-regard, there will be those who will step forward to support his right to form a bond." He hesitated before adding, "Two of the Council members are healers. I think it is likely they will come to our side in this as well. Especially when they learn of Kaylee."

Worry for her daughter choked Ariel so that it was no longer enough to have them simply holding her hands, and as if sensing it—or needing more themselves—both Komet and Zeraac turned so their bodies pressed against hers, their wings pulled forward so that Ariel felt as if she were in a cocoon of masculine skin, velvet suede and soft feathers. "Can't we just leave and go to where Kaylee is?" she whispered, hoping for a different answer than the one she knew they would give.

"I would love nothing more than to do so," Zeraac said. "But this fight would only be delayed, and in leaving we might well lose the support of some who would side with us."

She shivered. "Can they really take me away from you and give me to other men?"

Komet's hold on her tightened. "They might come to rule this bonding should not stand, but they cannot force you to mate with other males, Ariel. Even if they find another who matches the Fallon marker you carry, the choice to accept him or not would be yours."

"What about Kaylee?"

Komet brushed a kiss along Ariel's shoulder. "Nothing has changed, beloved. The healers will tend her and then she will be treated by the scientists while in our—your care. Though Galil did not mention her, it was never our intention to hide Kaylee's existence. But now the Council will learn of her sooner than they might have otherwise, and will probably involve themselves—though perhaps in the long run, that will be better for her, since they have more resources at their disposal than we do."

The fissures of worry in Ariel's chest expanded into a chasm. She hadn't once considered the cost of curing Kaylee. On Earth she'd been more fortunate than many. The insurance Colin had been entitled to had paid for the majority of Kaylee's medical care, but even then, what was left for her to pay had forced them to live on such a tight budget. What if…

Do not worry about such matters, Ariel, Zeraac said, covering her mouth with his own, kissing her. *Kaylee's health is critical to all of us. There is no "fee" to cure her. By resources, Komet means only that when it is time for the scientists to begin their work, it might be best if the male whose gene marker matches Kaylee's Fallon one has been located. I do not pretend to understand what will need to be done, but I do know that for her future happiness, it is important that nothing be done which might interfere with her ability to have healthy children.*

Ariel closed her eyes and relaxed against them, momentarily focusing only on their scent, their warmth, the contrast of hard muscle hidden under soft textures. "I don't want other husbands. Just you two. You're both perfect for me. And I don't want other fathers for Kaylee."

Komet rubbed his cheek against her hair. "You know we will do all in our power to keep the bond intact. And even if the Council rules against us, there is always the possibility that neither the Vesti justices nor the Amato priests will be able to enforce the edict by separating the Ylan stones and calling them back so they reside on their original wristbands. I have never seen such a mixing, where not only did our Ylan stones move to the bracelets you and Kaylee wear, but Zeraac's moved to mine, and some of mine moved to him, and the ones on your bands or Kaylee's, or perhaps both, moved to ours."

"What will happen next?" Ariel asked.

Komet sighed. "I believe the Council will wait until Kaylee is well before they meet. When they do so, we will be present and allowed to speak, then, much like your Supreme Court does, they will first vote on whether or not to consider the challenge."

"But there's no choice. I have to go with Galil."

"There is no choice in that," Zeraac said. "But it does not have to be a terrible thing, Ariel." His body firmed underneath her cheek, as though he would fill her with a new resolve. "You are free to explore, to learn more about our people and our ways. To make friends here. We will visit you as often and for as long as we are allowed. And when we are not with you, then we will be doing all in our power to see that the challenge to our mate-bond is put aside."

For a second his words filled Ariel with confidence and courage, but just as quickly a cold fear intruded as Galil's words repeated themselves in her mind. *They question secondly whether she came here willingly, accepting both of you as her mates before being transported here — as is required by Council law.*

Both Zeraac and Komet stiffened as Ariel's memory spread out like a dangerous pit between them. Uneasiness moved through her at the prospect of being interrogated. An intention formed, but the way their hearts jumped made her hesitate long enough for Komet to say, "You are a treasured addition to our world, Ariel. None will question you formally until the Council has decided whether or not to consider the challenge. Even then, you would not be expected to answer questions mind to mind, without the protection of the spoken word. But in our world, a lie is easily discovered and the liar's honor left tarnished, their company judged undesirable."

Ariel nodded, hearing both his spoken and unspoken words. "So be careful about *exactly* what I say—or don't say."

The tension left Komet's and Zeraac's bodies, and for several long minutes the three of them stood, knowing they couldn't put off the inevitable much longer. *I just have one favor to ask*, Ariel said. *I believe you when you say Kaylee is okay, but would one of you go and check on her? I need to hear you say that you've seen her. That the Council hasn't had her taken away from the healers.*

I will go, Ariel, Zeraac said. *Perhaps while I am there I can speak with the Council members who are also healers.*

Ariel nodded, hugging him to her before lifting her face, meeting his kiss fully, the rub of their tongues against each other both comforting and arousing. *I love you*, she said before pulling away and turning, her hands going to Komet's sides, her eyes going to his, seeing past the beauty of his features to the need he had for her to love him as well.

Tears welled up in Ariel's eyes as unbidden, images from the butterfly house came to mind, Komet rubbing Kaylee's back, pressing his own handkerchief to her mouth and urging her to spit. He'd known their marriage—their bond—might be challenged, that he might lose not only a mate but a daughter, and yet he'd still risked his heart—maybe even some of his honor in order to get them here.

I love you, she whispered in his mind, pressing her lips to Komet's, coaxing him into opening his mouth, to twining his tongue with hers. How could she not love them when the bond forged by the Ylan stones allowed her to feel the intensity of their emotions, the depth of their caring for both her and Kaylee. *I never expected to have two husbands, but there's more than enough room in my heart for both of you.*

His arms pulled her to him them, holding her tightly as he deepened the kiss, pouring his emotions into her soul, raw and painfully honest.

With the need for breath came the need to face what had to be faced. It was Zeraac who went to the door this time, opening it and mentally summoning Galil and his companions. "We are ready," he said when they arrived at the door, this time stepping inside the living quarters.

Galil pulled a small instrument from his pocket and offered a smile to Ariel. "If you will give me your hand then I will take a few drops of blood. That is all I require."

She offered her hand and an apology along with it. "I know you'd prefer not to be doing this. I'm sorry I was hard on you earlier, Galil."

He nodded, placing the instrument on the back of her hand where the vein was obvious, and within seconds the small clear chamber was red. "Thank you," he said, pulling the instrument away, his gaze meeting hers, soft with sympathy. "Shiraz and Paraisio will take you now."

For a second Ariel's heart felt as though it had seized. Her lungs burned and a knot formed in her throat, blocking sound and air alike. She felt rooted to the spot, unable to move, to respond.

Then Kaylee's sweet voice filled her mind and filled her with courage and pride, just as it had in the moments before her little girl's back had straightened and her sure steps had led her to the elderly healers who were waiting to take her away.

It'll only be for a little while, Mommy. We can both be brave.

I know, baby, we can be. We can be brave, and the next time we see each other, we'll think of something to do that we've never been able to do before.

Ariel took a deep shuddering breath then gave both Komet and Zeraac one last hug and kiss before nodding to the waiting women and saying, "I'm ready to go."

* * * * *

129

How many have gathered in Winseka? Zeraac asked, glad he could reach Galil's mind with his, sure that he would be unable to force the words through a throat that felt as if two hands were around it.

All but the healers and Miciah d'Vesti. He only recently returned to his home and now the rains have begun again. It will take time for the Council messengers to reach him.

Galil pulled two sample-gathering instruments out of his pocket and Zeraac stiffened at the sight of one of them, though he'd known a sample of his semen would be required. *I will take the blood first,* Galil said, *and allow you privacy, if you wish, for the second.* He turned his attention to Komet. *The same samples are required of you. Though you are not registered among those wishing to be matched with a human female, I assume you know how to use the equipment and provide a sample of your sperm.*

Komet grimaced and nodded.

* * * * *

Ariel was stunned by the beauty around her. She hadn't expected it—no, that wasn't right—she hadn't even thought about what this city might look like. "It's beautiful," she said, pausing to take in the buildings that looked as though they'd been done in a rainbow hue of crystal, one connected to another with elegant arches between them.

Everywhere she looked there were flowers reminding her of colorful tulips and trees reminiscent of palms, though that shouldn't have surprised her given the desert around them, the sense of being on an oasis surrounded first by dunes of yellow and red sand, and in the distance by towering, uncompromising mountains, their peaks ice-white and forbidding. She shivered, wondering why they seemed so inhospitable now when they hadn't seemed so from the window.

As if noticing her reaction, the Vesti—Shiraz—said, "The Amato call this part of Belizair the birthplace of the Goddess." Her hand swept toward the mountains. "And those are the

Arms of the Consort." She shrugged. "The Vesti have no special name for them, but we share a truth with the Amato. The mountains welcome us for only short periods of time, but then we sicken and must leave them."

"Except for the healers," Ariel said, remembering Komet's earlier words. *The mountains call to those with the talent to heal and they answer, separating themselves from the cities, living in small enclaves and serving all who ask for their help.*

Shiraz nodded. "Yes, only the healers make their homes in the mountains."

Ariel's eyebrows drew together. "So everyone else lives here?"

"No. There are three separate passes through the mountains. Two lead to fertile growing regions before reaching the sea. One leads to a jungle that only the Vesti have seen fit to live in."

The Amato female shuddered and fluffed her feathers, seeming to have come to some internal decision and now appearing more relaxed and approachable as she joined the conversation. "The bugs in that region relish our lighter skin and burrow into our wings. That is why you do not find us there."

Ariel touched one of her wristbands. "So when you want to go somewhere, you pop in and out. Except for when you want to go to another planet, then you use the portal chamber."

"You are correct in some ways," Paraisio said, once again fluffing her wings. "We can use our own Ylan stones to move about, but it drains them of energy, which then takes time to replace. So most often we choose to fly when we are within a city. Our distances are not so great that it can't be managed. The portal where you arrived was built by our ancient ancestors and much knowledge has been lost since the Fallon existed. Only those with permission to visit Earth use it. If it leads to other places, our scientists have yet to discover the pathways. And though the portal here cannot be moved, the chambers on Earth can be, as long as the stones are returned to their proper order. When we wish to travel to the planets we do business in, then we most often go to the city of Tarlifah where we have ships for that purpose."

Ariel couldn't help but shiver. It was real. *This* was real. And yet the thought of other beings, other planets, seemed momentarily *surreal*. "So Tarlifah is…like our Cape Canaveral? Or is it more like a huge airport where travelers come and go?"

Paraisio frowned. "I have not prepared for visiting your planet, so I do not understand your first term. But perhaps you would consider the place where our ships are an airport. Though a very small one. Only those whom the Goddess and Ylan embrace by allowing them to wear the stones are allowed to come here. There are no visitors to our world. The only ones here are Vesti, Amato, or human women like you, whose ancestors once mated with one of the Fallon."

"You don't let anyone else come here?"

"It is not for us to decide. It is the Goddess and Ylan who rule."

Ariel turned slightly to send a questioning glance at Shiraz. The Vesti woman shrugged. "We do not share the religion of the Amato. But what Paraisio says is true." She touched her own wristbands. "Without the Ylan stones, there is no entry or exit, no surviving here. Any who might try are rendered into particles so small that neither a healer nor Amato priest would be able to bring them back to their true form."

It was gruesome, something straight out of a horror movie, but Ariel had already noticed there didn't seem to be any way to remove the bands other than sever the hands or arms and then slide them off. She couldn't stop herself from saying, "But what's to prevent someone from killing one of you, or maiming you while you are on another planet and taking the bands?"

Shiraz shook her head. "The stones and those who wear them are one being. There is no way to separate the two."

Ariel's eyebrows drew together, but her heart jerked in recognition of the truth. She remembered the strange, disorienting sensation she'd experienced when Komet and Zeraac had first slipped the bands on her wrists. The even more profound one that had occurred when they were on Earth, linked together by joined hands in what she now knew was a binding ceremony.

And yet, they looked like stones, and stones weren't alive. At least not on Earth. But then again, on Earth it wasn't possible to use stones as a source of energy in order to disappear and reappear. "So the Ylan stones are symbionts?"

Shiraz frowned, "I am not sure that is the correct word. They are necessary for our survival, and yet..." She shrugged. "Perhaps Paraisio can take you to visit one of the Amato priests or priestesses and they can better explain. The Vesti have never been a race to question as the Amato have. We accept what the god provided for us before he moved on to other worlds, and we use it wisely."

Ariel shook her head, amazed that even here — among beings straight from the religious teachings of her own world — two separate belief systems had emerged from a common ancestor.

"Would you like to walk around now and see more of Winseka?" Shiraz asked. "Or would you prefer that we try and arrange a visit with another from Earth?"

"Let's walk and talk some more," Ariel said, realizing the tightness in her chest had faded, and despite being away from Zeraac and Komet, despite the trouble that lay ahead, she was enjoying learning about and exploring this new world.

* * * * *

Even in the mountains, Zeraac could feel the ascent of the third sun. He would shelter and take his rest among the healers. But first he wanted to visit with Kaylee.

His daughter. He already thought of her as such.

You have heard? he asked the elderly Amato healer who had come to the portal for Kaylee.

Yes, word reached us long before you did. The old man smiled. *Those of us who share this enclave give thanks to you and Komet for bringing Kaylee among us. She is like a rare Ylan stone, an exquisite treasure we are privileged to hold for even a short while.*

I felt as you do from the first moment I saw her.

Her mother has asked you to ensure that the Council has not taken her away? At Zeraac's surprised expression, the healer laughed. *Mothers are the same regardless of race. Come, your daughter is resting but will welcome your visit.*

Without another word, he guided Zeraac through the ancient, twisting, underground passages, their walls deep tones of Ylan stone set in symbols and patterns that had once held significance for the Fallon.

"Zeraac!" Kaylee yelled when she saw him, her body jerking into a sitting position before a spasm of coughs bent her over her knees.

He moved to her bed, his hand immediately going to her back, rubbing, offering comfort. Memories from Earth rushing in and leaving him feeling helpless, momentarily afraid for her.

"Take it easy, little one," the healer admonished, his voice unworried, "or you will undo all that we have accomplished this day."

The coughing stopped and Kaylee threw herself into Zeraac's arms as he sat on the edge of the bed, hugging him in a grip that would do a warrior proud. "I knew someone would come to check up on me."

His arms encircled her, pulling her tight as he buried his face in her soft hair, overcome with love for her. Other than

Ariel, she was the most precious thing in his world. Before the two of them had come into his life, he'd never imagined he could feel such a depth of emotion.

When the hug ended he said, "You had better lie down or the healer will tell me that I must leave before we have had a chance to visit."

Kaylee giggled and repositioned herself on the bed, modestly pulling the sheet up to cover her bare chest, the sight of the scars on it still stabbing at Zeraac's heart.

"I already feel a lot better," she said. "I even ate today without having to take medicines to help me digest it." Her nose wrinkled. "Is it really true? There are no Happy Meals here?"

Zeraac's eyebrows drew together. "You may be happy at meals if you wish. In fact it would please your mother and Komet and I to see you enjoy yourself all the time."

Peals of laughter escaped and Kaylee grabbed her sides before curling up and coughing again. Perplexed, Zeraac looked up at the elderly healer to find him also smiling.

"I am missing something here?" Zeraac asked.

An image flowed through his mind and pride filled him when he realized it was Kaylee, already adapting to their world, explaining what a Happy Meal was in terms he could see and understand.

"I fear it is true, Kaylee," he said, when she was once again on her back, this time with his hand held in hers. "I saw this place known as McDonald's when I was on your world. But I did not sample the food there."

"Maybe sometimes we can 'pretend' we're on Earth and you can hide a prize under my plate," she teased, though he sensed there was a deeper intent behind her words.

He squeezed her hand. "Perhaps. It is an idea that I will present to your mother and Komet when I return to Winseka."

The laughter faded from her face, her eyes growing serious, and yet still holding a child's vulnerability. "Are you and Komet going to be my new daddies?"

Zeraac's lungs seized, freezing him in place, slowing the moment so that eternity seemed to span between one heartbeat and the next, with only the words drawn from the deepest part of his soul allowing him to escape. "That is my wish as well as Komet's."

Kaylee sighed, the tension flowing from her body and releasing his as well. "I'd like that," she said. "I'd like that a lot."

He squeezed her hand gently, the feel of it in his large one both empowering and humbling, the gift of her trust and approval one he would never cease to appreciate or fail to deserve.

She turned onto her side, her fingers plucking at the edge of the sheet, her eyes suddenly fascinated by what she found there. "It'll be different once I'm well. We can do all kinds of fun things together. You won't be sorry if you become my daddy."

The haunting words Zeraac had first heard in the San Francisco fog reached across time and space. *Do you think it'll be different when I see Daddy the next time? Do you think he'll want to be with me if I'm not sick anymore?*

Zeraac's free hand went to her face, cupping it and turning it so that he could meet her gaze. "I would never be sorry to have you as my daughter, Kaylee. Even when we were back on Earth, and your pain tore my heart into shreds, I wanted to be your father."

Her too-old eyes bored into his, looking for the truth — finding it. "Sometimes my real...my other daddy would come in when he thought I was asleep," she whispered. "He used to kneel down next to the bed and just...cry. Only he never made a sound. And then in the morning he'd be gone, for weeks and weeks, so it seemed like I didn't have a daddy at all."

Chapter Ten

❧

Ariel woke to find the crystal walls around her still darkened against the intensity of Belizair's third sun, making it a time for sleeping on Belizair since it was both too hot and too bright to venture outside. What an amazing world. What an amazing place to be, to study, to explore. She could spend a lifetime just investigating the Ylan stones.

She rolled to her back, her heart swelling with a mix of happiness and melancholy as she thought about once again being able to do the things she used to do, only this time with Kaylee and Zeraac and Komet, as she remembered how much she'd loved hiking and camping and looking for rocks—how many weekends she and Colin had done just that. Escaping from their postage stamp-sized apartment in the city, from the demands of their day-to-day lives. He'd been a newly minted cop, she'd just started college. They'd been young, untested—their confidence that they could handle any challenge exceeded only by their belief that nothing bad would happen to them now that they'd found each other.

Ariel wiped the tears from her cheeks as she saw Colin's handsome face, his eyes dancing with mischief. "These are the only rocks worth looking for, Ariel, come and check them out," he'd tease, cupping himself, luring her back to their sleeping bag, or to a soft bank of moss. And she'd go, laughing, teasing him, playfully comparing his rocks to some of those in her collection.

She kicked off the sheet, smiling as she remembered Paraisio's questions regarding Earth homes, her shock at learning the beds there not only had top sheets—which she found strange enough—but often had heavy blankets as well.

"Don't your dwellings maintain a comfortable temperature for you?"

"We have air conditioners to cool rooms down and furnaces to heat them up, but they're expensive to run."

Paraisio's mouth had gaped. "You build with materials that do not react to the outside temperatures, reflecting or absorbing the sun's heat as necessary?"

"Most of our buildings are wood or steel or brick," Ariel had said, torn between amusement and outrage when Shiraz muttered, "I have heard others claim Earth was a backwater planet, but I found it hard to believe it could be so. Not when all hope of avoiding extinction seems to live there."

In the hours she'd spent exploring Winseka with them, she'd come to think of Paraisio and Shiraz as friends rather than guards. And she'd come to accept that they really were present to ensure her safety and comfort, and do their best to see she was happy. Well, as happy as she could be given she'd been separated from Zeraac and Komet.

Her nipples tightened and her cunt pulsed at the thought of the men, need building between one breath and the next, and Ariel's hands skimmed over her chest, settling on her breasts. She almost laughed out loud as she remembered Paraisio's horrified expression when Shiraz had offered to secure loin clothing, of a size for a boy, to serve as a sleeping garment should Ariel desire to wear something while she slept—Shiraz's voice suggesting that wearing sleeping clothes was yet another indication Earth was indeed a backwater planet. Ariel had elected to wear nothing, as was both the Vesti and Amato custom—though she had pointed out, with their wings, they had ready covering should they need it, while she did not.

Naked. Ariel closed her eyes, taking pleasure in the feel of the bottom sheet against her body, in the feel of her own hands on her breasts. It had been so long since she'd slept this way. Since she'd felt this way. Fully alive, ready to once again enjoy her sexuality.

One hand left her breast to trail over her abdomen and cup her bare mound. Colin had asked her to do this, and she'd found she liked it so much she'd never even considered allowing the hair to grow back.

She let herself think again about those early years, but there was too much pain between the present and the past for her to linger over the images of their sex life. There would always be a place in her heart for Colin, where she cherished the memory of him—of them as they once were. She'd made that promise to herself when she'd seen him closing up, walling himself off as their infant daughter became sicker and sicker. She'd promised not to allow bitterness and hate to destroy the memory of those good times and take a part of her soul along with them. And she hadn't, despite the times she'd felt mad, hurt, alone—when she'd screamed and cried and raged inside at the unfairness of it all. When she'd prayed for a miracle for Kaylee and offered her own life in exchange.

A miracle.

Kaylee's health.

But she'd gotten more than just one miracle.

She'd also gotten Zeraac and Komet.

Ariel's breath caught in her throat as her fingers began manipulating her nipple, her clit, swirling, stroking, wishing it was Komet's mouth on her breast, Zeraac's mouth between her legs.

A small moan escaped as her efforts grew more concentrated. As she tried to relive the moments she'd been with them. Her body responding, but warning that she'd only find minimal relief.

She accepted what was offered, cresting, a tiny hill instead of a mountain. But maybe it would be enough until they could visit her.

* * * * *

The healers will stand with us, Zeraac said, taking a seat at the table of what was supposed to be their home while Ariel and Kaylee settled in to life on Belizair.

Komet joined him, setting a bowl of fruit down between them. *How is Kaylee?*

Zeraac's smile was a bright flash of love and happiness. *Already much improved. Even the healers are in awe of her progress. Perhaps thanks to you. The Tears of the Goddess glitter brightly in her wristbands.*

Truly? Komet looked down at his own wristbands, then at Zeraac's. They looked as they had the previous day, changed, merged, gold and blue with green flecks and only a hint of glitter submerged in their depths.

Truly. They think she might well be strong enough to return before the third sun rises, but have suggested she remain in the mountains with them until a match is found for the Fallon gene. I agreed to allow it. His face was troubled as he met Komet's gaze. *The healers who serve on the Council took samples of Kaylee's blood and left when I did, promising to do all in their power to hasten a match.*

It is for the best.

Zeraac sighed. *I know and yet I cannot help but regret the loss of free will, free choice, especially when it comes to the selection of a mate. Both of our races have always valued it, claimed it as a right. Kaylee is only nine Earth years old. It seems unfair to…*

Komet laughed. *Spoken like a father who loves his daughter. The choice will remain hers, Zeraac. This is not like the betrothal customs the humans once widely embraced. Kaylee will accept the one who is genetically compatible with her, or not. Who knows what the future will bring. Perhaps there will be other answers to the Hotaling virus by the time she is old enough to bind herself to another and desire children.*

Zeraac picked up a piece of fruit and bit into it. *You are right. I worry about things in the future when there is plenty in the present to concern me. Did you meet with the scientists who sit on the Council?*

Yes. Both believe another genetic match could be found for Ariel. Both subscribe to the theory that perhaps there is both a potential Vesti and a potential Amato match for each human female with the Fallon gene marker. Komet shrugged. *I think it a reasonable idea given we still cannot explain why the combination of one matching mate and another of a different race are required in order to produce offspring.*

So they are looking for a Vesti mate for her?

I do not know. Perhaps. But even if they find one, they will tread carefully. Think of what it would mean to our cultures if suddenly the unmatched men began looking at another's bond-mate and wondering if she could have been theirs?

So the scientists on the Council will stand with us?

I don't know. The possibility of a second match is not something they want to become common knowledge. Not yet anyway. The human females are still too scarce. But... Komet shrugged. *We are threatened with extinction.*

If you were to guess?

Then I would say Jati d'Vesti will stand against and Gabri d'Amato will stand with us. Between the twelve Council members, we have accounted for half of them in the time since Ariel left, and three are with us, three against.

Zeraac stood and walked over to the window, the view clear now that the third sun had set, leaving the ever-present first sun alone with only a short time before the second would join it, officially starting the day on Belizair. Confusion rushed through him so fiercely that it escaped through his mouth. "I do not understand why Zantara set this thing into motion by going to her uncle! It was she who put me aside! She who decided she would rather wait for the scientists to find a solution—or failing that, at least take mates where one day there might at least be the *possibility* of having children."

Komet rose from his chair, unable to remain sitting in the face of Zeraac's pain. He closed the distance between them, placing a hand on the other man's shoulder. "I think we cannot truly understand the depth of suffering our women are experiencing. Both of our cultures have revered motherhood since the very beginning, when we were Fallon and not separate races. And now our women are stripped of what they have come to value in themselves and view as their most important purpose. Zantara is…perhaps she is confused and hurting…angry at herself for throwing you away…especially when she sees you have found happiness…that there is a possibility of happiness even without producing children." Komet shrugged. "I do not know, Zeraac, but I would guess she lashes out in reaction to her own pain, and in the final analysis it has very little to do with you."

Emotion swelled within Zeraac. Appreciation and caring, a bonding that was not carnal, but based in friendship, in the hope of a shared life together, a shared mate. It was no doubt what his brother, Adan, shared with Lyan, though their friendship had existed longer than their bonding with Krista. *I thank you for your words and your support.*

You would offer the same to me, Komet said, moving back to the table and picking up a piece of fruit. *Do you wish to visit Ariel separately, or together?*

You go and pass on the news about Kaylee. I will try and hunt down some of the other Amato Council members before visiting with her.

* * * * *

Zeraac entered the building where the Council members maintained offices. Where in a few short days, he would find himself in their judgment chamber, a place he had seen but never been called to—unlike his brother Adan's co-mate, Lyan, who probably had the room memorized. A small smile formed on Zeraac's face, the earlier warmth returning. He and Komet were well suited to share a mate. And if they managed to overcome the challenge to their mate-bond, he could see great pleasure in the years ahead as they cared for Ariel and shepherded Kaylee to adulthood.

His eyes closed briefly in a silent prayer to the Goddess and her consort. By all that the Amato held holy, he'd never known how powerful, how all encompassing a parent's love could be.

What he felt for Kaylee…it was beyond words. Beyond anything he could have imagined. And that she'd opened her heart so readily…it was a priceless gift. Just as the gift of Ariel's love was nearly overwhelming.

Zeraac's body tightened with thoughts of Ariel, though his mind shied away from what she might soon be doing with Komet. When he'd left the living quarters, he hadn't intended to seek out the one who'd initiated the challenge, Zantara's uncle, Raym d'Amato. But as he'd approached the building which served as the Council's seat in the desert region, he'd pushed his own painful emotion aside, facing the truth of what needed to be done. If Raym could be convinced to drop his challenge to the bond… Zeraac rounded the corner, his footsteps nearly coming to an abrupt halt when he saw Zantara emerging from her uncle's office.

It will do you no good to speak to him, she said, her voice harsh in his mind, her expression equally so, and yet, was there also a hint of guilt there?

Zeraac came to a stop in front of her, asking the same question he'd put to Komet earlier. *Why, Zantara? It was you who cast me aside. You who decided to pursue another path.*

And how quickly you acted to find another mate, even knowing that there would be no children! If you were suddenly so desperate to bond, why not choose from an Amato or Vesti female, one who wanted the life of a bounty hunter, one who had put aside dreams of motherhood?

I did not go to Earth seeking a mate. Surely you know that by now.

But you took one anyway! And not only that, but you took an Araqiel as a co-mate!

Confusion filled Zeraac as he tried to determine the true source of her anger. Did she not know that her own brother was friends with Komet, that Jeqon had been instrumental in seeing that Komet gained a bond-mate in Ariel?

He refrained from mentioning either, saying instead, *Komet is a scholar, a scientist. He is innocent of all blame for what has befallen Belizair. And regardless, what difference does it make? Are we not entitled to find a measure of happiness?*

Tears formed in Zantara's eyes, stabbing at Zeraac's heart despite all that had happened between them. But she quickly brushed them aside, her face hardening. *You find your happiness at the expense of others.*

Ariel is my match.

And what if there is another who could claim her?

The Council scientists have not found a second match for any of the human females carrying the Fallon marker.

Only because they have not continued to look once a first match was made.

Zeraac's chest tightened. *Ariel is my match, and both Komet and I have formed a bond with her, Zantara. We are…a family.*

As you and I could have been if you had not kept putting it off in favor of being a bounty hunter.

Guilt settled in Zeraac's stomach. An acknowledgement that what she said was true. If they'd bonded before the Hotaling's attack… If they'd started a family… But it was pointless to revisit the past. *I am sorry,* he said, the words inadequate.

And that means nothing now.

For an instant Zeraac thought he saw the hint of guilt appear on her face again. Then she added, *You will find my uncle will not be swayed by your arguments or your pleading,* before turning and striding away.

Zeraac hesitated, watching her disappear around the corner, emotion twisting and churning in his gut. But once again he braced himself, touching his hand to Raym's door though he suspected the Council member was well aware of what had taken place outside his private chambers.

Enter, came Raym's response, and Zeraac did so. Wishing now that he'd gotten to know the members of Zantara's family better. He had spent little time with her uncle.

You know why I am here, Zeraac said, seeing no point in delaying the confrontation or masking the purpose of his visit. *I ask that you drop your challenge to my mate-bond.*

Raym steepled his hands in front of his face. His expression holding no clue to his thoughts. *You will stand before me and say you broke no Council law when you brought the human female to Belizair?*

Zeraac knew then that it had been a mistake to seek out Raym. He had broken Council law on Earth in order to save Kaylee's life and he would do it all over again, but he would not stain his honor on Belizair by lying. *Ariel is my match, as the scientists have no doubt informed you. And we are bonded. If you ask her, she will say she is happy to be here, mated to Komet and me.*

That is not what I asked. I asked if you were willing to stand before me and say you broke no Council law when you brought the human female to Belizair.

I will not answer that question.

Then I will not drop my challenge.

Zeraac nodded and turned to leave. But as his hand touched the door, Raym said, *I would find the match less objectionable if you did not have an Araqiel as a co-mate. I suspect my nephew had something to do with Komet's selection, but if another Vesti stood in Komet's place…*

I am content with my choice of a co-mate. As is Ariel.

You can so easily accept him? Even knowing that because of his clan-house, there will be no children for you?

Zeraac masked his surprise, Raym's comment making him think the Council member didn't yet know about Kaylee. *What is done is done. Now is the time for working together so we may all thrive again.*

I was not one who voted in favor of no further sanctions. Had it been left to me, I would have banished the Araqiel clan-house from

Belizair. I would have sent every member of their house chasing after the Hotalings, unable to return until they found a way to undo the devastation they brought down on us all. But as you cannot vow that you have broken no law, or choose another Vesti as a co-mate, then I agree it is a time to look to the future. Where every human female carrying the Fallon gene marker must be placed in a mate-bond where offspring will result. The challenge stands.

* * * * *

Ariel moved around the room, restless, her body still on edge, needy.

"One, if not both of your bond-mates will arrive soon," Paraisio said from where she and Shiraz were playing a strategy game called Fett, which resembled chess.

Shiraz snickered. "And if not, there are toys in the bed drawer to ease the need. They are new, provided for you by the Council itself."

Ariel's face flamed, but curiosity halted her pacing. "You have sex toys here?"

Both Paraisio and Shiraz jerked their heads up, sharing a look before turning their attention to Ariel. It was Shiraz who said, "Has Komet told you anything of the business his clan-house pursues?"

Ariel thought back over the conversations she'd had with Komet and shook her head. "He said he was a scientist and a scholar, uninvolved in the business his family is in." Her eyes met theirs. "Though he did say it was because of his family that the virus making you...that these are such terrible times here." Ariel hesitated before adding, "I've come to think of you both as friends, but I've wondered how you can be so nice to me given that Komet is my bond-mate."

Paraisio sighed, pushing away from the table, pain in her face, in the way her soft white wings drooped, sweeping low to cover more space on the floor than they had only a moment before. "I was prepared to resent you," she admitted. "Even though the path of motherhood was not one I planned to follow, at least not for many years to come, I have a sister and am not immune to her suffering as she waits for the scientists to offer some hope of a child, and watches as our men line up for a human bond-mate. A mate we would have considered...deformed...only a short while ago. One not created in an image pleasing to our Goddess—the one we see in the sky around us and who gave us wings so that we might be close to her. But I have found we are more alike than different. And the pain you have endured is as great as any that we have suffered—though such a sickness as your child has experienced is unknown to us. The priests and priestesses claim the Goddess and Ylan are at work here. Perhaps they are correct." She smiled. "But regardless of what those on a higher plane may desire, I am happy you consider me a friend, Ariel. You are one I have already come to value as such."

"As do I," Shiraz said. "I volunteered when I heard what the Council planned to do. Your world interests me, and I harbor no ill-will toward the Araqiel clan-house." She sighed and looked away. "If they are to blame, then all who looked forward to seeking their pleasure with the artificial mates are also to blame."

At Ariel's questioning glance, Shiraz shook her head, her face filling with uncomfortable color. "The Araqiel clan-house is in the business of pleasure. They produce toys, along with the ritzca oil, and other such concoctions. In the course of their travels, they discovered...a toy...that was part machine and part humanoid, programmable for a wide range of pleasure—and one the women here would welcome. Only later did we learn it was a carefully designed weapon arranged for us by the Hotalings."

"Like a Trojan Horse," Ariel murmured, forestalling their questions with a picture from Ancient Greece, then a much fuzzier one of a computer virus sent in a harmless looking email.

Shiraz nodded. "Yes, like one of your Trojan Horses."

For a few minutes Ariel was able to let the subject drop, but then curiosity got the better of her. "You said these 'artificial mates' were programmable and would be welcomed by the women here, but from what I've learned so far, and seen so far..." her cheeks reddened, "and experienced so far, your men seem perfectly equipped for pleasure."

Shiraz and Paraisio exchanged glances before breaking into smiles and then laughter. It was Shiraz who finally answered, admitting with a grin, "Oh yes, our men are certainly equipped for pleasure. But unless you are prepared for motherhood, you enjoy them at your own risk. There is no birth control here except for the wash of a man's seed across your belly as he pulls from your body and comes." She sobered. "Or so it was before the virus."

Ariel allowed the subject to drop, pacing over to eat a purplish-colored fruit that tasted like an Anjou pear. Her friends returned to their strategy game, only stopping as a chiming sounded, indicating a visitor.

Komet.

Ariel was in his arms before he'd even stepped foot through the door. And he responded, holding her against his body tightly and covering her mouth with his. Raw emotion flowing back and forth between them.

All is well? Komet asked.

Yes. Have you heard from Zeraac about Kaylee?

He returned a short while ago. Kaylee has made amazing progress. The healers say they will bring her back for the last part of her cure as soon as a match is found for the Fallon marker she carries.

When they finally pulled away from each other, Shiraz said, "By Council order we must remain in the room with you, but I think it fair to say that with the door to Ariel's quarters open, it becomes part of the greater area." Her eyes danced as she glanced toward the table where the crystal game pieces sparkled in the sunlight coming through the window. "If you have need of either Paraisio or me, then call loudly as our attention is consumed by Fett. We are both slow players, so it is quite possible that by the time our game is finished, we will have erred and allowed you to stay past the time designated by the Council."

Ariel smiled, pulling away from Komet long enough to hug Shiraz, before grabbing his arm and leading him to her room, her hands going almost instantly to his loin covering, his rushing to remove her trousers, both of them groaning as naked flesh touched naked flesh.

Komet tumbled her to the bed and came down on top of her, his cock jerking at the feel of the smooth flesh between her legs. She wrapped her legs around him, so hungry for the feel of him that it was almost impossible to form a thought, much less words.

His penis slid into her, joining them together, and emotion ruled. Intense. Blistering. Leaving no room for anything except sensation, movement. Shared pleasure.

She came, crying into his mouth. Shivering as the hot wash of his orgasm filled her channel, her womb.

Only then could they talk. Their bodies still joined, the Ylan stones pulsing subtly in the rhythm of a contented purr as their sweat-slick bodies pressed against each other, his wings a warm blanket affording them privacy.

I love you, he said.

Ariel kissed him, teasing along his mouth, spearing her hands through his hair, *I love you, too.*

He returned the kiss, savoring the intimacy, savoring this first joining when it was only the two of them.

His mating fangs ached to drop from their hidden sheaths and sink into her neck, his mind and heart demanded that this time she be aware of them, that she accept this part of him openly and not recoil as though he was a demon from one of the human legends.

Reluctantly he lifted his lips from hers and met her gaze. She traced his nose with her finger, her eyes dark and sultry.

"You're so beautiful," she whispered. "When I look at you, I just want to eat you up."

His laugh was husky, his voice teasing. "I believe my clan-house produces a number of delicious body coatings..." His nostrils flared and his cock swelled in her channel as he remembered the feel of her hot, wet mouth on his organ. "But I am afraid that I am little more than a beast when your mouth is on me."

"And that's a problem?" she teased, her hands going to his shoulders, and then around to stroke the undersides of his wings, to explore their velvet texture and firm muscle, to caress the places where they attached to his body. He groaned in response, shuddering against her, his cock growing larger, more insistent. "They're sensitive, aren't they?" she whispered, her own body tightening at the expression on his face.

"Only to a lover's touch," he answered, lifting his wings, repositioning them, letting her see how they could attach to his arms and along the sides of his body and down the outside of his legs.

Her fingers moved to explore the new connections, sending another rush of blood to his penis and with it, a seductive smile to her lips. "Is there anything else you want to show me?"

Komet gave up the battle and let his mating fangs slip from their sheaths, allowing her see them—his heart nearly stopping at her expression of excited lust. "You bit me before, that first time when we made love."

His nostrils flared as the scent of her increased arousal reached him. "Yes."

She tilted her head back and arched her upper body, making an offering of her neck and breasts as she whispered, "Do it again."

And he did. Letting the veneer of scholar and scientist slip away, to be replaced by what he truly was, a Vesti male in the throes of the mating fever. He took her repeatedly, pinning her to the bed at first, then positioning her on her hands and knees, mounting her from behind, reveling in the way she was submissive, in the way her body shivered in anticipation of his touch, reveling in her cries of pleasure as he mated with her, his fangs sinking into her time and time again, his own ecstasy heightening with each climax as he injected her with the serum that once helped bring about pregnancy as well as make a female easy to track.

Wild, primitive urges assailed him even after his body was sated and they lay together under the cover of his golden-brown wings. He wanted to defy the Council and leave with her, to take her to his home and keep her there, to continue mating until some miracle occurred and she grew heavy with his child.

"I love you," she whispered, running her finger along his side, smiling at the knowledge that this man—who was so beautiful, so desirable, who could be both a gentle scholar and lust-ridden primitive—was hers.

Komet chuckled. Her thoughts reaching him and making his heart and cock swell. *Only for you, Ariel. No other has seen both sides of me.*

She gave a small embarrassed laugh, not meaning for him to hear *everything* she was thinking and yet when she was with him—or Zeraac—self-control was the last thing on her mind. Her color deepened a moment later, when she was reminded of just how uncontrolled she'd been, just how much of their unrestrained passion Paraisio and Shiraz *might* have heard when Shiraz's overloud voice reached them, reminding them of the open doorway and the others present, saying, "You win, Paraisio, and it's just as well the game is over. We have failed to pay attention to the time. Komet should have been long gone from here."

"Let me get a drink of juice first," Paraisio's voice was also a shout mixed with laughter, "and then I will ask him to leave."

We'd better get up, Ariel said, her arms tightening around Komet's waist in contradiction to her words.

He returned the hug. His body tense, as though a great struggle was taking place inside of him. But finally he sighed, rubbing his cheek against her hair as he repositioned his wings so they were folded behind his back. *Yes. They have allowed us more time and privacy than I hoped for.* He rose to his feet, pulling her along with him.

They were naked, kissing when Paraisio arrived at the doorway. *He's just leaving,* Ariel said, flushing—still not completely accustomed to the comfort the people on Belizair had with both nudity and the naturalness of sexual activity— but unwilling to pull her mouth from Komet's in order to speak out loud.

Yes, it looks that way, Paraisio said in a droll voice, making Ariel laugh and end the kiss.

"If I may have a moment in the cleansing chamber before I leave?" Komet said.

"Alone or I will no doubt have to call Shiraz in order to assist me with your—removal."

Ariel laughed when Komet's cock jumped against her abdomen—wondering whether it reacted in worry about being removed from Komet's body or whether it anticipated the challenge of being removed from her cunt. She gave him a quick kiss. "You can use the cleansing chamber in this room, I'll use another one."

And all too soon she was saying goodbye at the front entrance. Wishing she could go with Komet to the quarters she'd only been in briefly but already thought of as home. Wanting desperately to see not only Kaylee, but Zeraac. To have them all together in one place. A family.

"Zeraac will visit you when he is done with his tasks," Komet said, reluctantly pulling away from Ariel.

"If we're not here, we'll be at the market. We didn't have time to fully explore it before your third sun drove us inside yesterday."

"I will tell him."

Ariel nodded. The tears in her eyes making it hard for Komet to turn away and leave. But he forced himself to. There were a few Vesti he could call upon and ask to intercede with the Council, and beyond that, he wanted to meet with the scientists whose care Kaylee would soon be in. He needed to understand what they planned so he could prepare Ariel and Kaylee for what was to come.

"Shall we leave as well?" Shiraz asked, placing a friendly arm around Ariel's shoulder, trying to lighten the mood by adding, "Even from the back, he is beautiful, is he not?"

"More than just that," Ariel said, remembering her thoughts as they'd left the butterfly house on Earth. "How about heart-stopping, soul-stealing, body-pleasing desirable."

"I do not often think of the Vesti in such a way," Paraisio said, joining them at the doorway. "But your description of Komet, and the others of his clan-house, is accurate. Long ago, in the times written about but not well remembered, in the days before we found a way to live among each other without constant strife, it is said that whenever one of the Araqiel clan-house arrived in a city, the Amato men hid their mates and children for fear that they would be lured away by the beauty of the Araqiel."

"A demon leading the unwary into temptation," Ariel said, excited all over again by the culture and history of Belizair, and how it blended with that on Earth.

Shiraz twitched her wings in mock aggravation. "A demon, is that how you see me?"

Ariel laughed, her arms going around both of their waists. "As friends first." Then she teased, "And as an angel and a demon second."

Paraisio fluffed her wings, preening in fun. "Yes, I have always seen myself as one of your mythical beings. But would I truly be expected to play the golden instrument if I were to visit your planet? And would your men be so overcome by my beauty that they would be unable to perform sexually?"

Shiraz choked, laughing, surprise on her face as she turned to look at Paraisio. "You would lie with one of them?"

Paraisio shrugged. "Perhaps. Now that I have gotten to know Ariel, it has forced me to rethink my prejudices. To better understand why the Fallon and even some of our Vesti and Amato ancestors found those on Earth desirable." She grinned. "Or perhaps being in the same quarters while Komet and Ariel *conversed* has simply made me a little...out of sorts. Shall we go to the market before what is there has been picked over?"

They went, the sights and sounds and smells so intriguing that Ariel was able to put her worries and thoughts on hold as what she would have considered "morning" passed.

"Shall we eat here or return to our quarters?" Shiraz finally asked.

Ariel's stomach provided an answer. As did her mouth, watering at the mention of food, her hunger already primed by the hours spent both seeing and smelling a variety of breads and pastries and fruits. "I vote for here," she said, partially turning, a destination already in mind.

But just as quickly, all interest in food vanished as she spotted Zeraac, his attention fixed on a stall containing gems and stones. Laughter and joy raced through Ariel, along with tenderness at the thought that perhaps he was buying a gift before visiting her. She didn't wait for him to look up and see her, or for him to come to her. She raced over to where he was, taking only enough time to whisper his name before wrapping her arms around him and pressing her mouth to his.

He stiffened, actually taking a step backward and bumping into the stall, rattling the display of stones. His hands going to her hips, not to pull her more tightly against him, but to push her away.

He didn't need to.

Ariel jumped back, embarrassed color racing to her face, an apology tumbling out. "I'm sorry, I thought you were Zeraac."

The man she'd attacked actually grinned then, his attention going to someone behind her before returning to Ariel. His arms extending in the greeting she'd learned from Paraisio and Shiraz. "You must be my brother's bond-mate. I am Adan d'Amato."

She grasped his arms, briefly pressing her wristbands to his, almost instantly aware of a presence behind her in addition to Paraisio and Shiraz's. Her heart already thundering with the knowledge of who it was.

My brother, Adan, is involved in law enforcement. The man who murdered your husband was killed by Adan's partner, Lyan d'Vesti, in a cabin where Krista was being held prisoner. But rather than free Krista from fear, she knew Alexi's death would only make his family members want to avenge him, striking out at both her and those she cared about. She sought protection and my brother and his partner offered it.

Ariel took a deep, shuddering breath, trying desperately to suppress the sudden pain, the sudden return of the nightmare images she'd tried to put behind her in the last year. When she felt as though she wouldn't break down, she turned to meet the woman who had witnessed Colin's murder.

Chapter Eleven

೮

The two women stood, immobilized by the unplanned meeting, each looking for some clue as to what the other was thinking, each trapped for a moment by the events of the past. And yet, whatever Ariel might have thought or felt had she encountered Krista on Earth, it was irrelevant against the miracle of Zeraac, the explanation for his presence that he'd given in the police car near her apartment—*My brother's wife suggested I visit San Francisco*—suddenly filling her with certainty, making her say, "You sent Zeraac to check up on Kaylee and me."

Krista relaxed, her arm going around Adan's waist, a smile forming on her face. "Yes, though I admit, I had no idea the two of you would hit it off so well." She pinched her bond-mate's side. "I'd offer to show you around and tell you all about this place, but this is the first time *I've* been allowed to leave our living quarters."

Ariel laughed, her face heating with color, and knowledge. If the Council hadn't ordered her separated from Komet and Zeraac, she doubted she would have seen much of Winseka either.

"We were just on our way to grab a bite to eat," Ariel said, pausing to introduce Shiraz and Paraisio, "then we were going to continue exploring the market."

"Perhaps Adan and I can join you?"

"I'd like that," Ariel said, realizing it was true, realizing that in spite of the fact she already felt at home on Belizair, a small part of her longed to be with someone like her, human, without the grandeur of wings.

They ate, the conversation entertaining, friendly, and then afterward, as if reaching some unspoken agreement, Adan, Shiraz and Paraisio fell back as they moved through the market, allowing Ariel and Krista time with each other.

"Where is your other mate?" Ariel asked.

Krista grinned, her hand going to her abdomen. "Lyan is off somewhere plaguing the Council scientists for answers—or maybe just having a nervous breakdown in private."

"You're pregnant?" Ariel guessed, remembering the times when she'd placed a hand on her own abdomen, marveling that a life was growing inside of her.

Krista's eyes teared up, but she laughed. "Ignore me. I'm totally out of control emotionally—though I don't think I can blame it on hormones." She waved her arm, embracing their surroundings. "It's just everything—and finally being able to stop running from Alexi."

The name hung in the air for an uncomfortable moment, until Krista said, "I'm sorry. I had no idea what he was when I was dating him. But he's dead now—not that it changes the past."

Ariel took her hand, squeezing it. "It destroyed your life, too. But you've moved on, and now you have a child to look forward to."

Krista squeezed Ariel's hand in response. "Not one child, two. The scientists are fairly certain there will be both a Vesti and an Amato, but they aren't positive. The first women who were brought here are close to delivering. All of them are carrying twins and apparently each fetus contains the distinctive markers for *both* races, which was unexpected, but not alarming. It also strengthens the argument that the children will turn out to be one Vesti and one Amato since usually there are no Amato children when a Vesti is involved in a pairing."

"Every pregnant woman is carrying twins? A child of each race?" Ariel could only gape in amazement.

"Every one of them." Krista grinned. "Genetics isn't my specialty, math is, and for better or worse, Lyan and Adan are both bounty hunters—and not inclined to talk about scientific topics—" a snicker escaped "Actually they haven't been inclined to talk much at all since we got here. But from what history I have been able to gather, I'm guessing that we poor, wingless humans probably contain a purer sample and wider range of the Fallon genes than the Vesti and Amato here on Belizair do. I mean, we only mixed it up with other humans for thousands of years while their ancestors went out of their way to suppress some forms and emphasize others. Which makes one wonder exactly *what* form they took when they were creating the next generation. For some reason, I keep thinking about the myth of Leda and the swan. You know the one I'm talking about? Where Zeus took the form of a swan and had sex with Leda and she later gave birth to Helen of Troy. What if that was a common occurrence here way back when?"

Ariel choked on a laugh, trying to keep her mind from veering off into thoughts of kinky interspecies sex. "What about the wings? Don't the scientists have monitors? Aren't they able to tell the race of the babes that way?"

"They've got tests so they know the babies are healthy. And they've got monitors. So they know the sexes of the babies as soon as the pregnancy gets far enough along—but the wings don't manifest until after birth, when the wristbands are put on and a portion of the parent's Ylan stones migrate to the child's bracelet." Krista laughed. "You've got a daughter, so you know more about giving birth than I do, but I'll tell you one thing, the thought of trying to push out two kids, both with wings…" She shuddered dramatically. "Let's just say I was in a total state of freak-out just thinking about it!"

Ariel couldn't help but like Krista. "I think I'd feel the same way. Kaylee's birth was easy compared to some, but I still screamed and cursed and swore I'd never go through it again." She paused, the long-ago words forming a hollow place in her heart. "But I would, if God granted me another miracle. I'd gladly suffer through it all over again in order to give Zeraac and Komet children."

"Maybe you'll get your miracle," Krista said. "Being here makes me think anything is possible." She laughed. "Other than getting a Big Mac and fries...which I desperately crave— much to my bond-mates' horror. And ice cream—hah! I can already tell it's going to be a long, miserable pregnancy, at least for Adan and Lyan! Meat here is an expensive delicacy and the idea of keeping animals around for their milk is almost sacrilege if they're to be believed."

"There's no ice-cream?"

"None. Nada. Zilch. Though they swear they've got something similar to chocolate—which is part of the reason Adan and I were trolling the market today."

Ariel grinned. "Chocolate is definitely a good reason to shop."

And they did, spending much of the day together, searching and eventually finding what they were looking for in a small stall owned by an ancient Vesti woman.

"This is supposed to taste like chocolate?" Ariel said, skepticism in her voice as she and Krista leaned over a bin containing what both Adan and the Vesti stall owner called *yaschi*.

"It doesn't look very appetizing," Krista admitted. "Have you ever been to Santa Cruz?"

"Yes. And I know what you're thinking. Banana slugs. Yellow, squishy and slimy. Thankfully the yaschi appears to have the first two characteristics but not the third."

Krista snickered. "They're pretty shiny. That could be sunlight bouncing off moisture. So I wouldn't rule out slimy. Since I'm pregnant, with very delicate sensibilities, why don't you try them first?"

Ariel laughed. "Okay, but only because we've spent most of the day looking for this." Still she braced herself for the possibility that the yellow, sluglike "chocolates" were going to be slimy as she reached out, stopping before she actually picked up one of the yaschi. "I don't have any money."

Krista waved her hand. "You've probably got some. Didn't Zeraac tell you that the wristbands house a nanocomputer along with the Ylan stones? To pay for something—or so I've been told—you just present your right wrist and the vender scans over it, transferring the money from your account to theirs." She held her hand out to the vendor.

Adan laughed, pulling her arm back and saying, "Let me, beloved, it is slightly more complicated than that. You will empty our accounts if you are not careful." He smiled at the elderly Vesti vendor, offering his wrist. She touched her right band to his briefly. "All done. Now try the yaschi. I promise, you will find it almost exactly like the chocolates you claim to crave."

Krista pounced. "Almost?"

He hugged her to him. "Perhaps even better," he said, his mouth covering Krista's, her arms going around his neck as she returned the kiss.

Ariel couldn't help but smile, enjoying their company, happy for both of them. Her thoughts going to Zeraac and her body heating up, her nipples tightening and her womb fluttering. The sensation so intense that she though he must be nearby.

She turned, scanning the marketplace, a jolt of heat searing her belly and clit when her eyes connected with a Vesti male who stood several stalls away, staring at her intently, focused completely on her—scaring her with the intensity of his gaze and the way her body responded to it, desire coursing through her when there should be none.

Ariel turned back toward the yaschi, shaken. She enjoyed the sight of a handsome man as much as the next woman did, but she'd never been one to actively lust after strangers, especially when her heart was engaged elsewhere. And yet every cell in her body was humming in awareness of the unknown Vesti's presence, in awareness of his gaze caressing over her shoulders and down her spine, making her conscious of her bare breasts and tight nipples. It took all of her willpower to fight the urge to turn back around.

She tried to distract herself by picking up one of the yaschi, a mild relief filling her when she found it dry and slightly hard, like a caramel in cool air.

Krista pulled away from Adan, laughing and saying, "Well?" when she saw that Ariel had picked up one of the "chocolates".

"So far so good. It doesn't feel like a banana slug." Ariel closed her eyes, taking the plunge and biting into the yellow "candy", becoming completely distracted from her previous thoughts when a burst of flavor filled her mouth, the yaschi dissolving, coating her tongue with the taste of dark chocolate. "Wow," she said. Opening her eyes and reaching for a second candy, her body relaxing, her nipples going soft as she realized the disturbing male presence behind her was gone.

Adan had to offer his wrist to the vendor a second time before Ariel and Krista were done eating yaschi, and then a third time when Krista insisted she wanted to take some of the yellow candy back to their living quarters, laughing and saying, "I need to stock up. Who knows when you and Lyan will let me out again!"

They continued wandering, not just in the market, but the gardens around it, this time with Paraisio and Shiraz joining in the conversation, talking about some of the nearby planets and the inhabitants on them, only stopping when Zeraac appeared, obviously anxious for some time alone with Ariel.

Zeraac was grateful Paraisio and Shiraz did not expect him to linger or make polite conversation when they returned to the living quarters. Their muffled laughs as they retreated to where a game of Fett waited for play to begin were testament to the fact they had noticed the tenseness of his features and the erection making a mockery of his loin covering.

Ariel's soft laugh joined theirs, but where Paraisio and Shiraz's muted amusement brought a smile to Zeraac's face, Ariel's enflamed him, making his blood swirl hungrily through his body, making him wish for nothing more than to push her down on the cushioned bench only a few feet away from where they stood, and take her.

This way, she said, making his cock pulse with the urgency in her voice as she turned toward an open doorway, the sway of her long hair and hips entrancing him.

He followed, with little thought beyond getting them both out of their clothing. But her need was as great as his own. As soon as they were in her sleeping chambers, she pushed her pants off, letting them form a silky pool of blue at her feet.

Zeraac's gaze went immediately to her bare mound and his penis jerked, wetting the front of his loin covering with his arousal. By the Goddess, Ariel's smooth, flushed folds ensnared him.

"Get on the bed," he ordered, the need to dominate crashing down on him as soon as his eyes found the bite mark Komet had left on her inner thigh. A bite mark that even now glistened, coated with her juices.

She shivered, doing as he ordered, her ready obedience making the desire deepen in both of them. He stripped out of his clothing, taking his cock in his hand, remembering the sight of her pleasuring Komet with her mouth, how he had longed to feel her lips and tongue on him.

Later, he promised himself, the need to reassert his claim as her bond-mate more important than his own pleasure right now. He crawled up on the bed with her, positioning himself at her side, his hand between her already spread legs, exploring her wet inner thighs, her puffy cunt lips and erect clit.

She flushed under his regard, her face and breasts and mound deepening with color. Reminding him of their first encounter on her couch.

I've left you...hurting.

A little pain beforehand only heightens the anticipation and deepens the satisfaction.

There were things Colin and I liked to do, early on, before we were married, and then afterward, before we knew about Kaylee's illness. I think sometimes he blamed himself for her being born with a disease and having to suffer so much. He wouldn't talk about it, but I think he sometimes told himself it was God's way of punishing him for the things he – we – liked in the bedroom.

Zeraac had shied away from asking her for details then, though his imagination had reeled with images – the interlude in the shower making it even easier for him to guess at some of the things she might enjoy. And yet he wanted to please her, not frighten or offend her. But he feared some of the activities going through his mind would do just that.

His body grew rigid. He hated even the thought of her dead husband, though he knew the other man was no threat. He pitied the policeman for all he'd lost by his own actions – his wife and his daughter – even before he'd been murdered.

Zeraac's gaze found yet another one of Komet's bite marks, this one on her neck, near her hairline, and the need to claim her roared through him, overcoming his aversion to asking about her past.

His fingers plowed into her channel, his palm hard and dominant on her clit, making her whimper and arch even as he leaned in, kissing her roughly before asking, "Tell me what pleases you in the bedroom, Ariel."

"You do, Zeraac, anything you do pleases me."

He pulled his fingers from her sheath, removing his touch for only a second before bringing the palm of his hand down on her mound in a spank that had her breath catching and her body jerking, her legs widening before she whispered in his mind, *Oh yes. Please, Zeraac. Please.* And as if she too remembered their moments together in her apartment, she added, *Let me come, Zeraac. Make me come.*

Her cunt reddened, flushing with arousal and the sting of his spanks. The sight of it making Zeraac's cock swell and ache with need until he was no longer sure who was being sexually punished. Who was in control.

Lust raged through him, fierce and primitive, and he leaned over her, devouring her breasts, biting at her nipples, leaving them reddened and well loved as his hand drove her to her first orgasm, her screams filling the room as well as his soul.

And still it was not enough to satisfy the primitive craving in Zeraac. He levered himself off her just enough to open the bed drawer, hoping it contained the toys most kept for sexual play, his cock pulsing when his hand encountered the bindings and nipple rings.

He retrieved them, rising to his knees and taking Ariel's wrists, quickly fastening them to hidden ports in the bed. She jerked in reaction and his gaze flew to her face, watching as she nervously licked her lips, as her nipples tightened and her breath grew shorter.

Do you accept this? he asked.

She shivered—both feminine fear and carnal knowledge in her eyes—her husky *yes* confirmation of what he'd already guessed, that this was something she and her husband had once done.

Zeraac's nostril's flared in response, his cock growing fuller, his balls heavier. The combination of Komet's bite and her memories of her dead husband enflaming him further. By the Goddess, now it was his turn to possess her so thoroughly, so deeply, that there would be no room for thoughts of any other in her mind while he was pleasuring her.

He bound her ankles, leaving her spread, his to view, his to touch at will. Her mound beckoned, her lower lips glistening and parted, begging for his kiss, for the thrust of his tongue. But before he gave in to the siren call, he slipped the nipple rings created by the Araqiel clan-house around her areolas, watching as they tightened, making her arch upward and gasp as though twin mouths were suckling her.

When she was writhing with the stimulation to her nipples, he turned his attention to her bare woman's flesh, soft and pink, swollen, aroused, in need of his touch. "Zeraac!" she screamed at the first lap of his tongue, jerking violently against the ties keeping her from seeing to her own pleasure or hurrying him.

He teased her. Tormented her. Swallowed up her cries and pleas as ravenously as he ate her pussy. Reveling in every moment of it, uncaring of anything but the pleasure of being with her, of making her scream again and again in release until tears streamed from her eyes and she was whimpering, submissive, completely his.

Only then did he release her bindings and allow himself what he had wanted but not yet experienced, going to his knees with his wings spread out behind him, his body tense, aching with the need to plunge into her, and yet he had promised himself this. *Take my cock into your mouth, Ariel,* he ordered, his penis almost exploding just from seeing her move quickly to obey him, positioning herself on her hands and knees in front of him, her face lifting so that she could watch him from underneath her lashes as she put her mouth on his cock and pleasured him.

Zeraac nearly came at the first touch of her lips and tongue. He speared his fingers through her hair, telling himself he did so in order to control her, but knowing it was a lie even as he thought it, knowing that he held her in order to keep upright under the sweet torture of her mouth.

He was panting within seconds, fucking in and out of her mouth, out of control. His entire reality, his entire world, centered in his penis and what she was doing to it.

Ariel, he cried moments later, unable to stop himself, to delay his release as she worked him, giving him pleasure as he had never experienced before. His shout filled the room, his body shaking as he tumbled forward, taking her with him.

Desperation drove the blood back into his penis almost immediately, the knowledge that his visit with her would soon be over. *Ariel*, he said, and she responded, opening her legs, welcoming him into her sheath, their movements gentler this time, but no less urgent. Culminating in shared joy, shared release. A love Zeraac knew he would die without.

I love you, he whispered, slipping the nipple rings from her body, wanting nothing artificial between them.

I love you, too. You're my miracle, Zeraac. And Kaylee's.

His lips were soft on hers, his tongue languid as it stroked and twined with hers, as they both absorbed the emotion that swirled around and between them, the Ylan stones pulsing gently, echoing their heartbeats. *I would stay like this forever*, he said, his cock still in her body, reveling in her wet heat and tight muscles.

She laughed silently, her thoughts letting him know she enjoyed the feel of him inside her, even though she said, *Parenting is difficult enough without trying to maneuver around in a highly sexual version of Siamese twins.*

Her hands explored the top edge of his wings, making him shiver. The need for breath making him end the kiss.

"What's going on with the challenge?" she asked.

"Komet and I continue in our efforts to get the Council to set the challenge aside without addressing it directly."

Ariel bit her lip. Part of her wanted to just escape into sensual bliss, to ignore everything else but the feel of Zeraac's body on hers, in hers. But she could tell by the way the wall stones were darkening that soon the third sun would emerge, signaling that the Belizair "resting time" was drawing near. He would be required to leave before that happened, and then she would have no further news until either Zeraac or Komet or both of them visited again. "How many Council members are accounted for?"

Zeraac sighed. "Nine. Five who will probably vote to let the challenge to our bond stand, four who will argue to dismiss it."

Tension filled Ariel's body. "There are only three left to speak with. How do you think they'll vote?"

"I do not know."

"But if you were to guess?" she pressed.

He shook his head. "I cannot, Ariel."

She wanted to push harder, to *know* one way or the other. But she let it drop in favor of a subject that would lighten both of their hearts. "How long do you think it will be before Kaylee's DNA is matched and she can come back home?"

Zeraac laughed. "Not soon enough as far as we are concerned, but far too soon for the healers. They would keep her with them even past the time of adulthood if they could." He leaned down and kissed Ariel. *Like her mother, she is truly beautiful, inside and out. Her courage and spirit are a beacon, drawing all in her vicinity to her.*

Ariel's eyes grew misty with his praise, but she teased, "You'd better prepare yourself for the reality of childrearing. She's not always an angel, sometimes she can be a little demon."

He grinned. "Then what better place to raise her than on Belizair, where angels and demons have long coexisted, and now share the same human mate?"

Ariel laughed, kissing him, holding tightly to the moment, hoarding it, cherishing it. Praying there'd be a lifetime more just like it. Though all too soon, reality intruded—this time in the form of Shiraz's raised voice saying, "I am almost certain that move is against the rules, Paraisio, but I will concede defeat since we have once again failed to pay attention to the time. Do you break the news to Ariel or do I?"

I must go, Zeraac said, closing his eyes as he pulled his cock from her body and rose to his feet.

She rose with him, hastily donning her pants as he clothed himself. Both of them knowing by the color of the walls that there was no time to linger, to prolong their goodbyes.

"When the second sun rises," he said, kissing her at the doorway, "one of us will come to you."

And in me, Ariel teased, her eyes tearing up just as they had when she'd said goodbye to Komet.

In you, or on your beautiful, smooth mound, he said, returning her teasing, trying to make their separation more tolerable.

She flushed with color at the image his words provoked, the tears forgotten as her nipples tightened in repose. "I love you."

Zeraac couldn't resist one final kiss. *As I love you.*

* * * * *

The crystal walls had already cleared, allowing sunlight into the bedroom by the time Ariel woke, smiling as she stretched, her body pleasantly sore from the lovemaking with Zeraac and Komet.

A laugh escaped, her happiness shifting to a sense of exhilaration and anticipation as she got off the bed and dressed, choosing pants that matched the green swirls in her wristbands.

Kaylee. She had a feeling her daughter would return today.

Paraisio and Shiraz were once again engaged in a battle of Fett, the discovery that they were equally skilled feeding their love of the strategy game. Ariel received only a mumbled response when she greeted them before preparing herself a breakfast of fruit and bread.

Her stomach growled, not so much from hunger, but with the desire to bite into a strip of bacon, or better yet, a sausage biscuit—she snickered silently—maybe even go the whole hog and smother it in thick gravy. For a minute she let herself contemplate the extravagance of buying meat on Belizair, because despite how macho her new husbands were, she couldn't picture them hunting food down and killing it—well, didn't want to picture it, was more truthful. Meat came in tidy cellophane-wrapped packages in the grocery store, with little blood or anything else to hint it had come from a once living creature, and she was honest enough with herself to admit she wanted to keep it that way. No thoughts of Bambi left orphaned in the woods because hunters had killed his mother. No thoughts of big, gentle eyes.

Ariel sighed. Maybe it was just as well she would be eating from the non-mammal food group. Still, she couldn't stop herself from wondering if the meat available on Belizair would taste like beef or pork.

No. It would probably taste like chicken. She grinned, remembering the time she and Colin had been offered fried rattlesnake in Texas. "Tastes like chicken," the cranky waitress at the roadside diner told them. But they hadn't ordered the "house specialty", so Ariel didn't know whether the waitress had been telling the truth. In Louisiana they'd been offered nutria stew, but the thought of eating a rodent similar to a muskrat was not even a consideration, despite their host saying, "Eat up, tastes like chicken."

Ariel finished her breakfast, intent on dragging her companions away from their game, but before she could do it, the dwelling filled with chiming and she raced to the door, using the stones in her wristband so the wall reabsorbed a portion of itself, appearing to dissolve and form an opening.

"Mommy! I'm back!" Kaylee said, throwing herself into Ariel's arms, her soft cheek sliding against Ariel's wet one as they hugged each other fiercely.

"Oh baby," Ariel said, closing her eyes, unable to say anything else, her throat clogged with emotion, not just at having her daughter back, but at seeing Kaylee glowing with health and energy, at feeling Kaylee's small heart pounding with the promise of a future, thundering against her own chest and blending in with the fierce roar of maternal love that filled her. "Oh baby," she whispered again, choking back a laugh as she felt Kaylee begin to squirm, anxious to talk and demonstrate all that she could now do.

Reluctantly Ariel released her daughter, a fresh wave of joy rushing through her when Kaylee held her hands only inches away from Ariel's face. "Look, Mommy. They fixed them!"

Ariel took Kaylee's hands in hers, fresh tears forming at the corners of her eyes as she looked down at fingers which were no longer clublike from lack of oxygen, fingers that Kaylee would no longer ball into a fist in order to hide them from sight.

For an instant, the past overlaid the present, and Ariel was once again sitting up in a long-ago hospital bed, staring down at her beautiful newborn daughter, counting the tiny fingers and toes, perfectly formed miniatures of her own.

Just as she'd done that day, she brought Kaylee's hands to her mouth, turning them over and kissing each palm before forcing herself back under control, though she was unable to keep from giving Kaylee one more hug before she straightened, finally greeting and thanking the elderly Amato healer who stood in the doorway.

He smiled, his wrinkled hand going to the top of Kaylee's head. "Much lies ahead for this one. But it is I who was blessed with her presence in our enclave. She is like a rare Ylan stone, an exquisite treasure we were privileged to hold for even a short while."

Ariel stepped away from the doorway. "Would you care to come in for something to eat or drink?"

"No, thank you for your offer, but I must return to the mountains. I have already sent word of Kaylee's return to your bond-mates. I expect you will soon have company."

He started to turn away, but Ariel stopped him with a hand to his arm, then moved forward, hugging him. *Thank you for everything you've done for Kaylee.*

She will always be welcomed by the mountains, he said before leaving.

Kaylee's arrival had pulled Paraisio and Shiraz away from their game and now they stood side by side with amused expressions on their faces as a small human child took up a position in front of them and placed her hands on her hips, saying, "Mommy, how come we're living here with them instead of with Komet and Zeraac? I don't want three mommies, I want one mommy and two daddies."

Paraisio was the first to react, her laughter filling the room before she said, "And hopefully you will have just what you wish for, Kaylee, but until then, perhaps you can make do with one mommy and two...*aunties*...that is the word you would use on Earth, correct?"

Kaylee relaxed her stance and wrinkled her nose. "We can use that word if you want. But you don't really look like you could be Mommy's sister."

"But we can pretend, can we not?" Paraisio said, managing to suppress her mirth and offer her arms in greeting. "I am Paraisio d'Amato and your other auntie is Shiraz d'Vesti."

Pride filled Ariel as she watched Kaylee touch her wristbands to Paraisio's and then to Shiraz's, her manner so adultlike and serious, though as soon as it was done, Kaylee said, "Can you see if Komet and Zeraac are on their way here? I want to show them all the things I can do now."

"There is no need," Zeraac said, appearing at the doorway with Komet.

"Zeraac! Komet!" Kaylee launched herself at them and Zeraac lifted her in his arms, throwing her skyward before pulling her to his chest and hugging her.

Komet hugged Ariel to him, kissing her before turning his attention to Shiraz and Paraisio, his hold tightening on Ariel. "The scientists wish to begin preparing for Kaylee's treatment immediately. We are here to accompany both her and Ariel to the scientists' work area."

Ariel's heart jerked in her chest. Even though she'd known... "Kaylee only just got here."

Komet brushed his lips against hers. *I know, beloved. But the sooner she begins, the sooner it will be finished. Something to remain forever in the past.*

A different thought rushed in, and with it a fresh wave of worry and uncertainty assailed Ariel. *The scientists have found a match for her.*

His immediate tension did nothing to unwind the knot in Ariel's stomach. *Yes.*

There's more.

Yes.

The truth, Komet, not some sugarcoated lie you think would be best for me right now.

They have found two matches for the Fallon gene Kaylee carries. One Vesti. One Amato.

The knot in Ariel's stomach tightened. *So there may be a Vesti match for me as well.*

Yes.

Chapter Twelve

ഇ

"I want to hug Komet," Kaylee said, her demand for Komet's attention forcing the conversation with Ariel aside.

But when Kaylee would have wrapped her arms around Komet's neck and transferred herself to his arms, Zeraac laughed and moved away, saying, "Not yet, or you will crush the surprise Komet has for you."

"You brought me a surprise?" Kaylee asked, her eyes widening and her face glowing with childish joy, though her eyebrows drew together and a teasing scowl formed almost immediately as her gaze moved over Komet. "It must be a tiny surprise and not a big one. I don't see anything. Where is it?"

Komet laughed, letting go of Ariel in order to pull his curls back and turn, revealing a small, light green creature clinging to the back of his neck.

"What is it?" Kaylee asked, her voice an excited whisper.

Komet coaxed the small hitchhiker onto his hand and Ariel couldn't keep from smiling, amazed by the delicate-looking animal. "It looks like a miniature flying squirrel," she said.

"Only the ones on Earth aren't green," Kaylee added. "And look, Mommy, it has lines, just like a leaf has."

"Exactly right," Komet said. "It's called a banzit, and it lives in the trees, using the leaves as camouflage." His eyes sparkled. "Now perhaps if I get that hug, I will allow you to take charge of this female I have named Sabaska."

Kaylee opened her arms wide, allowing Komet to pull her into his and give her first a hug then a kiss on her forehead. "It is good to have you home and see you feeling well."

"Not home yet. How come Mommy and I can't live with you and Zeraac?"

"We will talk about that later. The scientists are waiting for you, though they have agreed to allow us to spend some time together before they begin their tests. And they have agreed that Sabaska can remain with you in the examination room."

Kaylee's gaze flew to his, then to Ariel's, her small features showing a moment of fear and worry. "Will you get to stay with me, too?"

"We all will," Komet said.

Ariel placed her head on Komet's shoulder and rubbed her daughter's still too-thin back. "It'll be okay, baby, just a little bit longer now and you'll be done with being sick."

"But I wanted to spend the day doing fun things," Kaylee whined.

Zeraac joined them, his hand going to Kaylee's head and tangling in her baby-fine hair. "And you will. The visit with the scientists will not take the entire day. Komet has talked to them and they have devised a plan. Today they desire to take samples from various parts of your body so they can know where to strike at the disease and how best to do so. The majority of their work will take place after they have gathered what they need from you."

"Will it hurt?" Kaylee asked, her bottom lip trembling.

"There might be moments when you are uncomfortable," Komet said, "but the procedures shouldn't be painful."

"Will they stick needles in me?"

"No. We do not use such things here."

"Okay then. Okay. But you said I don't have to go right away."

Komet smiled, moving his hand to Kaylee's shoulder and urging the banzit to take up a perch there. "Not right away. I thought perhaps we might spend some time outside."

Kaylee giggled, her attention diverted by the small mammal on her shoulder. "It's got sharp toenails!"

"For climbing up and down trees," Komet said, gently setting Kaylee to her feet. "Though banzits can glide for fairly long distances, most of their time is spent either sleeping or looking for food. I found Sabaska on the forest floor when she was a baby, but could not locate the nest so that I could return her to it."

Kaylee slowly stroked the tiny green animal, jumping a little when its front claw gripped her finger. "She's beautiful. Are you going to take her with you when you go back home?"

"We do not own pets, as you do on Earth, but I hoped you would be interested in sharing the duties of caring for Sabaska with me," Komet said, his expression so tender that tears flooded Ariel's eyes.

"Really?"

"Yes, if your mother allows it."

"Can I, Mommy?"

Ariel smiled. "Yes, though Komet will have to instruct us so we can be good caretakers."

Kaylee gave a small squeal and jump, toning down her excitement so she wouldn't scare Sabaska. "Can we go outside now?"

They went, Komet and Zeraac taking up positions on either side of Ariel, with Kaylee racing ahead, laughing and giggling when she found that the banzit was happy to burrow under her hair and cling to her neck. "Look, Mommy! Look how fast I can run!" She went as far as the archway leading to the next cluster of living quarters, before turning and sprinting back, nearly knocking Ariel over when she came to a halt, her arms around her mother's waist. "I love you, Mommy."

Ariel kissed Kaylee's upraised cheek. "I love you, too."

Kaylee moved to Zeraac, hugging him. "I love you, Zeraac."

He kissed her. "I love you as well."

Komet also got a hug, one so fierce it made him say, "I fear she is going to grow up to be a bounty hunter, she is about to bring me to my knees with her grip!"

Kaylee giggled. "I love you. Thanks for sharing Sabaska with me. I've never had a pet before." Her eyes flew to his. "I mean, an animal to help care for."

Komet smiled, brushing a strand of Kaylee's hair back from her face. "I am sure Sabaska does not mind if you call her a pet. What matters is that she is seen as both a privilege and responsibility, and not as a possession."

She gave him another fierce hug. "I'll take good care of her and never think of her as belonging to me." She released him, turning her attention to Shiraz and Paraisio. "On Earth, aunties play tag or hide-and-seek with their nieces so that mommies and daddies can have some time alone."

Both Paraisio and Shiraz laughed. Paraisio said, "I think we can be counted on to do our best when it comes to being aunties. Two courtyards over is a place designed with children in mind. I will count to twenty and allow you and Shiraz a chance to hide."

"Count slow!" Kaylee said, already racing away with Shiraz loping after her.

When Paraisio was also gone, Komet said, "I should have spoken with you first about Sabaska..."

Ariel squeezed his arm. "You want to be her father, Komet, and I want her to have one—" she laughed, "well, not just one, but two, and Kaylee has definitely settled on the idea of claiming both you and Zeraac. I'm sure there will be times when we disagree about things, but I also know the two of you will always be acting from your hearts."

Komet's hand covered hers where it rested on his arm. "The boys who carry the matching genes are with their parents in the courtyard where Kaylee goes to play."

A bolt of fear rushed through Ariel as reality crashed down on her. In a heartbeat, the thought Kaylee had derailed earlier returned in an avalanche of worry, threatening to suffocate her. "So now the Council will think there's another match, a Vesti, out there for me."

Komet's answer was stark. "Yes."

"So they'll vote to break the bond? And then what? Force me to marry this other Vesti when they find him, along with someone else that he chooses?"

"We have always valued free will," Zeraac said. "I do not believe it will come to that."

"But you can't be certain."

He sighed. "No. These are difficult times. Nothing is certain—other than we are faced with extinction—and our ways will change as a result."

Komet squeezed her hand. "I am not without hope. The Council and their scientists are treading carefully. To let it be known there is both a Vesti and Amato match for each human female could cause social upheaval here. The parents of the boys who match Kaylee's Fallon marker were asked to bring *all* their children and told only that our scientists think some of the genes their children carry could aid a human child."

Ariel's eyebrows drew together. "And they dropped everything to come here?"

Zeraac nodded. "Yes, children have always been important to us. Most on Belizair would offer aid to Kaylee without any thought of gaining from it." He shrugged. "Perhaps they suspect the truth behind their being asked, but it is just as likely they carry hope alone, and pray that should their children's genes be used, then Kaylee's will somehow be altered so that she will eventually be the mother of their grandchildren."

It truly hit Ariel then, a great river of pity crashing through her at how desperate the situation was on Belizair, how heart-wrenching. How similar, in some ways, to her own

177

nightmare on Earth. When she would have done anything in her power to ensure a future for Kaylee. Just as these parents had come, pinning their hopes for their sons, and their clan-house, on a nine-year-old girl who was years and years away from adulthood.

"When will the Council decide whether or not they'll hear the challenge?" Ariel asked, forcing the question out.

Zeraac answered, "They have been waiting for Miciah d'Vesti to arrive. Now they wait for Kaylee to be completely well." He brought her hand to his mouth, kissing the back of it. "They are not without hearts, Ariel."

"And if they were to vote today, how do you think it would go?"

"The first part of the challenge has already been eliminated. The Council's scientists have verified that you carry the marker matching mine." His wings drooped, only a tiny bit, but enough to warn Ariel she wouldn't like the rest of his answer. "I think there will be six who vote to allow the remaining parts of the challenge to go forward, six who vote to let it drop. In the end they will compromise. I believe they will address the second part—whether you came here willingly, accepting both Komet and me as your mates before being transported here, as is required by Council law—but will decide to put aside the third part of the challenge because the cost to our world would be too great if they begin to question who is entitled to a mate, given that our females can produce no children, and those already in bonded arrangements also suffer a similar fate."

"And if we lose and the Ylan stones on the wristbands can be separated, would that be the end of it?" Ariel asked, feeling as though her heart was being squeezed by a merciless hand.

Zeraac answered, "No. They would most likely forbid either Komet or me from seeing you, perhaps even exile us for a time, in the hopes you would take other bond-mates. All is not lost. They have yet to meet you or Kaylee, to hear what you have to say. There is still room for hope."

"For a miracle?"

He laughed softly. "Your coming into my life at all was one of these miracles you speak of."

"And mine as well," Komet added, also bringing Ariel's hand to his mouth, kissing the back of it. "Now let us put aside worries about the future and enjoy these moments that are ours to share right now."

Bittersweet emotion choked Ariel. The last nine years had prepared her to do just that, to savor every good moment and hoard it in preparation for the bad ones ahead.

Meeting the parents of the boys who might one day be Kaylee's bond-mates was initially awkward—for all of them—and yet the antics of the children and the sight of Kaylee playing tag, running and screaming, part of a group of three boys and three girls, made it impossible for Ariel to be anything but thankful, joyous. She could barely stand to take her eyes off her daughter, and as if sensing how miraculous it was for her, the other parents allowed her space, engaging each other along with Zeraac and Komet in discussion.

As Paraisio had said, the courtyard was designed with children in mind. And yet done with the aid of nature and not the equipment found on an Earth playground. Rocks had been piled into "mountains", allowing children to test their skill in climbing, while a smooth, gently sloping surface provided a fast "slide" down. Hollowed out pits of sand, each with a miniature oasis, made it possible to both dig and create forms. And of course, there were trees, some with branches close together and easy to navigate, while others provided more of a challenge.

They are handsome boys, are they not? Zeraac asked later, after Ariel's attention had finally returned to the adults and she'd joined their conversation, all of them getting to know one another until they'd eased into a companionable, comfortable silence.

Very, she agreed, her eyes going to the boys in question. On Earth they would probably be twelve or thirteen. Large for their age, and surprisingly serious—though perhaps that was a result of the situation on Belizair.

They'd spent much of their time climbing on the rocks, conversing with each other and ignoring the younger children's call for them to come play tag. And yet more than once Ariel had seen their eyes stray to Kaylee, but then again, her daughter was so outgoing, so full of life—even in the days when she'd been fighting for each breath—that it was hard to ignore her.

And as if on cue, Kaylee yelled, "Mommy, look! Sabaska climbed all the way to the top of the tree. Watch me! I'm going to go get her."

Ariel's hands gripped both Komet's and Zeraac's as she bit down on her lip to keep from saying anything, fear for Kaylee's safety warring with a happiness, and amusement—directed at herself. Nine years of having a daughter who had never been able to do anything risky had left her in danger of being an overprotective mother now that she saw how easy it was for a child to get hurt!

Zeraac's fingers stroked over Ariel's whitened knuckles. "I think you are right, Komet, our daughter will be a bounty hunter when she reaches maturity."

Komet's hand tightened on Ariel's as he too offered a silent gesture of comfort. "Perhaps I spoke in haste. She has the makings of a scientist and scholar. Many a time I have pursued knowledge in just such a manner. She looks as though she has been climbing trees all of her life."

Ariel laughed, letting the tension leave her body. "I'm sure there are more choices for Kaylee than becoming either a bounty hunter or a scientist."

"True," Zeraac answered, his own body becoming suddenly tense when the two older boys launched themselves from the "mountain" and flew directly at the tree where Kaylee was climbing. The young Vesti aimed high, swooping Sabaska up, while the young Amato plucked Kaylee from the tree before gliding to earth.

For an instant, Kaylee's reaction teetered on being thrilled—not only at flying, but at being the center of an older boy's attention—but then he made the mistake of scolding her, his serious voice making the adults hide their smiles, as he said, "You are too small to be climbing so high. Too helpless without wings. What would happen if you fell? Splat! That is what would happen. It cannot be allowed."

For a heartbeat there was complete silence. And then Kaylee responded.

"You are not the boss of me!" she said, her small spine ramrod straight as she reached over and yanked a feather from the boy's wing in order to drive home her point.

He let out a howl of protest, but the sound of it was nearly obliterated by the laughter that escaped from the adults present.

She marched over and collected the banzit from the Vesti boy, who jerked his wings backward as though making sure she couldn't get to them—and set off a fresh wave of laughter as a result.

Then, in a move that brought a rush of love to Ariel's heart, Kaylee came over—a little girl needing a hug of reassurance. "I could have climbed that tree all the way to the top, Mommy."

"I know, baby, and we'll come back another day and you can do just that."

"Perhaps we will even race to the top," Komet said, tweaking her hair. "But in the meantime, you should say goodbye to your new friends. We have kept the scientists waiting long enough."

The goodbyes dragged, Kaylee's reluctance to leave obvious to all, though no one hurried her. But eventually she could put off the inevitable no longer. Her hand slid into Ariel's, her mouth firmed—with only a small tremble. "Okay, I'm ready to go see the scientists now. But you promised we can come back here."

Ariel bent over, giving her daughter a hug. "We'll come back as soon as we can."

Kaylee looked up, somber and much too old for only nine years old. "With Zeraac and Komet?"

"I hope so, baby. I want that, too."

"Then why aren't we living with them?" Kaylee asked, coming full circle now that her attention wasn't distracted by the banzit or her new friends.

Ariel cupped Kaylee's chin and brushed her thumb over her daughter's bottom lip. "Let's take care of you first, then we'll worry about what happens next. Okay?"

For long moments they stared at each other, then Kaylee sighed. "Okay, Mommy. But I want us to be a family."

"Me too, baby. I want that more than anything except knowing you're completely well."

* * * * *

The testing was tedious, boring, with stretches of waiting in between, making Kaylee cranky and contentious when it seemed to her that the scientists wanted to take one sample after another, some of them in the exact same place.

"Aren't we almost done yet?" she finally asked, her voice holding an unmistakable whine.

"Almost," the male Amato taking the latest sample said. "You need to slip out of your pants next."

Modest color flooded Kaylee's face. "Then only Mommy can be in the room, and the other scientist, the lady Vesti. You're not my doctor so you can't see the rest of me."

The scientist looked up, startled, but Komet interceded, saying, "Kaylee makes a reasonable request. She has already been through many changes." He rose, kissing Ariel, then Kaylee. "I will wait in the other room for you."

Zeraac did the same, his heart flooding with tenderness, his mind spinning at how overwhelming it could be to have a daughter.

The scientist disappeared as well, leaving Ariel and Kaylee alone. "Are you mad at me?" Kaylee immediately asked.

Ariel took her daughter's small hand, running her thumb over Kaylee's perfect fingers. "No, I'm not mad. But can you do something for me?"

Kaylee gave a dramatic sigh, the slump of her shoulders indicating she already knew what her mother would ask. "What?"

"Be patient for just a little while longer. You know the scientists are working for *your* benefit."

"I know, Mommy," Kaylee said, sounding duly chastised. "But I'd rather be outside playing."

"And the quicker the scientists get their work done, the quicker that will happen."

Kaylee moved closer and Ariel couldn't resist. She pulled her daughter into her arms for a hug, burying her face in the soft hair that was exactly the same color as her own. "We're so close now, baby, so close. Just a little longer, then you'll be completely well."

Chapter Thirteen

ℬ

Ariel's mind wouldn't sleep. Her thoughts and emotions chased around in an endless roller-coaster loop. Another day, two at the most, and Kaylee would be entirely free of the disease that had nearly killed her. Another day, two or three at the most, and the Council would address the challenge to her "marriage".

None will expect you to answer questions mind to mind, without the protection of the spoken word. But in our world, a lie is easily discovered and the liar's honor left tarnished, their company judged undesirable, Komet had said, and yet what would she do if she was asked point-blank whether or not she'd agreed to come here, whether or not she had accepted both Zeraac and Komet as her bond-mates beforehand?

"Mommy," Kaylee's voice sounded in the dimly lit room, interrupting Ariel's worry. Out of habit she pressed a kiss to the top of her daughter's head. "I thought you were asleep, baby."

Kaylee snuggled closer to Ariel, but reached out, plucking at the edge of bed where they were both lying, the wall crystals darkened against the intensity of the third sun. "Do you think Daddy is watching us from Heaven?"

The question pierced straight through Ariel's heart. "I don't know. Have you been thinking about him lately?" she asked, smoothing the baby-fine strands of Kaylee's hair.

"Yes."

"Because of Zeraac and Komet?"

"Yes."

Ariel continued to gently untangle and straighten the pale blonde hair as she waited for Kaylee to find words for what she was feeling and thinking. Her heart aching as she watched her daughter's fingers pluck at the edge of the bed—the telltale sign a subtle indication of distress.

"Sometimes I can hardly remember what he looks like," Kaylee finally said. "Do you think Zeraac and Komet can bring the pictures that were on our bookcase?"

"Yes. I've already talked to Zeraac about our things. When there's time we'll ask Zeraac and Komet to bring them to Belizair."

"Okay. That would be good. Especially the pictures. And maybe some of my games. And my books. I don't want to forget about the animals on Earth." They slipped into silence again, this one heavier than the previous one, only broken when Kaylee asked, "Do you still love Daddy?"

Tears rushed to Ariel's eyes. "Yes, baby, I still love him. He gave me you. He was my husband, the first man I loved." She dropped her arm over Kaylee's side, gathering her closer. "But that doesn't mean I don't have room in my heart for Zeraac and Komet. And if your daddy is watching from Heaven, then I think he would understand. I don't think he would want either of us to never love anyone else just because we loved him first."

Some of the tension left Kaylee's body, and yet her fingers still plucked at the sheet. "Zeraac said that even when we were back on Earth and I was so sick, he still wanted to be my father." *How come Daddy couldn't feel like Zeraac does?*

Whether intentional or not, the question Ariel had struggled with for nine years settled between them, the words not spoken out loud, and yet heard all the same. "He loved you and wanted to be a good father to you, but he just couldn't handle—the disease. It hurt him to see you suffering. And he blamed himself. So he closed himself up, he went away—and after awhile, I think he couldn't find a way back to us."

"I wanted him to come back."

"Oh baby, so did I. But we made it. And he's in a better place now, and if he's watching, then he knows we are, too."

Kaylee sighed, pulling her hand back from the edge of the bed and snuggling. "Are we going to go and live with Zeraac and Komet?"

"If we can."

"Why can't we?"

"There are rules here. I don't understand them all myself. But in a few days we've got to go in front of the Council and talk to them." She hugged Kaylee. "But no more questions on that, okay? Let's just concentrate on getting you well."

"I want Zeraac and Komet for my daddies."

"I know you do. I think you've made that *very* clear to anyone who'll listen."

"Will I get to tell the Council what *I* want?"

"Kaylee…" Ariel chided, reminding her daughter that they weren't going to talk about a future beyond getting her completely well.

"Okay, Mommy, no more questions. But I want to have my say."

Pride filled Ariel, though she masked it with a soft laugh. "And I wouldn't have it any other way. You can talk to Zeraac and Komet about letting the Council know what you want."

"Okay then," Kaylee said, rolling to her back so she looked into her mother's face. "You want to know something interesting?"

Ariel gave an exaggerated sigh. "Aren't you sleepy yet?"

"Not yet." She paused for a minute. "Mommy, I can talk with my mind, but I like talking with my mouth better. Do you think that's okay?"

Ariel laughed. "I'll tell you a secret. I like talking with my mouth better, too."

"That's good. We can stick together. So do you want me to tell you something I learned from the Healers?"

"Okay, one interesting fact, then we'll try and get to sleep."

"Well, it's more than one. But they all go together." Kaylee held her arm up so her wristband was directly in front of her mother's face. "Can you see the animals?"

"Not in the dark," Ariel answered, momentarily distracted by the way Kaylee's band glittered — different from her own or Zeraac's or Komet's — as though a constellation of stars had taken up residence in the Ylan stones.

"Well, if you could see, then you'd see one animal looks like a saber-toothed tiger and one looks like a...well, a unicorn with a horn on its forehead and two shorter horns on its nose, kind of like a rhinoceros. The saber-toothed tiger is the device of Zeraac's clan-house and the kind-of unicorn is the device of Komet's. But — this is the first interesting fact, Mommy — the saber-tooted tiger *isn't* extinct here like it is on Earth! And the animal that looks kind of like a unicorn, it really exists, too. Only its coat isn't white unless it goes high up in the mountains where the snow is. Most of the other time it's brown or reddish. Can you believe that?"

Ariel laughed. Knowing just by the excitement in Kaylee's voice that however close she might have been to sleepiness before, it was long past now. "Are you sure the Healers weren't telling you a tall tale?"

"Mommy! Healers don't lie!"

"Okay. So these almost-unicorns and saber-toothed tigers exist. What else?"

"Well, you know how when you greet someone, you touch your wristbands to theirs?"

"Yes."

"And haven't you wondered how come they introduce themselves by saying they're Vesti or Amato, even though it's *obvious* because of the wings?"

Ariel laughed again, leaning down and rubbing Kaylee's nose with her own. "I'll confess, I did wonder. So it's my good luck I have such a brilliant and beautiful daughter to explain things to me."

Kaylee giggled, raising up enough to kiss her mother. "You *are* lucky to have me."

"So how come they introduce themselves by saying d'Amato or d'Vesti?"

"I thought I could only tell you *one* interesting fact," Kaylee teased.

Ariel kissed her. "For you, I'll make an exception."

"Okay. But there are *two* parts to the answer. First. When they touch each other's wristbands, even without looking at what's engraved on them, they know automatically what clan-house the other person belongs to. The Healer said once we've learned more about Belizair and learned how to listen to the Ylan stones, then we'll know too, and we'll be able to do what everybody else can do—except fly. What do you think about that, Mommy?"

"I think that sounds wonderful," she said. "Before you were born I used to collect rocks. So I can hardly wait to learn more about the Ylan stones. Now what's the second part of your answer?"

"The second part is not as interesting as the first. The Healer says it's really hard to make your wings disappear here. It takes a lot of energy. So introducing yourself as d'Amato or d'Vesti is more a habit than anything else— because when they go to other planets, they don't usually show their wings, and they know their clan-house names will be hard to remember, so they just tell what race they are. That way if someone from Belizair arrives after they do, then that person will know not only that they're not alone on the planet, but they'll know whether it's a Vesti or Amato that's there with them." A giggle escaped. "So I guess that means from now on you're Ariel d'Human and I'm Kaylee d'Human."

Ariel laughed. "Hmmm, sounds a little like Conan the Barbarian."

A peal of giggles followed, along with more humorous suggestions, then easy conversation plus several trips to see if the banzit was still content to hide among the leaves in one of the potted trees in the main living area. But eventually sleep found both Ariel and Kaylee. Settling over them like a comforting blanket. Content to hold them until the crystal walls cleared to allow the muted light of a single sun to form an artificial dawn.

Komet and Zeraac arrived soon after, and though Shiraz and Paraisio had been told they didn't need to stay with Ariel given she would be with the Council scientists, they elected to go, walking well behind the small family group in order to give them privacy.

"What's going to happen when we get there?" Kaylee asked, walking between the men with Sabaska perched on her shoulder.

Komet answered, "The scientists have already prepared the cells containing the corrected genes. They started out with your own cells, then adjusted them, using some of the DNA your friends from yesterday volunteered. Now they just have to put the cells back in you and..."

"Not from the older boys," Kaylee interrupted. "I don't want anything belonging to them inside of me."

Zeraac was the first to react, making a strangled sound even as his face reddened in fatherly embarrassment. Komet following suit, whatever he'd been about to say, dead on his tongue as his gaze sought Ariel's—though before she could comment, Kaylee asked, "What's wrong with Komet and Zeraac?"

Ariel laughed, leaning over to tweak her daughter's nose. "I think they're just surprised you didn't like the older boys." She moved her eyebrows up and down in a comical gesture. "You have to admit, they were both very handsome boys."

"M-o-m-m-y," Kaylee said, dragging the word out in exasperation. "I'm too young to have boyfriends. And besides, those boys were bossy. I don't like bossy boys."

Ariel laughed again, thinking how much fun bossy men could be in the bedroom, but she said, "I'm glad to hear you're too young for boyfriends. Once you're completely well, you're going to be too busy to think about boys."

"Except as friends. I can have some boys who are just friends."

"I would vote for such a thing," Zeraac said. "For many, many years to come—well into adulthood in fact."

Komet nodded. "As would I."

Ariel grinned. "Then it's settled. Only boys as friends until Kaylee is one hundred years old."

Kaylee giggled. "Not that old, Mommy. I might want a husband one day. But no more than two. There was a healer in the mountains who had three wives. And they were all sisters. Can you believe that?"

Ariel shook her head, but declined to comment for fear of where the conversation might lead. The last thing she wanted to do was begin a sex-education discussion. Though it did make her smile to realize how easily both she and Kaylee had adapted to the idea of marriages that didn't involve only a single man and woman.

They walked in companionable silence until the building housing the scientists came into sight.

"How long will it take?" Kaylee asked.

"A day, perhaps two," Komet told her.

"Will it hurt?" This time there was a slight quiver in Kaylee's voice.

"It shouldn't," Komet said, thinking to reassure her by adding, "You will sleep through most of it."

Kaylee stopped abruptly, real fear in her face, and immediately both men knelt down so their faces were close to hers. "They're going to make me go to sleep?"

"They will do so without needles," Zeraac said, remembering the words that had drifted to him in the San Francisco fog, Kaylee's panicked voice, *I don't want a shot. I don't want to go to sleep. Please don't make me go to sleep.*

Ariel leaned over, kissing the top of Kaylee's head. "It's okay, baby. You don't have to worry about not waking up. Just be brave for a little bit longer."

Komet's heart stilled for a beat, gripped in a fist of pain, hating that Kaylee had ever been so close to death, had ever known the fear of dying. His thumb smoothed over her sparkling wristband. "Remember when we met in the butterfly house?" She nodded. "Trust us. We will watch over you while you sleep. And when you wake, we will be there."

Kaylee's lips trembled, but she whispered, "I trust you."

For two days they stayed with Kaylee, helpless to do anything other than watch and wait, and occasionally hold her hands in theirs when the scientists paused the treatment long enough to gather fresh samples. Ariel struggled to remain free of worry, but the tears escaped often, the sight of her daughter lying in something that resembled a glass coffin almost unbearable.

"It is almost over," Komet said, gathering Ariel into his arms, positioning her so that her face was turned away from the chamber housing Kaylee. "When I last checked, the scientists said the new cells had very nearly replaced all of the old ones. Just a little longer now."

Zeraac joined them and Ariel reached out, taking his hand. He smiled and said, "It is amazing, is it not? I have never had much interest in science, but I am awed by what has been accomplished here, and in such a short period of time."

Ariel squeezed his hand. "It's nothing less than a miracle. That you came into our lives. That the two of you risked so much to bring us here. That Kaylee will be like any other child." She laughed, trying to lighten the mood. "Except for having no wings—unless your scientists can also provide those."

Komet laughed. "No. Those she will do without, and perhaps it is just as well. I imagine Kaylee will get into enough mischief and trouble without flying to and from it."

Ariel wanted to deny the charge, but the image of her tiny daughter climbing a tall tree in order to retrieve the banzit, then plucking a feather from her future mate's wing, made her smile instead. "You might be right. She is so...courageous... but her body has always kept her from even attempting anything that might lead to trouble."

They moved to a small table, loaded with food and drink on one end, and where Shiraz and Paraisio were engaged in another heated battle of Fett on the other end. "Play the winner?" Paraisio asked when Zeraac sat down next to her.

He chuckled. "Do you never tire of the game? And getting beat by me?"

Ariel rolled her eyes, her attention going to Paraisio. "I hope one of you beats him soon. His ego is swelling and he's going to be impossible to live with."

As soon as the words were out, a new heaviness settled in Ariel's heart. Automatically her hand reached for Komet's, and across the table, for Zeraac's. "How come the Council is letting you both be here and yet as soon as Kaylee's well, they're going to try and tear our bond apart?"

Zeraac sighed. "They are not without hearts, Ariel. And the happiness of those brought from Earth is of great importance to all of us. But they cannot ignore the challenge."

"Could it be withdrawn?"

"Raym d'Amato will not do so," Paraisio said, shooting a sympathetic glance at Komet, then Zeraac. "His clan-house

192

suffered greatly when the virus struck. Most in it have more daughters than sons. In Raym's own family, both of his daughters were newly pregnant and lost their babies. There are no sons in his home."

Anger rushed through Ariel, hatred for this unknown Amato. "So he'll persist in trying to destroy our bond despite the fact that Komet had nothing to do with the virus? That Zeraac had nothing to do with it?"

He is Zantara's uncle and they are close. He feels her...pain...as well, Zeraac said, directing his thought to Ariel alone, cringing at the necessity of mentioning the other woman's name, though Ariel's expression only grew fiercer at hearing it.

That just makes it worse! If she hurts from losing you, then it is a suffering she brought on herself! Ariel said, feeling suddenly as though a lifetime of suppressed despair and rage—toward a disease that had taken her daughter day by day, and destroyed her marriage—had coalesced, threatening to fill and consume her.

It was Shiraz who steadied Ariel, her hand going to Ariel's shoulder, her voice holding deeply felt pain—and truth. *The Council has not yet heard your words, or those who will speak in favor of setting the challenge aside. We are a just people, despite what is happening on our world. Find it in your heart to forgive, to try and understand that we, too, suffer. Our culture, though allowing free choice, has always revered childbearing and childrearing. And now our women are without hope, struggling with despair and feelings of worthlessness, while our men must take a human mate even as they watch helplessly while those they love become less than they once were. Have faith that your love will prevail. This is your world now. Your home.*

Ariel nodded, her anger drowned by the sorrow in Shiraz's dark eyes. Resolve and strength of purpose settling in her heart—not just to fight the challenge, but to do what she could for Belizair.

A short time later the scientists returned, removing the shielding from around Kaylee and taking another round of samples, so optimistic they were finished with their work that they allowed Zeraac to lift the sleeping child and carry her to a bench, where he placed her in Ariel's arms. He and Komet sitting on either side of her.

Joy rushed through Ariel, a happiness that escaped in tears. "I used to pray for a day like this one. Promising all kinds of things to God if only a cure could be found and Kaylee would get well. It's hard not to believe that somewhere out there, he heard me—sending angels, not from Heaven above, but from *the* heavens."

Zeraac smoothed the tears from one of Ariel's cheeks, his heart so full of love that he too felt close to crying. "We do not believe in the same divine being, and yet I also feel as though a prayer that lived in my heart—unacknowledged in my pain— has been answered by the Goddess and Ylan."

"As do I," Komet said. "Perhaps the god who created us and wandered on to other places, still looks in on Belizair, offering small rays of hope to help us endure."

The scientists arrived en masse, their smiles infectious, their message a miracle. "She is free of the disease now. We will take samples periodically, merely as a precaution, but we do not truly worry that the disease will resurface.

A simple injection done with a needle-free instrument, and Kaylee was awake—bursting with energy—her limbs nearly shaking with the need to run and play and get rid of two days worth of sleep.

"I will take her to the courtyard," Zeraac volunteered. "At this time of day there will be other children for her to play with should she wear me out." To Ariel he said, *If it is not against what orders Shiraz and Paraisio must abide by, take this time alone with Komet. No doubt we will face the Council tomorrow.*

Ariel's gaze swung to Shiraz who said, *We are not to leave you except while you are here. But once we have returned to the living quarters, the old rules apply. I have no orders denying them a visit today – as long as you are not 'alone'.* She grinned. *And as luck would have it, an unfinished game of Fett awaits Paraisio and me.*

Thank you, Ariel said, truly grateful her guards were her friends. It would have been almost unbearable if they hadn't been.

"M-o-m-m-y," Kaylee said, having already squirmed out of Ariel's arms and collected Sabaska from a tree the scientists had allowed in to serve as a temporary habitat, "can we go now?"

Ariel looked at her daughter, torn, wanting to go to the park and yet needing some time alone with both Zeraac and Komet.

Kaylee resisted slightly as Ariel pulled her into her arms, an indication of her high energy level and not a show of bad temper. "Would it be okay if only Zeraac went to the park with you? I'd like to go back to our living quarters for a little while."

Ariel blushed when Kaylee immediately asked, "So you and Komet can be alone?"

"Yes."

"I told you I'd share our angels with you, Mommy. As long as one of them goes with me to the park, you can have the other one."

Laughter and snickers met Kaylee's comment. Ariel gave her daughter a quick kiss before releasing her. "Thank you for sharing, baby."

Zeraac was still chuckling several minutes later as he watched Kaylee demonstrate how quickly she could run. The banzit sat on his shoulder, grooming itself with one hand while it clung to a strand of his hair with the other.

Just in case I run so fast that Sabaska falls off, Kaylee had said. *I don't want her to get hurt. It wouldn't be any fun if we had to turn around and go right back to where the scientists are.*

Still, the small animal scrambled, nearly losing its balance when Kaylee crashed into Zeraac, giggling and saying, "I was running so fast that I couldn't stop in time. Did you see me?"

"I saw you. If you had wings you would have taken off like one of the airplanes you have on Earth!"

"Can we fly the rest of the way to the park?" Kaylee asked, bouncing so eagerly that Zeraac thought she just might gain enough height to slam the top of her head into his chin.

"Only if you are very still so we do not both end up visiting the healers."

"I will be," Kaylee promised, but nearly deafened him with her squeal when he gathered her in his arms and ran a few steps before launching upward, the golden-veined wings expanding to their full span, fighting against gravity until a balance was achieved.

Kaylee clung to him, for a moment too fearful to look down, but finally finding her courage, her grip tightening when she did, her body shaking just slightly, but her voice was still excited. "I used to dream about what it would be like for an angel to carry me away. To Heaven. But this is much, much better." She giggled. "Because we're only going to the park. And in a little while we'll go back home. Well—back to where Mommy and Komet are. Do you think the Council Mommy was telling me about is going to let us come and live with you and Komet?"

"I want that more than anything else."

"Z-e-r-a-a-c," she said, and he laughed at hearing the same exasperation in her voice, only directed at him instead of her mother. "You didn't answer my question."

He kissed the top of her head. "I do not know the answer to your question, Kaylee, and I have no wish to lie to you."

"Okay," she huffed. "That's a good thing. Mommies and daddies shouldn't lie to their children."

He made a gentle landing, glad to see the courtyard had a good number of children in it. "Do you wish to play with some

196

of the others and have me watch, or would you like for me to accompany you as you explore?"

Her eyes moved from the children, many of them already noticing her, back to Zeraac, her expression torn until her eyes widened and she reached out and touched his wristband. "Look, Zeraac, now you have the sparkles!" She quickly glanced at her own bands. "And there are only a few of them left in mine!"

Zeraac looked down, unable to look away from the glitter, the swirl of a small galaxy at home in an inexplicable mix of Ylan stones. "The Tears of the Goddess," he murmured, remembering the awe he had felt when he first viewed them in the bands Komet had fashioned for Ariel and Kaylee.

Kaylee rubbed the tips of her fingers over them. "That's what the healer called them, too. And he said it just the way you did. Only I never got to ask him. Are they happy tears or are they sad tears?"

Chapter Fourteen

℘

Emotion assailed Ariel, bombarding her with so many different feelings that not one of them filled her completely or lasted for more than a moment. She still felt torn, on edge, as though she needed to be in several places at once—alone, with Kaylee, with the men who had changed her world.

Komet sat on the edge of the bed, her hand in his, though he made no move to pull her down or remove their clothing. "You're overwhelmed," he said, his expression gentle. "Perhaps a few moments in the cleansing chamber will relax you. I have often found it helps me when I am unable to settle otherwise."

He opened his hand, prepared to release her, but she tightened her grip, her focus suddenly finding a center—him. She saw now that despite his calm expression and easygoing manner, his body was tense, the small loin covering tented with an erection it was impossible to hide.

Love filled her, for this man who was so desirable that he could easily have been egotistical, and yet who had turned out to be generous, sensitive, willing to adapt in order to ensure that those around him were happy. That she and Kaylee were happy.

She couldn't resist leaning down and kissing him, luring his tongue into her mouth after only a few short probes with her own. He groaned, dropping her hand and moving his own to her hips, pulling her forward so that she stood between his legs.

When they came up for air she decided to test her luck, ordering him to move up on the bed and lie down. He obeyed, spreading his wings out like a dark comforter, making her vulva swell and her nipples tighten in anticipation of giving back to him, of thinking of *his* pleasure first. "No touching," she whispered, pinning his hands to the bed in a symbolic display as she straddled him. "If you touch me, I'm going to stop."

His laugh was husky, full of masculine pleasure and anticipation. "I will be good."

She closed the distance between their faces, rubbing his nose with her own. "Oh, I don't doubt you'll be good, Komet. You're always very, very good." She kissed him again, a slow, lingering kiss as her lower body rubbed against his, her clit pulsing with pleasure with each inch of his erection that it stroked.

He jerked in response, his hips coming off the bed, his cock grinding against her, the sheer fabric of her own pants already wet with arousal. "That's close to cheating," she teased, nipping his bottom lip then licking over it, enjoying the way his face tightened and a small groan escaped.

She pressed his wrists to the bed again in a symbolic gesture. "No touching," she warned for a second time then released him so that her fingers could spear through his thick, honey-brown curls. "How come you weren't already claimed?" she asked, the question springing from nowhere, and yet one she'd considered often.

A hint of color settled on his cheeks. "I have always found my studies more interesting than those pursuing me."

This time a laugh escaped from Ariel and she couldn't resist teasing. "So you *do* know just how desirable you are."

His color deepened, but his eyes were liquid-soft, full of love and honesty. "I am a scientist and a scholar so I understand more than most, the importance of appearance in attracting a mate—and also how external beauty is a product of genetics. But looks are only a small portion of who I am. You were the first to see me with your heart, to care for me regardless of appearance or clan-house." He dared to cheat again by lifting his head so that he could kiss her. *I am glad my body pleases you, Ariel. You are the only one I wish to be desirable to.*

She returned the kiss, cupping his cheeks before trailing her hands down to measure his shoulders. *I love you,* she whispered in his mind.

I love you as well.

His control nearly snapped when her hands moved to tease his tiny, hardened nipples and then her mouth followed. *Ariel!* he said, his cock jerking against her still-covered mound, the thought of her smooth bare flesh causing beads of arousal to escape from the tip of his penis.

She nipped him in response, her intention suddenly becoming clear when she left his nipple, her wet mouth traveling downward. "Ariel." This time it came out as a pant— of denial, of longing, of anticipation. His hands released the sheet and she stilled, biting the tight flesh of his abdomen in warning. *No touching or I'll stop.*

He shivered, his chest already heaving with the struggle to breathe, but he couldn't prevent himself from lifting his hips off the bed in a silent plea for her to remove his loin covering.

Feminine power and pride rushed through Ariel. Love. Desire. A need to please this man who'd already given so much of himself. A desperate urge to make this time together enough to see them through if things didn't go well when the Council met.

She relented, baring him to her touch, the sight of his erection making her cunt tighten and clench, making her womb flutter and her own nipples ache. He nearly came off the bed when she put her hands on his hips and her mouth on his cock. His penis jerking and pulsing under the lashes of her tongue, his fingers tightening on the sheets.

She moved her hands, cupping his heavy testicles with one and surrounding his penis with the other, controlling how deeply he could thrust into her mouth, the sight of his taut wings and body making her want to crawl up his body and impale herself on his cock.

Ariel knew she was lost when he began to beg, to plead, telling her with words and thoughts that he wanted his seed to jet into her tight sheath, that he wanted to feel her holding him tightly in the depths of her body as he thrust into her, became one with her.

With a whimper she yielded, crawling up his body, her own hand guiding his cock to where they both wanted him to be, the feel of his suede-textured wings against her knees and thighs incredibly erotic as she settled into a rhythm, riding him, fucking him, loving him, pleasuring him, only forgetting her earlier command at the very end, when his hands released their grip on the sheet, finding her nipples as his mating teeth sank into her neck in the instant before he rolled them over, taking command until they were both crying out in exquisite ecstasy — the hot wash of orgasm burning a path from womb to heart, from shaft to soul, the Ylan stones in their bands echoing the joy of their union.

The sleeping chamber reeked of sex — as Zeraac had known it would. He didn't bother with words, but stripped out of his loin clothing, glad that Kaylee had been thrilled by an outing with Komet, hadn't even needed to see her mother before leaving the dwelling again.

Zeraac's cock hardened at the vision in front of him, Ariel lying naked on the sheets, her smile sultry, her body already well loved, the sight of her bare mound making his nostrils flare and his body tighten. By the Goddess, he would never have imagined such a thing could make him rage with desire, with need, with the primitive instinct to claim.

As if sensing his thoughts, she shifted, widening her legs so he could see the swollen folds of flesh, the clit that stood erect, begging for his attention, her glistening, inner thighs, coated with her arousal and the perfumed residue left from her visit to the cleansing chamber.

"Fuck me," she ordered, still riding a wave of power left over from her encounter with Komet—and Zeraac knew he would, but only on his terms, only after she submitted to him.

He joined her on the bed, covering her body with his, enjoying the feel of her soft feminine flesh, craving the look of love in her eyes even as he needed more from her—something he'd never desired of any other woman, something so primitive that he would have shied away from it had it horrified Ariel.

But it didn't.

Her eyes darkened and she shifted, rubbing her smooth flesh and wet crevice against his straining cock, enticing him, tormenting him, the look in her eyes begging him to take charge, to dominate her, to claim her.

Zeraac pinned her wrists to the bed, answering her whimpers by covering her lips with his and plunging his tongue into her mouth, teasing her by withholding the part of him she'd ordered inside of herself.

Please, she whispered, opening her legs wider and coating his penis with her juices, not a command this time but a plea. He rose on his arms, just far enough so that his mouth could find her breast and suckle, swallowing the taste of her along with her cries as she arched into him, willing to let him swallow her whole.

He laved and bit and sucked, first one nipple and then the other, knowing he could spend a lifetime doing more of the same, wanting to spend forever with her.

She came, the keening sound making his cock jerk in warning and Zeraac could no longer resist the lure of her velvet-soft mound. But rather than shove himself into her, he moved down her body and latched on to her clit, sending another shudder of orgasm through her body and leaving her helpless under him, weak with desire and submission.

He drove her up again, hoarding her whimpers and mewling cries, her whispered pleas for him to take her, fuck her, love her. He'd intended to tie her to the bed again, to put a pleasure device up her anus, making her channel so tight that the pleasure would border on pain when he finally worked his cock into her, but she'd already made him desperate, needy, nearly unable to keep from spewing on flesh and sheets.

"Ariel." It was a hoarse cry coming from the depths of his soul, his heart, a scream from every cell in his body that no other woman would ever exist for him now that he had bonded with her.

Please, Zeraac. I can't stand being apart from you, she said, tears of need slipping from the corners of eyes filled with love.

He rose over her then, his wings extended, full, taut, quivering, seeming to fill the room with their glittering gold-veined presence, and she welcomed him, as he knew she always would — into every part of her being — clinging to him, taking his strength and comfort while she offered him the same. Taking his love as she gave her own. Their bodies moving in an ancient rhythm, allowing them to find a gateway into a heaven that existed regardless of beliefs.

Afterward they held each other. Both dreading the moment when they would have to separate. Both knowing the limit on their time together might extend beyond this visit.

"When do you think they'll meet?" Ariel finally asked.

"Tomorrow, with the rising of the second sun."

She tightened her grip on him. "You sound sure."

He adjusted his wings so that they could lie on their sides and face each other. "Paraisio told me when I arrived with Kaylee."

"What will happen tomorrow?"

"We will be summoned to the Council chambers and allowed to speak. Then each Council member will make a brief comment before a vote is taken as to whether or not to allow the challenge to our mate-bond to stand. If the vote is tied, the Council members will speak privately until they have reached an agreement as to how to proceed. If the challenge is allowed, then the Council members will be allowed to ask us questions. If the challenge fails, then we will be free to leave, to begin our life together."

"And if the challenge is allowed and we lose?"

"Then a Vesti justice along with an Amato high priest or priestess will try to call the Ylan stones back to their original bands." He leaned forward, sealing her lips with his. *Our time together is almost over. Komet and Kaylee are approaching. Their conversation hovers at the edge of my mind, just out of hearing range. We have done what we can, Ariel, the rest is in the hands of the Goddess and the consort.*

* * * * *

Sleep was impossible. For Ariel because she was worried. For Kaylee because she was both worried and full of pent-up energy from her two days of enforced sleep. But the third sun finally set, and a short time later the second one rose, bringing with it the summons they'd been expecting.

"How come Zeraac and Komet didn't come and get us?" Kaylee asked Paraisio, who was walking next to her.

"The Council probably summoned them first," she grimaced, "in order to lecture them on rules and protocol as some of the more rigid members are prone to do."

Kaylee's hand tightened on Ariel's. "Will I get to have my say?"

Shiraz, who was walking at Ariel's side, said, "It is unusual for children to appear before the Council, and in fact, your presence was not specifically requested. But after the protest is read, one of the Council members will ask if any directly involved or affected by the proceedings would care to speak, before the Council members themselves weigh in. There is no specific order for speaking, as long as it is done in a manner that does not disrupt the proceedings. But I can think of no law or rule preventing you from offering your thoughts."

"Then I'm going to have my say," Kaylee's said, her chin going up in a gesture that made Ariel's heart squeeze with pride, even when her daughter's bottom lip trembled slightly as she added, "Will they ask me questions afterward?"

Shiraz's face became solemn. "It depends. They are allowed to ask some questions, but not others—at least not right away."

Paraisio took over, reaching for Kaylee's hand and taking it in her own. "Just tell the Council members what is in your heart. And if they should ask you a question, tell them only what you know is the truth. Do not be afraid to tell them if you do not know the answer. And if you are afraid to give an answer, then tell them you cannot do so without talking to your mother first."

"Okay," Kaylee said, her voice subdued as she read Paraisio's worry, the seriousness of what was about to happen suddenly scaring her so that she halted in her tracks, forcing the adults to stop with her.

Ariel immediately knelt, pulling her daughter into her arms. "Be brave, baby," she whispered. "We can get through this. Let's make Zeraac and Komet proud of us."

"I'm trying to be brave, Mommy, but I want them to be my daddies."

Tears rushed to Ariel's eyes when Kaylee began crying, her sobs like small gasps for breath, reminding Ariel of all the times pain had racked Kaylee's frail body and she hadn't cried. Ariel rubbed Kaylee's back, holding her tightly, but not offering platitudes or false promises—their shared battle against disease had long ago stripped them of the ability to find comfort in pretense.

Eventually Kaylee calmed, raising a tear-stained face and saying, "I love them both, Mommy."

"I know you do. And you can tell the Council that's how you feel."

"Is that what you're going to tell them?"

Yes." Ariel rubbed her nose along Kaylee's. "They're our angels and we're not giving them up without a fight. Are we?"

Once again Kaylee's chin jutted out. "Not without a *big* fight, Mommy. A big one. When we were at the park yesterday, Zeraac showed everyone some bounty-hunting moves. If I have to, I'll use them on those Council members!"

That brought laughs from Paraisio and Shiraz, as well as Ariel, though Ariel knew her daughter well enough to add, "Be careful not to give them a piece of your mind by broadcasting your thoughts, Kaylee. And it would be best if violence was avoided—including plucking feathers in order to make a point. Okay?"

"Okay, Mommy," Kaylee said, giving an exaggerated sigh before snickering. "But that boy *was* bossy."

"And will one day be quite a handsome man," Paraisio teased, making Kaylee roll her eyes and say, "Not you, too!"

Ariel stood, keeping Kaylee's hand in hers, the moment of teasing quickly fading as they continued toward the chambers where the Council members were already gathered.

Zeraac's heart rose to his throat, threatening to suffocate him with emotion when Ariel and Kaylee arrived and he saw they had been crying. He and Komet both stood, intending to go to them, but before they could take a step, Kaylee broke away from her mother and rushed over, throwing herself against them. "Mommy and I are going to fight to keep you!" she told them, the easily heard words making some of the Council members smile, while others frowned.

Ariel joined them, unsure of the protocol, but unable to keep from touching them, from offering them each a quick kiss. *Are we allowed to sit together?*

Yes, Komet said in the instant before one of the Council members intoned, "Let us begin."

In a lot of ways, the room resembled a courtroom—though there were no benches for spectators and no seats for jurors. The twelve Council members—six Vesti, six Amato, nine men and three women — sat behind a long, slightly raised judge's bench made of crystals so varied in color that it made Ariel think about the mix of Ylan stones on her own wristbands.

But what really surprised her was the set of scales placed in the center of the long table, the carved base and arms a collage of winged creatures. *The Scales of Justice?* she asked Komet.

Yes — a symbol from our shared ancestor — though here each Council member holds a token, a representation that no one opinion has more weight than another, but when joined together they control the balance. The images on the scales are the forms the Fallon once took. After we have spoken, each Council member will stand individually and place their token on the scale. They can choose to speak, though it is not required. A token on the left is a vote to hear the challenge to our mate-bond. A token on the right is a vote against letting the challenge stand.

Ariel's gaze traveled along the row of Council members who held so much power over her "marriage". It appeared as though they had taken their seats at random, men and women, Vesti and Amato, with no obvious order or grouping.

They were somber, unsmiling, their thoughts hidden, the focus more inward than outward. Except for the last Council member. Her heart rate jumped at the sight of the Vesti male, the same one she'd seen in the market, his golden-colored eyes boring into her here just as they'd done there, demanding that her body acknowledge his and piercing through her attempts to remain calm, making her panic inside.

She shivered, moving closer to Komet. *Who is he?*

Komet followed her gaze and immediately tensed, his body going rigid, making Ariel think of a primitive male getting ready to battle another for the right to mate. Though they were both Vesti, where Komet was sleek and beautiful, the other man was rugged, fierce, raw — as though his genes passed to the next generation by conquering a female rather than luring her.

Who is he? Ariel repeated.

Miciah d'Vesti of the Danjal clan-house.

An Amato Council member stood, drawing Ariel's attention away, though she could still feel the intensity of Miciah's gaze moving over her in an almost sensual regard. Her nipples tightened in reaction though her mind rebelled, coloring her chest and neck and face with a red nearly as bright as the standing Council member's hair.

"I have offered a challenge to this mate-bond," the Amato said, and Ariel knew immediately that he was Zantara's uncle, Raym, "so I speak on the matter now that we are gathered. Our scientists have addressed the first issue, so that question no longer stands before the Council. Zeraac d'Amato of the clan-house Gadreel has been found to have the Fallon gene matching that of the human known on Earth as Ariel Ripa. I acknowledge that under the Council's own laws, he has the right to choose a Vesti co-mate and claim her. But I challenge whether or not she came here willingly, accepting both men as her mates before being transported here—as is required by Council law. He was not matched to her before he went to Earth and no others have succeeded in bringing a mate back so quickly—much less a woman with a very sick child." He paused long enough to meet the gaze of the other eleven members of the Council before adding, "Regardless of the outcome of that challenge, I believe we need to consider what actions best serve both of our races in the event that a human female with the Fallon gene is matched with a male when there is no possibility of children coming from the bonding— especially when we now know a second match might be found for her on Belizair. I ask that the Council decide to allow this challenge so these concerns can be addressed."

He sat down and another Amato rose, this one a woman. "She's a healer," Kaylee whispered, squeezing Ariel's hand.

"Do you know what to expect in these proceedings?" the woman asked Ariel.

"Yes."

"Then let us move forward." She sat down and her attention shifted, as did Ariel's, a thin layer of sweat breaking out on her skin when she realized that beside Komet, Zeraac, Kaylee and herself, there was only one other person in the room to speak on their behalf—another Amato she'd seen only briefly—on Earth, in the moments before Komet and Zeraac had rushed her into the transport chamber.

It was that man who stood, going to the center of the room and standing in front of the scales. "I am Jeqon d'Amato of the Lahatiel clan-house. Though it is my uncle who has questioned whether this bond should be allowed, I speak in favor of it and ask the Council to let it stand without further harassment. Our world now has many bonded matches with no children. We do not question their right to find happiness with each other. Why should we question this bond? Though it may yield no additional children of Ariel, it has provided one in the form of Kaylee." He paused, extending his hand toward the scale. "In the balance of things, is that not enough? The daughter for the mother? And if you do not believe so, then know this. Because of Ariel and Kaylee we have identified another child with the Fallon gene marker, a child whose mother has no mate and who might also prove to be a match for one of us."

Raym d'Amato stood, challenging his nephew. "What proof do you bring of this additional child and mother?"

Jeqon opened his closed hand and put a small stuffed animal on the table, directly underneath the scale arm that would soon hold any tokens in favor of setting the challenge aside. But before he could say anything, Kaylee's excited voice carried to the Council members, "That's the koala Kendall gave me! Is she going to come here and live? She's my best friend." A pause. "Other than you, Mommy."

Most of the Council members smiled, unable to remain somber in the face of Kaylee's excitement at the prospect of her friend being brought to Belizair, of her obvious closeness to her mother. Even Jeqon was grinning when he answered,

"Ariel told Zeraac about a friend Kaylee had who claimed to see imaginary beings—including an angel now and then. Zeraac passed on the information and when the things from Ariel's home in San Francisco were gathered and brought to the Council house there, I found several strands of hair on this bear—probably belonging to the daughter. I tested them. They contain the Fallon marker, though we have not found its match yet."

His uncle nodded, accepting Jeqon's words as truth, then sat down. Jeqon turned to leave, but hesitated—his grimace an indication that one of the Council members was speaking to him. He reached over and picked up the bear, handing it off to Kaylee before exiting the room.

I will speak next, Zeraac said, rising from the bench they shared, his words heavy with a pain he hated to so publicly face, making Ariel want to cry. Instead she reached out as he passed, touching him, telling him without words that she loved him.

He too stopped in the center of the room, in front of the scales. "I would ask the Council to set aside the challenge to my mate-bond. While I did not go to Earth seeking a mate or a daughter, as soon as I met Ariel and Kaylee, I was lost. I would have remained at their sides for as long as I could, even forsaking a task I had volunteered for on behalf of our world." He took a deep breath before forcing the rest of his words out. "I was to bond with Zantara d'Amato of the Lahatiel clanhouse. After the effects of the Hotaling virus became known to us, she asked that I submit to testing, hoping perhaps…" He shrugged. "I cannot speak for her hopes. But I had no reason to object, and so I allowed myself to be tested, only to learn that…there would be no children for me, even with a human bond-mate and a Vesti co-mate. I have come to terms with that knowledge. Ariel and Komet have both accepted it. We are already blessed with a daughter, one restored to health by our healers and scientists. One I love deeply. We are a true family and wish only to remain so."

He returned to his seat and Komet moved to stand before the Council. "What Zeraac has said is true. We are a true family and wish only to remain so—to live together and raise a daughter, to do what we can to aid Belizair in these painful times. I would remind the Council that they have already addressed the issue of sanctions against the Araqiel clan-house and found we have suffered enough for our part in Belizair's devastation. Like Zeraac, I ask that this challenge be set aside."

When he sat down, Kaylee scrambled to her feet. "I want to go next," she said, taking a step before stopping and turning back, uncertainty in her face. *Will you go with me, Mommy?*

Ariel joined her, the two of them holding hands as they faced the Council. *Do you want me to go first?* Ariel asked.

Kaylee's chin jutted out. *No I'll go.* To the Council she said. "I love Zeraac and Komet and I want them to be my daddies. I don't want you to take them away from me. They came to Earth for Mommy and me and I said I wanted to go with them." She looked directly at Raym d'Amato, giving him a fierce frown. "So none of your rules were broken."

Zantara's uncle stood once again, his focus on Kaylee. Ariel tensed when he asked, "And did your mother also say she wanted to go with them?"

"That's between my mommy and my two daddies," Kaylee said, and at least one of the Council members snickered.

For a moment Raym looked at Ariel, and she could see the desire to question her in his eyes, but Zeraac's voice whispered, *He cannot do so since it was Kaylee, and not you, who brought the subject up.*

Raym's mouth tightened, his attention going back to Kaylee, but in the end he returned to his seat, perhaps deciding that questioning a child would only serve to weaken his challenge.

Your turn, Mommy.

Ariel forced herself to meet the gaze of every Council member, included the heavy-lidded stare of Miciah d'Vesti, before saying, "Since I arrived on your planet, I have been told repeatedly that the happiness of human bond-mates is important, that *my* happiness is important. If that is the truth, then I ask you to set aside this challenge. I love Komet and Zeraac. I consider myself married to them. I want them at my side. I want them to be the men who help me raise my daughter. I have already lost a husband, just as Kaylee has already lost a father, please don't add to what we have already suffered by threatening to set the bond we have with Zeraac and Komet aside."

They returned to their bench, sitting between Zeraac and Komet, holding hands.

The Amato healer who'd first addressed Ariel rose again, her gaze sweeping over the other Council members as she spoke. "Once the Amato and Vesti warred with each other, becoming less than we had been with each new generation, finding peace only with the establishment of order and the acceptance of laws that governed us both while allowing us our differences. Since that time we have prided ourselves on our fairness. The matter before us is a serious one, not only for those whose bond has been challenged, but for the future of Belizair. Whether this particular mate-bond stands or is set aside, I do not believe it is fair to apply a standard to them that has not been applied before. The issue of who can claim a human descendent of the Fallon needs further thought and discussion and should be addressed at a separate time and without regard to the matter before us." She turned to Raym d'Amato. "I would ask Raym to withdraw his request that we consider it as part of his challenge."

Raym d'Amato stood, his gaze also sweeping over the assembled Council members, assessing their expressions before saying, "Withdrawn."

The female healer nodded and took her seat while Raym remained standing. "If all have spoken, then I move we take a vote on whether to proceed with the challenge before us—a challenge now limited to whether or not Ariel Ripa of Earth came here willingly, accepting both Zeraac d'Amato of the clan-house Gadreel and Komet d'Vesti of the Araqiel clan-house as her mates before being transported here—as is required by Council law. I believe this bond bears further investigation because Zeraac was not matched to Ariel before he went to Earth and no others have succeeded in bringing a mate back so quickly—much less a woman with a very sick child."

He leaned over and placed a token on the scales—tipping it downward in favor of allowing the challenge to proceed.

Two others quickly followed, their tokens joining his, only to be balanced by three on the other side.

A Vesti stood. "We have based our society on free will and have made laws in support of it. Despite the fact that those in front of us appear content with their mate-bond, if we ignore this challenge, then how can we then take action the next time we question whether a human bond-mate has been brought here without first gaining consent?" The scales tipped back in favor of addressing the challenge.

Another joined, countered by two on the other side, leaving the scales balanced, five in favor of proceeding, five in favor of dismissing.

Ariel swallowed, her eyes going to Miciah d'Vesti, whose token was on the judges' bench in front of him.

He gave a small, nearly feral smile as the Vesti with the other remaining token stood.

Komet tensed, warning Ariel in advance, *He will vote against us.* But rather than moving toward the scale, the Council member said, "Though it is unusual to do so, it is not against our rules. My conscience dictates that I yield my vote to another." With the flick of his wrist, he sent his token sailing.

Miciah d'Vesti stood, calmly plucking it from the air. "I would speak to Ariel privately before I place these tokens on the scale."

Zeraac and Komet's instant denial rang in Ariel's head, but she stood, kissing them both and Kaylee before silently following the Council member out of the chambers. He led her to an office—or at least that's what she would have called it on Earth—though it lacked stacks of paper or equipment, instead boasting an assortment of plants throughout, and what was probably some type of flat computer on the desk.

She expected him to take a seat. Instead he closed the door and moved into her personal space, filling her nostrils with his scent and warming her body with his heat.

"You are my match," he growled without preamble, momentarily stunning her with his words. But when his fingers speared through her hair, she reacted instinctively, flinching away from him and making him scowl.

"I'm Zeraac's match."

"And mine as well. You know it is possible. So do not deny the truth, nor what your body is telling you. What it told you the other day when you were in the market." His eyes roved over her, narrowing when they encountered Komet's bite marks, but heating when they saw her tight nipples. She shivered in reaction and his nostrils flared.

"I've already got bond-mates," she reminded him, hating it that her body *did* respond to him.

"I could make you desire me. I could make you crave my touch."

She saw no point in lying to him, or to herself. "Yes, you could. But you couldn't make me love you, or forget about them. You'd always wonder if I was thinking about them while having sex with you. You'd grow to hate both me and yourself."

His head jerked up and he released her, taking a step back. "Love and caring are not essential in order to produce offspring. Look at your own planet, you breed so freely that you threaten to destroy yourselves by using up and polluting your resources."

"And is that the type of a world you want? One like Earth? Where children too often end up unwanted, torn between parents who hate each other—or worse. There are places where children can be found foraging in the streets, abandoned for the most part by parents who don't love each other or them. Is that what you want for Belizair? It seems like just another kind of devastation to me."

He growled, pacing over to the window and stopping, his body radiating such tension and anguish that Ariel found it impossible to resist going to him—though she didn't touch him.

"Do you truly love him? A man whose clan-house has caused so much suffering here?" Miciah asked.

She started to argue that Komet had nothing to do with his family's business, but something stopped her, making her take a different tack instead. "You have never used any of the pleasure items the Araqiels provide?"

He jerked as though she'd struck him, then surprised her by conceding, "Your point is well taken. Do you truly love him?"

"Yes. I love both of them. I want to live with them, sleep with them, be with them. I want to share the joy and pain that comes with rearing a child and have them at my side when that child finally leaves to make her own home."

His shoulders hunched forward, just enough for Ariel's heart to go out to him. "Surely you are not without...male friends." He stiffened and she quickly added, "An Amato who would choose you as a co-mate."

That brought a snarl as he wheeled away, pacing the length of the room and making her regret saying anything. With a sigh, she forced her thoughts away from the two tokens he controlled and looked out the window, at a courtyard full of flowers and sparkling fountains.

He calmed, returning to her side. "Do you tell me the truth? Are there places where children fend for themselves, unclaimed, unwanted?"

It was Ariel's turn to jerk in reaction, suddenly worrying about those children being taken from what they knew and brought here. Her concern not just for them, but what impact they might have on a world so different than their own. She was not so naïve as to think a change of environment was always enough to change the course of a child's life, to change who and what they were at their core. "And if there are?" she hedged.

He laughed softly. "Though it may sometimes seem a complex contradiction, we do value free will. Perhaps those who have no hope now, would find a measure of peace in going to Earth and becoming surrogate parents, raising a generation that might then come to Belizair of their own free will when they are old enough to form mate-bonds." His hand reached out, cupping Ariel's face, forcing her to meet his gaze—his own intense, seeking—as though he wanted to see her very soul. Then without a word, he turned away, leaving the chamber.

She followed, her heart pounding. Wild emotion rushing through her as she watched him stride over to the scales and drop the tokens on the crystal plate—the weight of the two new tokens changing the balance, the challenge to the mate-bond disappearing as the plate lowered, heavier by the votes Miciah cast.

Epilogue

ഇ

"Did Zeraac come here for the surprise?" Kaylee asked, her innocent expression belying the fact that she was still hunting for clues and trying to get Komet to reveal the secret the adults shared.

Komet looked around the marketplace, frowning as though he was in serious contemplation while Kaylee's eyes followed his, watching for any sign of his gaze settling on an object, even for a second. "Maybe," Komet said after a torturous silence, not completely managing to hide his smile or his amusement.

"K-o-m-e-t. No fair. Just a hint. Please. Zeraac wouldn't mind if you gave me a tiny hint. Right, Mommy?"

Ariel laughed. "On no, leave me out of this."

Kaylee started to say something but Komet's expression made her turn and follow the direction of his gaze. Ariel's attention shifted also, tension and foreboding instantly assailing her when she saw Zantara d'Amato.

The flame-haired woman stopped in front of them, her gaze dropping momentarily to Kaylee.

"You have caused enough pain and suffering, Zantara," Komet said. "Neither Zeraac nor I will allow you to inflict more of it on either our bond-mate or our daughter."

Zantara flinched slightly, her gaze meeting Ariel's as she said, "I did not realize there was a child involved when I spoke so bitterly to my uncle. Had I known that Zeraac...had I known...it would have been easier to accept."

Kaylee pressed her back to Ariel's front, her body tense. Ariel put her hands on her daughter's stiff shoulders, thinking to give her reassurance, but instead Kaylee sought her own. Her small chin jutted out like a pugilist ready to take on an opponent. "You can't have Zeraac back, he belongs to Mommy and me now," she said, going to the heart of the matter—as she interpreted it—her boldness making the woman who even now reminded Ariel of an avenging angel, take a step backward.

"Kaylee..."Ariel began, only to have Zantara shake her head and say, "No, I will answer your daughter's challenge and hopefully put her fears to rest. I came to apologize for the part I played in the separation of your family. I am sorry and though I ask for your forgiveness, I do not expect it." She smiled slightly as her glance shifted to Kaylee. "Rest easy, I make no claim on Zeraac, either now or in the future."

For a long moment Kaylee remained tense, but then she relaxed and nodded, leaning her back against Ariel's front, so that Ariel couldn't resist the urge to lean over and place a kiss on the top of her daughter's head. "I'd like to speak to Zantara alone for a few minutes. Why don't you and Komet see if you can find some of the fruit that tastes like bananas, along with some sweetbread, and some nuts for Sabaska. It's almost time to stop and eat."

Kaylee nodded, her posture saying she was uncertain about leaving her mother alone with Zantara. Komet's protest was not so subtle. *No,* he said, worry and protectiveness heavy in the one small word.

She turned, meeting his gaze, acknowledging with her own that she appreciated his concern before pressing a kiss to his lips. *Please, Komet. Stay close if you wish, but give me a few minutes with her.*

He relented. Finally. Both he and Kaylee moving so slowly it would have been funny had it not been so touching.

When they were far enough away to allow for a private conversation, Ariel turned her attention to Zantara. She wanted to hate the woman in front of her. But when Zantara had looked at Kaylee, Ariel had seen such a deep well of suffering in Zantara's eyes that she'd felt compassion instead.

Hadn't she once experienced similar emotions as she'd looked around and seen others enjoying what was not even possible for her? In her darkest moments, when she'd felt alone, helpless, hadn't she sometimes become overwhelmed, filling with pain and despair, and envy for those who had healthy children and good marriages?

Shiraz's earlier words echoed through Ariel's mind. *Find it in your heart to forgive, to try and understand that we, too, suffer. Our culture, though allowing free choice, has always revered childbearing and childrearing. And now our women are without hope, struggling with despair and feelings of worthlessness, while our men must take a human mate even as they watch helplessly while those they love become less than they once were. Have faith that your love will prevail.*

And her love had prevailed. Her love for Kaylee had seen her through to a miracle—and would have sustained her had there not been one. The memories as cherished as they would have been painful had Kaylee died. Her love for Zeraac and Komet had given her a new future, new possibilities, a new world to explore. And even without the promise of additional children, Ariel's heart was full, her spirit soaring just as high as any Amato or Vesti might fly.

"I can't say I've felt exactly what you feel," Ariel said, her gaze finding Kaylee, "but there were times when I hated, when I raged inwardly at the unfairness of life—when I listened to parents complain about their children's minor illnesses or threaten to sue their neighbors over broken bones, and I thought of my own child who had never climbed a tree or played on a sports team, who had never learned to swim or to ride a bike because each breath was a struggle for her. Each bite of food was a battle her body waged to gain enough nutrition to exist. Each day a victory, and yet a defeat. There were times when I wished my hardship on others, when I even disliked some of the children—spoiled and whiny—unaware of just how lucky they were. It ate away at me, like an acid stripping away my soul, taking the best parts of me and threatening to leave me bitter—until I resolved not to let it." Ariel turned her attention back to Zantara, noting the tears in the other woman's eyes. "I forgive you," she said, holding out her arms in greeting. "Let the past stay in the past while we work together toward something better. I can think of this as the first time we've met, if you can."

Zantara nodded, raising her hands and gripping Ariel's forearms so their wristbands touched for just an instant. "Thank you," she said, her voice hoarse. "May you find happiness on Belizair."

* * * * *

Zeraac stood in the Council's San Francisco house and looked at the boxes containing what remained from Ariel and Kaylee's apartment, feeling hesitant now that he was faced with the task of deciding which of their possessions held value and should be taken to Belizair. It had seemed like a good surprise for Kaylee, and a way to bring closure to Ariel's life on Earth, but now…

"It's not as difficult as it looks," Jeqon said, pushing away from the doorway with a smile that immediately had Zeraac tensing. "Take this box for example." He leaned down and rummaged around, tossing out articles of clothing that would be ill-suited to the desert city of Winseka. "I think you can agree, it would be a waste of energy to transport them."

"True," Zeraac agreed, hearing the laughter in Jeqon's voice and bracing himself.

Jeqon stood, each hand on a thin strap, a sheer garment of pale blue shimmering as it unfurled, the sight of it—and the image of it covering Ariel's body—making Zeraac's cock grow hard.

"But this might be interesting," Jeqon said, grinning, his eyes dropping to Zeraac's loin covering. "Agreed?"

"Agreed," Zeraac growled, suddenly ready to get the task done and return to Belizair, to Ariel, so that she might put the garment on and allow him to torture them both by removing it—slowly.

"I will leave you to your sorting then," Jeqon said, laughing has he left the room.

Much of it was easy. The photographs that had once lived on Ariel's bookcase. The books themselves along with a collection of photo albums. The sheer, impractical sleep clothing that no winged creature could wear but which would be arousing on Ariel. The toys belonging to Kaylee, and the games, some of which were similar to those on Belizair, and some that Kaylee would no doubt enjoy introducing to her new world. Zeraac smiled at the vision of his small, bossy daughter instructing others and informing them about the rules of play.

Those were easy for him to deal with and he did so by repacking them and placing the boxes outside the transport chamber door. But the last box he opened caught him off-guard and brought tears to his eyes. Ariel had kept some of Kaylee's baby clothing, tiny sleepers and frilly dresses with matching socks and small polished shoes.

For long moments Zeraac looked at them, his heart aching for what he would never experience. But then he set the emotion aside, repacking the box and moving it directly to the transport chamber before carrying the rest of them inside. The Goddess had blessed him with a bond-mate and child when he had expected neither. It was enough. More than enough.

The lights pulsed as the Ylan stones gathered energy, the ancient chamber breaking everything into tiny molecules before opening the portal door between one world and the next, just as it had once done in the days when the Fallon walked on Earth.

* * * * *

The fruit that had looked delicious and smelled delicious and tasted delicious, sat heavily on Ariel's stomach, making her feel nauseous — nauseous to the point of needing to escape so she could vomit without an audience.

"Do you want some of my sweetbread, Mommy?" Kaylee asked, waving a piece of it in front of Ariel's nose and nearly breaking Ariel's control over her stomach.

Are you okay? Komet asked, rising from his own seat and moving around, his knuckles skimming over Ariel's suddenly clammy cheek. *You do not look well.*

I think maybe the fruit was bad.

He frowned. *It tasted as it always does.*

Ariel lowered her head, intending to put it down on the table, but instead, her attention fixed on her own wristbands. They glittered, just as she'd once seen them sparkle on Kaylee's wrists, and later on Zeraac's. *Look,* she directed Komet, and he looked, his eyebrows drawing together in puzzlement as he did so.

Kaylee squealed with delight, picking up on their actions though their conversation had been private. "Look, Mommy, the Goddess is crying for you now!"

Is it normal for the stones to keep changing? Ariel asked Komet.

I do not know. The Tears of the Goddess are rare, their power unknown, though I thought...I hoped...

What?

That they might aid in healing.

Kaylee?

Yes.

Ariel's mind raced, her nausea gone in her excitement as she remembered these same bouts of hunger for a particular food, followed by queasiness, when she was first pregnant with Kaylee. *And Zeraac? You thought that maybe they would allow him to father a child?*

Komet took Ariel's hand in his, squeezing it even as his other trailed along her neck, sliding under her hair and stroking the place his mating teeth had repeatedly marked her. *I hoped, Ariel – but for Kaylee's health alone, I would have given up not only the Tears of the Goddess, but every Ylan stone in my possession. As would Zeraac. It is enough for both of us if she is the only child we ever have.*

Can you run a pregnancy test?

He didn't answer immediately and she could see his reluctance, his fear of disappointing both of them with bad news. Ariel squeezed his hand, trying to impart some of her own sudden confidence. *What other explanation can you offer as to why the Tears sparkled on Kaylee's bands until she was healed, and then on Zeraac's, and now on mine – just as I am feeling as though I'm going to be sick – just when I might need them to ensure a safe pregnancy?*

Komet gave a shaky sigh. *I can think of none.*

For a moment they sat in silence, holding hands as hope filled them both, visible in their expressions. Finally Komet said, *My equipment is not as sophisticated as that of the Council scientists, they would be willing to...*

Ariel shook her head. *No. This is...private. I don't want to involve the Council or their scientists – not so soon after what we just endured. Can you do the test?*

He laughed softly. *I have brought a large number of intriguing specimens home in order to learn more about them. I think I can manage such a test on a willing bond-mate.*

Let's do it then, before Zeraac gets home with his surprise. But let's see if one of Kaylee's many "aunties" will look after her for a while. In case we have reason for an adult celebration.

* * * * *

Zeraac emerged from the portal building, glad he'd already made arrangements with several youngsters eager to earn credits. But instead of finding them waiting for him, ready to retrieve the boxes he'd moved to the outer chamber and carry Ariel and Kaylee's belongings back to the living quarters, he found Zantara—though her expression indicated she had not expected to find him.

"Zeraac," she said, tentatively offering her arms in greeting. And when he hesitated, torn between past and present, she gave a small, sad smile. "If it eases you, I have already offered my apology to Ariel, and she found it in her heart to forgive me. As I hope you will."

He nodded, briefly touching his bands to hers, but found he had no additional words for her. She filled the awkward silence by saying, "I have asked the Council to allow me to go to Earth as one of their agents, letting me take up the task of searching among the unwanted children in an effort to find those carrying the Fallon gene—and should any be found, to help raise them until they are old enough to be matched with bond-mates and come to Belizair of their own free will."

Zeraac's heart squeezed in his chest, surprising him at how clearly he felt Zantara's pain, even after all that had happened. And yet, wasn't this similar to how Ariel felt about her dead husband—where once there had been good times, a sharing of bodies and dreams. Love.

"May the Goddess and her consort bless you with a... May they bless you with happiness, Zantara. As they have blessed me."

Tears sparkled in her eyes and he could see words of love trapped in her throat. But he was glad she didn't speak them. It was too late now for them to emerge. For him, the love they shared was a thing of the past. And he didn't regret that it was.

He had Ariel and Kaylee. They made him a different man, a better man than he had been before. They were his miracle.

Zantara took a ragged breath, nodding, accepting the course their lives had taken, then turned and moved forward without a backward glance.

Zeraac watched her go, but there was no lingering doubt, no lingering desire—other than to get home and entice Ariel to put on one of the sheer sleeping garments.

He turned, grateful to see that the youngsters had arrived, though he was too anxious to wait for them beyond assuring himself they knew where to deliver the remaining boxes. Grinning, Zeraac picked up the one containing Kaylee's things and headed home, hoping its contents, followed by the arrival of other young people, would soon lead to some privacy for the adults.

* * * * *

Ariel looked around the small office, a room stuffed to the brim with rocks and samples of vegetation, as well as bones, feathers and things in crystal containers that she had no intention of inquiring about. "This is where you work?" she asked, finding it hard to picture him outside of the role of husband and father.

Komet laughed. "Not really. This is a place where colleagues can leave me messages and where I can store items of interest that I find in this region, at least until I take them back to Phlair, the home city of my clan-house."

"That's where you've lived up until now?"

"Yes. In quarters not unlike the ones we have here, though all of those around me are family members."

"What about Zeraac?"

"His clan-house calls Shiksa home."

"That's why you say you're members of a clan-house, because you actually live close together, even when you're adults."

"Perhaps that is the origin of the name. And yes, we usually live near others in our family, but it is not uncommon for us to stay with friends when we visit other regions." He grinned. "Until you came into my life, I most often roomed with Jeqon when I was in this region, though because he is also

225

a scientist and a scholar, we found early on that it was best not to mingle the things we collected."

She laughed. "Because you ended up fighting over them?"

"No, because it made movement around his living quarters nearly impossible. He is worse than I am when it comes to bringing interesting specimens home."

Ariel scanned the cluttered, tightly packed office. A memory surfacing of the first apartment she and Colin had shared, her collection of rocks on every windowsill, every countertop, as well as on tables and dressers. For a moment sadness lingered, but Komet's fingers chased it away as they stroked down her cheek, his concerned gaze making her feel foolish for visiting the past.

Don't, beloved. It is a part of you, of what makes you what you are today. His smile quirked upward. *And aren't pregnant women often weepy? If what you believe is true, then Zeraac and I will have to learn some new skills for dealing with our bond-mate.*

A small laugh escaped from Ariel. "Remember a single, important word. Yaschi. When all else fails. Bring me yaschi. And if we can find a way to roll it in bread, like a chocolate croissant, that'd be even better."

Komet grinned. "I will remember. Now then, let me find my sampling kit. What I have here in my office is just a simple yes or no test for pregnancy. But down the hall there is more sophisticated equipment. I might be able to gain access to it if…" He pulled her into his arms, kissing her, touching his nose to hers afterward. *Ariel, if the results do not come back as we desire…*

No tears. I promise.

He held her for a long moment before releasing her, retrieving an instrument identical to the one Galil had used to take a sample of her blood. Ariel offered her hand and Komet placed the crystal chamber above the most prominent vein. Within seconds the small space was filled with blood. He pulled the instrument away, placing it on top of a nearly identical crystal cube, except a thin layer of blue "dust" rested on the bottom. As Ariel watched, the blood from the upper chamber filled the lower one, the "dust" disappearing.

Without asking, Ariel knew what the results signified. She could feel Komet's joy rushing through the bond they shared. Its confirmation coming in the crushing hug he gave her and the tears she felt on his face.

No tears, she teased, gaining a laugh and a kiss. *Shall we go down the hall now and see if I'm carrying twins like the others? An Amato and a Vesti child?*

* * * * *

Zeraac knew a moment's disappointment when he found the living quarters empty. He'd been anticipating Kaylee's reaction to having her belongings brought from Earth, to meeting a new group of youngsters and perhaps introducing them to her games. Instead he gave those carrying the boxes the credits he'd promised them and saw to the unpacking himself—except for the boxes containing Kaylee's baby things. Those he left for Ariel.

It surprised him how much he felt the absence of Ariel, and Kaylee, even Komet. In such a short time, they'd become a family.

His cock stirred thinking about the pale blue sleeping garment that even now was spread on their bed, waiting for Ariel, as he was. He would enjoy seeing her wear it just as much as he would enjoy seeing her shed it.

In truth, he enjoyed everything about her. He craved her. Needed her. Could live on her smiles and love alone. And yet now he counted the moments until he could feel her body against his, could join with her, singly and at the same time Komet was lodged inside her.

When the Ylan stones hummed, signaling that they both were near, Zeraac's heart sped up even as his gaze went to his wrists and his eyebrows drew together. The Ylan stones on his bands had changed again. The glitter of the Tears remained present, more so than they had been at first, but less than the day he had flown Kaylee to the courtyard after she'd left the scientist's care. He shook his head, perhaps the bands would always change because of the Tears of the Goddess.

The door opened and Ariel walked in, followed by Komet. "No Kaylee?" Zeraac asked, confused by her absence, given her excitement about an upcoming "surprise". But when Ariel moved over, winding her arms around his neck, pressing her body to his and rubbing sinuously against his erection, Zeraac could find no fault in this new plan.

"Komet and I thought to turn the tables and give you a surprise instead," Ariel murmured, her eyes dancing with emotion, though for once she was containing her thoughts so that Zeraac could glean nothing from them.

His arms went around her, his hands trailing down her spine, unable to resist the temptation when he got to her pants. They slid off, becoming a pool of gold at her feet.

She laughed, a husky sound that had him swinging her into his arms and saying, "Shall we seek our pleasure in the bedroom?"

"Perhaps it would be best if you were lying down. It would prove embarrassing should you faint," Komet teased, his comment causing Zeraac's heart to jerk and race, so that instead of going into the bedroom, Zeraac sat down on the benchlike couch, with Ariel on his lap.

"What surprise do you and Komet have for me?"

Ariel took one of Zeraac's hands in hers, pressing her band to his, Komet moving to stand next to them, his hands joining theirs so that the Ylan stones hummed, a subtle hymn of joining. "Look what's happened to mine," Ariel said and Zeraac looked, seeing the tiny constellation in her stones, just as he'd once seen it in Kaylee's and his own.

"I noticed it when we were in the market, right after I felt queasy. It made me start thinking, Zeraac, and asking questions."

She stopped, her emotions swelling, nearly swamping Zeraac, the dam to her thoughts breaking, her message clear though he shook his head in denial. His own heart shuddering painfully under the impact of hope and joy he felt in hers. "Beloved, it cannot be. I have been tested — more than once."

Ariel squeezed his hand. "It is true, Zeraac. That's where Komet and I have been. To his office. And then to a shared laboratory. He ran the tests two times and then had another do it just to be sure. Each time the results were the same. Twins. Just like all the other mate-bonds formed with Human women."

Raw emotion rolled through Zeraac, intense, a lightning bolt resurrecting hopes and dreams he'd accepted as dead. He looked to Komet, unable to force the words past a throat that was nearly too tight to breathe.

It is true, Komet said. *I swear it. Perhaps a gift from the Goddess of the Amato, through her Tears.* He sent an image of the equipment used to gather sperm. *But if you would prefer to give a sample for testing…*

A laugh escaped, followed by tears as Zeraac buried his face in Ariel's hair, struggling to control the wild surge of emotions rushing through him, crashing in on him, overwhelming him with their intensity.

For a moment he was once again standing in front of the old apartment building on Earth, the fog rolling around and over him, wet and clinging, his heart heavy with despair, his mind resolved to hunting for the Hotalings, to dying for Belizair if that was to be his fate. His life had seemed empty, unbearable, until Ariel and Kaylee had come into it like a shaft of sunlight piercing the darkness.

And now this. A miracle.

Ariel's soft laugh filled his mind, her love filled his heart and soul. *We'll see if you still consider it a miracle when you're changing diapers and getting no sleep at all. Not to mention dealing with an emotional, pregnant woman.*

Zeraac lifted his face from her hair, finding a smile though he still felt nearly overwhelmed by the brightness of the future in front of him—them. *I believe I am up to the challenge.* He pressed a kiss to her mouth, the touch of his lips to hers transforming into a deeper need, to celebrate with the joining of their bodies, the stones on their bracelets pulsing as the desire traveled through each of them. *I, too, arranged for a small surprise for Komet and a treat for all of us.* He flashed them an image of the pale blue sleeping garment laid out on the bed.

Ariel laughed, feeling Komet's and Zeraac's anticipation at both seeing her in the sexy nightgown, and removing it from her—slowly—and only after teasing her into begging for them to do so. *Men!*

Your men, Zeraac said, rising to his feet with her still in his arms.

Your bond-mates, here to see to your protection and your pleasure, Ariel. Always. Komet grinned. *And to provide you with yaschi when all else fails.*

Why an electronic book?

We live in the Information Age—an exciting time in the history of human civilization, in which technology rules supreme and continues to progress in leaps and bounds every minute of every day. For a multitude of reasons, more and more avid literary fans are opting to purchase e-books instead of paper books. The question from those not yet initiated into the world of electronic reading is simply: *Why?*

1. *Price.* An electronic title at Ellora's Cave Publishing and Cerridwen Press runs anywhere from 40% to 75% less than the cover price of the exact same title in paperback format. Why? Basic mathematics and cost. It is less expensive to publish an e-book (no paper and printing, no warehousing and shipping) than it is to publish a paperback, so the savings are passed along to the consumer.

2. *Space.* Running out of room in your house for your books? That is one worry you will never have with electronic books. For a low one-time cost, you can purchase a handheld device specifically designed for e-reading. Many e-readers have large, convenient screens for viewing. Better yet, hundreds of titles can be stored within your new library—on a single microchip. There are a variety of e-readers from different manufacturers. You can also read e-books on your PC or laptop computer. (Please note that Ellora's Cave does not endorse any specific brands.

You can check our websites at www.ellorascave.com or www.cerridwenpress.com for information we make available to new consumers.)

3. *Mobility.* Because your new e-library consists of only a microchip within a small, easily transportable e-reader, your entire cache of books can be taken with you wherever you go.

4. *Personal Viewing Preferences.* Are the words you are currently reading too small? Too large? Too... ANNOYING? Paperback books cannot be modified according to personal preferences, but e-books can.

5. *Instant Gratification.* Is it the middle of the night and all the bookstores near you are closed? Are you tired of waiting days, sometimes weeks, for bookstores to ship the novels you bought? Ellora's Cave Publishing sells instantaneous downloads twenty-four hours a day, seven days a week, every day of the year. Our webstore is never closed. Our e-book delivery system is 100% automated, meaning your order is filled as soon as you pay for it.

Those are a few of the top reasons why electronic books are replacing paperbacks for many avid readers.

As always, Ellora's Cave and Cerridwen Press welcome your questions and comments. We invite you to email us at Comments@ellorascave.com or write to us directly at Ellora's Cave Publishing Inc., 1056 Home Avenue, Akron, OH 44310-3502.

erridwen, the Celtic Goddess of wisdom, was the muse who brought inspiration to storytellers and those in the creative arts. Cerridwen Press encompasses the best and most innovative stories in all genres of today's fiction. Visit our site and discover the newest titles by talented authors who still get inspired - much like the ancient storytellers did, once upon a time.

CERRIDWEN PRESS

www.cerridwenpress.com